WHAT HURTS THE MOST

MARY MILLS MYSTERY - BOOK 1

WILLOW ROSE

Books by the Author

MYSTERY/THRILLER/HORROR NOVELS

- Sorry Can't Save You
- In One Fell Swoop
- Umbrella Man
- Blackbird Fly
- To Hell in a Handbasket
- Edwina

HARRY HUNTER MYSTERY SERIES

- All The Good Girls
- Run Girl Run
- No Other Way
- Never Walk Alone

MARY MILLS MYSTERY SERIES

- What Hurts the Most
- You Can Run
- You Can't Hide
- Careful Little Eyes

EVA RAE THOMAS MYSTERY SERIES

- Don't Lie to me
- What you did
- Never Ever
- Say You Love me
- Let Me Go
- It's Not Over
- Not Dead yet

- To Die For

EMMA FROST SERIES

- Itsy Bitsy Spider
- Miss Dolly had a Dolly
- Run, Run as Fast as You Can
- Cross Your Heart and Hope to Die
- Peek-a-Boo I See You
- Tweedledum and Tweedledee
- Easy as One, Two, Three
- There's No Place like Home
- Slenderman
- Where the Wild Roses Grow
- Waltzing Mathilda
- Drip Drop Dead
- Black Frost

JACK RYDER SERIES

- Hit the Road Jack
- Slip out the Back Jack
- The House that Jack Built
- Black Jack
- Girl Next Door
- Her Final Word
- Don't Tell

REBEKKA FRANCK SERIES

- One, Two...He is Coming for You
- Three, Four...Better Lock Your Door
- Five, Six...Grab your Crucifix
- Seven, Eight...Gonna Stay up Late
- Nine, Ten...Never Sleep Again
- Eleven, Twelve...Dig and Delve

- Thirteen, Fourteen...Little Boy Unseen
- Better Not Cry
- Ten Little Girls
- It Ends Here

HORROR SHORT-STORIES

- Mommy Dearest
- The Bird
- Better watch out
- Eenie, Meenie
- Rock-a-Bye Baby
- Nibble, Nibble, Crunch
- Humpty Dumpty
- Chain Letter

PARANORMAL SUSPENSE/ROMANCE NOVELS

- In Cold Blood
- The Surge
- Girl Divided

THE VAMPIRES OF SHADOW HILLS SERIES

- Flesh and Blood
- Blood and Fire
- Fire and Beauty
- Beauty and Beasts
- Beasts and Magic
- Magic and Witchcraft
- Witchcraft and War
- War and Order
- Order and Chaos
- Chaos and Courage

THE AFTERLIFE SERIES

- Beyond
- Serenity
- Endurance
- Courageous

THE WOLFBOY CHRONICLES

- A Gypsy Song
- I am WOLF

DAUGHTERS OF THE JAGUAR

- Savage
- Broken

Published by BUOY MEDIA LLC

Cover design by Juan Villar Padron,
https://www.juanjpadron.com

Special thanks to my editor Janell Parque
http://janellparque.blogspot.com/

To be the first to hear about new releases and bargains from Willow Rose, sign up below to be on the VIP List. (I promise not to share your email with anyone else, and I won't clutter your inbox.)

- Go here to sign up to be on the VIP LIST :
http://readerlinks.com/l/415254

Tired of too many emails? Text the word: "willowrose" to 31996 to sign up to Willow's VIP text List to get a text alert with news about New Releases, Giveaways, Bargains and Free books from Willow.

Follow Willow Rose on BookBub:
https://www.bookbub.com/authors/willow-rose

Connect with Willow online:
https://www.amazon.com/Willow-Rose/e/B004X2WHBQ
https://www.facebook.com/willowredrose/
https://twitter.com/madamwillowrose
http://www.goodreads.com/author/show/4804769.Willow_Rose
Http://www.willow-rose.net
madamewillowrose@gmail.com

Prologue

COCOA BEACH 1995

THEY'RE NOT GOING to let her go. She knows they won't. Holly is terrified as she runs through the park. The sound of the waves is behind her. A once so calming sound now brings utter terror to her. She is wet. Her shirt is dripping, her shoes making a slobbering sound as she runs across the parking lot towards the playground.

Run, run! Don't look back. Don't stop or they'll get you!

She can hear their voices behind her. It's hard to run when your feet are tied together. They're faster than she is, even though they are just walking.

"Oh, Holly," one of them yells. "Hoooollllyyy!"

Holly pants, trying to push herself forward. She wants desperately to move faster, but the rope tied around her feet blocks them and she falls flat on her face onto the asphalt. Holly screams loudly as her nose scratches across the ground.

Get up! Get up and run. You can't let them get you.

She can hear them laughing behind her.

You can make it, Holly. Just get to A1A right in front of you. Only about a hundred feet left. There are cars on the road. They'll see you. Someone will see you and help you.

She tries to scream, but she has no air in her lungs. She is exhausted from swimming with her legs tied together. Luckily, her arms got free when she jumped in the water. They have pulled off her pants. Cut them open with a knife and pulled them off. Before they stabbed her in the shoulder. It hurts when she runs. Blood has soaked her white shirt. She is naked from the stomach down, except for her shoes and socks. Holly is in so much pain and can hardly move. Yet, she fights to get closer to the road.

A car drives by. Then another one. She can see them in the distance, yet her vision is getting foggier. She can't lose consciousness now.

You've got to keep fighting. You've got to get out of here! Don't give up, Holly. Whatever you do, just don't give up.

Their footsteps are approaching from behind. Holly is groaning and fighting to get a few more steps in.

So close now. So close.

"Hurry up," she hears them yell. "She's getting away!"

Holly is so close now she can smell the cars' exhaust. All she needs to do is get onto the road, then stop a car. That's all she needs to do to get out of there alive. And she is so close now.

"Stop her, goddammit," a voice yells.

Holly fights to run. She moves her feet faster than she feels is humanly possible. She is getting there. She is getting there. She can hear them start to run now. They are yelling to each other.

"Shoot her, dammit."

Holly gasps, thinking about the spear gun. She's the one who taught them how to shoot it. She knows they won't hesitate to use it to stop her. She knows how they think. She knows this is what they do. She knows this is a kick for them, a drug.

She knows, because she is one of them.

"Stop the bitch!" someone yells, and she hears the sound of the gun going off. She knows this sound so well, having been spearfishing all her life and practiced using the gun on land with her father. He taught her everything about spearfishing, starting when she was no more than four years old. He even taught her to hold her breath underwater for a very long time.

"Scuba diving is for tourists. Real fishers free dive," she hears his voice say, the second the spear whistles through the air.

It hits Holly in the leg and she tumbles to the ground. Holly falls to the pavement next to A1A with a scream. She hears giggles and voices behind her. But she can also hear something else. While she drags herself across the pavement, she can hear the sound of sirens.

"Shit!" the voices behind her say.

"We gotta get out of here."

"RUN!"

1

September 2015

Blake Mills is enjoying his coffee at Starbucks. He enjoys it especially today. He is sipping it while looking at his own painting that they have just put up on display inside the shop. He has been trying to convince the owner of the local Starbucks in Cocoa Beach for ages to put up some of his art on display, and finally Ray agreed to let him hang up one of his turtle paintings. Just for a short period, to see how it goes.

It is Blake's personal favorite painting and he hopes it will attract some business his way. As a small artist in a small town, it is hard to make a living, even though Blake offers paintings by order, so anyone can get one any way they want it and can be sure it will fit their house or condo. It isn't exactly the way the life of an artist is supposed to be, but it is the only way to do it if he wants to eat.

Blake decides to make it a day of celebration and buys an extra coffee and a piece of cake to eat as well. He takes a bite and enjoys the taste.

"Looking good," a voice says behind him. He turns in his chair and looks into the eyes of Olivia.

Olivia Hartman. The love of his life.

Blake smiles to himself. "You came," he whispers and looks

around. Being married, Olivia has to be careful whom she is seen with in this town.

"Can I sit?" she asks, holding her own coffee in her hand.

Blake pulls out a chair for her and she sits next to him. Blake feels a big thrill run through his body. He loves being with Olivia and has never had the pleasure of doing so in public. They usually meet up at his studio and have sex between his paintings on the floor or up against the wall. He has never been to her place on Patrick Air Force Base, where she lives with her husband, a general in the army. Blake is terrified of him and a little of her as well, but that is part of what makes it so wonderfully exciting. At the age of twenty-three, Blake isn't ready to settle down with anyone, and he isn't sure he is ever going to be. It isn't his style. He likes the carefree life, and being an artist he can't exactly provide for a family anyway. Having children will only force him to forget his dreams and get a *real job.* It would no doubt please his father, but Blake doesn't want a real job. He doesn't want the house on the water or the two to three children. He isn't cut out for it, and his many girlfriends in the past never understood that. All of them thought they could change him, that they were the one who could make him realize that he wanted it all. But he really didn't. And he still doesn't.

"It looks really great," Olivia says and sips her coffee. She is wearing multiple finger rings and bracelets, as always. She is delicate, yet strong. Used to be a fighter pilot in the army. Blake thought that was so cool. Today, she no longer works, not since she married the general.

She and Blake had met at the Officer's Club across the street from the base. He was there with a girl he had met at Grills in Cape Canaveral, who worked on base doing some contracting or something boring like that; she had invited him to a party. It was by far the most boring affair until he met Olivia on the porch standing with a beer in her hand overlooking the Atlantic Ocean. She was slightly tipsy and they exchanged pleasantries for a few minutes before she turned and looked at him with that mischievous smile of hers. Then she asked him if he wanted to have some fun.

"Always," he replied.

They walked to the beach and into the dunes, where they enjoyed the best sex of Blake's life.

Now it has become a drug to him. He needs his fix. He needs her.

"Congrats," she says.

"Thanks. Now I just hope someone will grab one of the business cards I've put on the counter and call me to order a painting. I could use the money. I only had one order last month."

"They will," she says, laughing. "Don't you worry about that." She leans over and whispers through those pouty lips of hers. "Now let's go back to your place and celebrate."

"Is that an order?" he asks, laughing.

"Is that an order, *ma'am*," she corrects him. "And, yes, it is."

2

September 2015

Being with Olivia is exhilarating. It fills him with the most wonderful sensation in his body because Blake has never met anyone like her, who can make him crazy for her. Not like this. But at the same time, it is also absolutely petrifying because she is married to General Hartman, who will have Blake killed if he ever finds out. There is no doubt about it in Blake's mind.

Yet, he keeps sleeping with her. Even though he keeps telling himself it is a bad idea, that he has to stop, that it is only a matter of time before he will get himself in some deep shit trouble. Blake knows it is bad to be with her. He knows it will get him in trouble eventually, but still, he can't help himself. He has to have her. He has to taste her again and again. No matter the cost.

Their lips meet inside Blake's studio as soon as they walk in. Blake closes his eyes and drinks from her. He doesn't care that the door behind him is left open. Nothing else matters right now.

"I thought you couldn't get out today," he says, panting, when her lips leave his. "Isn't the general on base?"

"He is," she mumbles between more kisses.

It has been two weeks since they were together last. Two weeks of constantly dreaming and longing for her. They communicate via

Snapchat. It is untraceable, as far as Blake knows. Blake wrote a message to her a few days ago, telling her about the painting being put up in Starbucks, knowing that she probably couldn't come and see it. He even sent a picture of the painting. It is also her favorite. She messaged him back a photo of her sad face telling him she didn't think she could get out, since her husband was home. Usually, she only dares to meet with Blake when her husband is travelling. Even then, they have to be extremely careful. General Hartman has many friends in Cocoa Beach and his soldiers are seen everywhere.

"I told him I was seeing a friend today. It's not like it's a lie. I don't care anymore if he finds out about us. I'm sick of being just the general's wife. I want a life of my own."

Blake takes off his T-shirt and her hands land on his chest. He rips off her shirt and several buttons fall to the floor. She closes her eyes and moans at his touches. His hands cup her breasts and soon her bra lands on the wooden floor. He grabs her hair and pulls her head back while kissing her neck. His heart is pumping in his chest just from the smell of her skin.

"You can't," he whispers between breaths. "You can't let him know about us. He'll kill the both of us."

Olivia lets out a gasp as Blake reaches up under her skirt and places a hand in her panties, and then rips them off. He pushes her up against a table, then lifts her up, leans over her naked torso and puts his mouth to her breasts. He closes his eyes and takes in her smell, drinking the juices of her body, then pulls his shorts down and gently slides inside of her with a deep moan. She puts her legs around his neck, partly strangling him when she comes in pulsing movements back and forth, her body arching.

"Oh, Blake…oh, Blake …"

The sensation is burning inside of him and he is ready to explode. Olivia is moaning and moving rapidly. His movements are urgent now, the intensity building. He is about to burst, when suddenly she screams loudly and pushes him away. Blake falls to the floor with a thud.

"What the…?"

Blake soon realizes why Olivia is screaming and feels the blood rush from his face. A set of eyes is staring down at him.

The eyes of Detective Chris Fisher.

"Blake Mills, you're under arrest," the voice belonging to the eyes says.

3

September 2015

"I'M SORRY, Mary, there's nothing I can do."

I stare at my boss, Chief Editor, Markus Fergusson. He is leaning back in his leather chair in his office on the twenty-eighth floor of the Times-Tower on the west side of mid-town. Behind him, the view is spectacular, but I hardly notice anymore. After five years working there, you simply stop being baffled. However, I am actually baffled at this moment. But not because of the view. Because of what is being said.

"So, you're firing me, is that it?" I ask, while my blood is boiling in my veins. What the hell is this?

"We're letting you go, yes."

"You can't do that, Markus, come on. Just because of this?"

He leans over his desk and gives me that look that I have come to know so well in my five years as a reporter for *The New York Times*.

"Yes."

"I don't get it," I say. "I'm being fired for writing the paper's most read article in the past five years?"

Markus sighs. "Don't put up a fight, will you? Just accept it. You violated the rules, sweetheart."

Don't you sweetheart me, you pig!

"I don't make the rules, Mary. The big guys upstairs make the decisions and it says here that we have to let you go for *violating the normal editing process.*"

I squint my eyes. I can't believe this. "I did what?"

"You printed the story without having a second set of eyes on it first. The article offended some people, and, well…"

He pauses. I scoff. He is such a sell-out. Just because my article didn't sit well with some people, some influential people, he is letting me go? They want to fire me for some rule bullshit?

"Brian saw it," I say. "He read it and approved it."

"The rules say *two* editors," he says. "On a story like this, this controversial, you need two editors to approve it, not just one."

"That's BS and you know it, goddammit, Markus. I never even heard about this rule. What about Brian?"

"We're letting him go as well."

"You can't do that! The man just had another kid."

Markus shrugs. "That's not really my problem, is it? Brian knew better. He's been with us for fifteen years."

"It was late, Markus. We had less than five minutes to deadline. There was no time to get another approval. If we'd waited for another editor, the story wouldn't have run, and you wouldn't have sold a record number of newspapers that day. The article went viral online. All over the world. Everyone was talking about it. And this is how you thank me?"

I rise from the chair and grab my leather jacket. "Well, suit yourself. It's your loss. I don't need you or this paper."

I leave, slamming the door, but it doesn't make me feel as good as I thought it would. I pack my things in that little brown box that they always do in the movies and grab it under my arm before I leave in the elevator. On the bottom floor, I hand in my ID card to the guard in the lobby and Johnson looks at me with his mouth turned downwards.

"We'll miss you, Miss Mary," he says.

"I'll miss you too, Johnson," I say, and walk out the glass doors, into the streets of New York without a clue as to what I am going to do. Living in Manhattan isn't cheap. Living in Manhattan with a nine-year old son, as a single mom isn't cheap at all. The cost for a private school alone is over the roof.

I whistle for a cab, and before I finally get one, it starts to rain, and I get soaked. I have him drive me back to my apartment and I let myself inside. Snowflake, my white Goldendoodle is waiting on the other side of the door, jumping me when I enter. He licks me in my face and whimpers from having missed me since I left just this morning. I sit down on my knees and pet him till he calms down. I can't help smiling when I am with him. I can't feel sad for long when he's around. It's simply not possible. He looks at me with those deep brown eyes.

"We'll be alright, won't we, Snowflake? I'm sure we will. We don't need them, no we don't."

4

September 2015

"Do you come here often?"

Liz Hester stares at the man who has approached her in the bar at Lou's Blues in Indialantic. It is Friday night and she was bored at the base, so she and her friends decided to go out and get a beer.

"You're kidding me, right?"

The guy smiles. He is a surfer-type with long greasy hair under his cap, a nice tan, and not too much between the ears. The kind of guy who opens each sentence with *dude,* even when speaking to a girl.

"It was the best I could come up with."

"You do realize that I am thirty-eight and you're at least fifteen years younger, right?"

Kim comes up behind her. She is wearing her blue ASU—army service uniform—like Liz. They are both decorated with several medals. Liz's includes the Purple Heart, given to her when she was shot during her service in Afghanistan. Took a bullet straight to her shoulder. The best part was, she took it for one of her friends. She took it for Britney, who is also with them this night, hanging out with some guy further down the bar. They are friends through thick and thin. Will lay down their lives for one another.

Liz's eyes meet those of Jamie's across the bar. She smiles and nods in the direction of the guy that Liz is talking to. Liz smiles and nods too. There is no need for them to speak; they know what she is saying.

He's the one.

"So, tell me, what's your name?" Liz asks the guy. She is all of a sudden flirtatious, smiling and touching his arm gently. Kim giggles behind her, but the guy doesn't notice.

"I'm Billy. My friends call me Billy the Kid."

"Well, you are just a kid, aren't you?" she says, purring like a cat, leaning in over the bar.

The guy lifts his cap a little, then puts it back on. "You sure are a lot of woman."

Liz knows his type. He is one of those who gets aroused just by looking at a woman in uniform. She has met her share of those types. They are a lot of fun to play with.

"Well, maybe I can make a man of you," she whispers, leaning very close to his face.

The guy laughs goofily. "You sure can," he says and gives her an elevator look. "I sure wouldn't mind that. I got an anaconda in my pants you can ride if you like."

Liz laughs lightly, and then looks at Jamie again, letting her know he has taken the bait.

"Well, why don't you—Billy the Kid—meet me outside in the parking lot in say—five minutes?"

Billy laughs again. "Dude! Whoa, sure!"

Billy taps the bar counter twice, not knowing exactly what to do with himself, then lifts his cap once again and wipes sweat off his forehead. He has nice eyes, Liz thinks, and he is quite handsome.

As stupid as they get, though.

He leaves her, shooting a finger-gun at her and winking at the same time. The girls approach Liz, moving like cats sliding across the floor. Liz finishes her drink while the four of them stick their heads together.

"Ready for some fun?" she asks.

They don't say anything. They don't have to.

5

September 2015

SHE WAITS for him by the car. Smoking a cigarette, she leans against it, blowing out smoke when she spots him come out of the bar and walk towards her. Seeing the goofy grin on his face makes her smile even wider.

"Hey there, baby," Billy says and walks up to her. "I have to say, I wasn't sure you would even be here. A nice lady like you with a guy like me? You're a wild cat, aren't you?"

Liz chuckles and blows smoke in his face. "I sure am."

Billy the Kid moves his body in anticipation. His crotch can't keep still. He is already hard.

What a sucker.

He looks around with a sniffle. "So, where do you want to go? To the beach? Or do you…wanna do it right here…?" he places a hand next to her on the car. "Up against this baby, huh?"

Liz laughs again, then leans closer to him till her mouth is on his ear. "You're just full of yourself, aren't you?"

"What?" he asks with another goofy grin.

"Did you really think you were going to get lucky with me? With this?" She says and points up and down her body.

The grin is wiped off his face. Finally.

"What is this?" he asks, his face in a frown. "Were you just leading me on? What a cunt!" He spits out the last word. He probably means it as an insult, but Liz just smiles from ear to ear as her friends slowly approach from all sides, surrounding Billy. When he realizes, he tries to back out, but walks into Jamie and steps on her black shoes.

"Hey, those are brand new! Dammit!"

Jamie pushes him in the back forcefully and he is now in the hands of Britney. Britney is smaller than the others, but by far the strongest. She clenches her fist and slams it into his face. The blow breaks his nose on the spot and he falls backwards to the asphalt, blood running from it.

"What the…what…who are you?" Billy asks, disoriented, looking from woman to woman.

"We like to call ourselves the Fast and the Furious," Liz says.

"Yeah, cause I'm fast," Kim says and kicks Billy in the crotch. He lets out a loud moan in pain.

The sound is almost arousing to Liz.

"And I'm furious," she says, grabbing him by the hair and pulling his head back. She looks him in the eyes. She loves watching them squirm, the little suckers. Just like she loved it back in Afghan when she interrogated the *Haji*.

Haji is the name they call anyone of Arab decent, or even of a brownish skin tone. She remembers vividly the first time they brought one in. It was the day after she had lost a good friend to an IED, a roadside bomb that detonated and killed everyone in the truck in front of her. They searched for those suckers all night, and finally, the next morning they brought in three. Boy, she kicked that sucker till he could no longer move. Hell, they all did it. All of them let out their frustrations. Losing three good soldiers like that made them furious. Liz was still furious. Well, to be frank, she has been furious all of her life.

Everybody around her knows that.

Liz laughs when she hears Billy's whimper, then uses two fingers to poke his eyes forcefully. Billy screams.

"My eyes, my eyes!"

Liz lets go of his hair and looks at her girls. They are all about to burst in anticipation. She opens the door to the car, where Jamie has placed a couple of bottles of vodka to keep them going all night. She lets out a loud howl like a wolf, the girls chiming in, then lifts Billy the Kid up and throws him in the back of the Jeep.

6

February 1977

When Penelope and Peter get married, she is already showing. It is no longer a secret to the people at the wedding, even though her mother does all she can to disguise it by buying a big dress. By the time of the wedding, Penelope has grown into it and her stomach fills it out completely. Peter's mother tells her she looks radiant and gorgeous, but Penelope's mother hates that people will talk about marriage as a necessity or *the right thing to do,* and their daughter is only getting married because she is pregnant. Because she has to.

But that is just the way it is, and no one cares less about what people think than Penelope and Peter. They are happy and looking forward to becoming parents more than anything.

Soon after the wedding, the bank approves a loan for them and they buy their dream house in Cocoa Beach. As a young lawyer who has just been made partner, Peter is doing well, and even though it is one of the most expensive locations in Cocoa Beach, Penelope doesn't have to work anymore. She quits her job as a secretary and wants to focus on her family and later charity work. It is the kind of life they have both dreamed of, and no one is more thrilled to see it come true than Penelope.

"I can't wait to become a family," she says, when Peter is done fixing up the nursery and shows it to her.

Seeing how beautiful he has decorated it makes her cry, and she holds a hand to her ready-to-burst stomach. Only two more weeks till she will hold her baby. Only two more weeks.

She can hardly wait.

Peter is going to be a wonderful father; she just knows he will. He has such a kind and gentle personality. She has done right in choosing him. She knows she has. This is going to be a perfect little family. Penelope already knows she wants lots of children. At least two, maximum four. She herself comes from a family of four children. Four girls, to be exact. There was a brother, but he died at an early age after a long illness. Being the oldest, Penelope took care of him, and it was devastating for her when he passed away. It is a sorrow she can never get rid of, and often she blames herself for not being able to cure him. Later in life, she played with the idea of becoming a doctor, but she never had the grades for it.

Peter, on the other hand, is an only child. His mother has spoiled his socks off all of his life. She still does every now and then. And she still treats him like a child sometimes. It makes Penelope laugh out loud when she spit-washes him or corrects his tie. But she is nice, Peter's mom. She has always loved Penelope, and there is nothing bad to be said about her.

It was always the plan that Peter would follow in his father's footsteps and go to law school, and so he did. He met Penelope right after he passed the bar and started working at the small law firm in Rockledge where she was a secretary. Soon he moved on to a bigger firm and now he had made partner.

Peter's career exploded within a few years, and now he is talking about going into real estate as well. He has so many plans for their future, and she knows he will always take care of them. She is never going to want for anything.

Two weeks later, her water breaks. Penelope is standing in the kitchen admiring the new tiles they have put in, with a coffee cup in her hand. The water soaks her dress and the floor beneath her.

Penelope gasps and reaches for the phone. She calls Peter at the office.

"This is it," she says, with a mixture of excitement and fright in her voice. "Our baby is coming, Peter. Our baby is coming!"

"I…I'll be right there."

Peter stumbles over himself on his way out of the office and the secretary has to yell at him to come back because he has forgotten his car keys.

Peter rushes her to the hospital, where the contractions soon take over and after a tough struggle and fourteen hours of labor, she is finally holding her baby girl in her arms.

"Look at her, Peter," she says through tears. "I…I simply can't stop looking at her. I am so happy, Peter. You made me so happy, thank you. Thank you so much."

7

September 2015

I SPEND the evening feeling sorry for myself. I cook chicken in green curry, my favorite dish these days, and sulk in front of the TV watching back-to-back episodes of *Friends* with Snowflake and my son Salter next to me.

"They can't fire you!" Salter exclaimed, when I told him as soon as he got home from school. He knew something was wrong as soon as he saw that I'd made hot cocoa for the both of us and put marshmallows in it.

That is kind of my thing. Whenever I have bad news, I prepare hot cocoa with marshmallows. I have also baked cookies. That is another diversion of mine. Nothing keeps me as distracted as baking or cooking.

"You're the best damn reporter they have!"

"I am, but there's no need to curse," I say.

I enjoy spending the rest of the evening with the loves of my life, both of them, and decide to not wonder about my future until the next day. Salter is so loving and caring towards me and keeps asking me if there is anything he can do for me, to make me feel better.

"Just stay here in my arms," I say and pull him closer.

He has reached the age where he still enjoys my affectionate hugs and holding him close, but lately he has begun to find them annoying from time to time, especially when it is in front of his friends.

I named him Salter because I have been a surfer all of my life, growing up in Cocoa Beach, and so is his dad. Salter means *derived from salt*. We believed he was born of our love for the ocean. How foolish and young we were back then.

It feels like a lifetime ago.

"So, what do we do now?" Salter finally asks when the episode where Phoebe fights with a fire alarm is over.

I take in a deep breath. I know he has to wonder. I do too, but I try not to think about it. Mostly to make sure he isn't affected by it.

"I mean, now that you don't have a job?" he continues. "Can we still live in this apartment?"

"I have to be honest with you, kiddo," I say. "I don't know. I don't know what is going to happen. I am not sure any newspaper will have me after this. I pissed off some pretty influential people."

"That's stupid," he says. "They're all stupid. Your article had more views than anyone's."

"I know, but that isn't always enough, buddy."

I sigh, hoping I don't have to go into details, when suddenly my phone rings. I let go of Salter and lean over to pick it up from the coffee table. My heart drops when I see the name on the display.

It's my dad.

"It's Mary," I say, my heart throbbing in my throat. I haven't spoken to my dad in at least a year. He never calls me.

"Mary." His voice is heavy. Something is definitely going on.

"What's wrong, Dad? Are you sick?"

"No. It's not me. It's your brother."

I swallow hard. My brother is the only family member I still have regular contact with. I love the little bastard, even if he is fifteen years younger than me.

"Blake? What's wrong with him?"

"It's bad, Mary. He's been arrested."

Arrested?!?

"What? Why…for what…what's going on, Dad?"

My father sighs from the other end of the line. "For murder. He's been arrested for murder."

8

September 2015

They take him for a ride. Billy the Kid is crying in the back when the girls take him first to the Super Wal-Mart in Merritt Island that is open 24/7. Placing a knife to his back, they walk through the store and pull bottles of wine, gin, and tequila from the shelves. They even find a fishing pole that they think could be fun to buy. Along with some chips Jamie wants, and sugarcoated donuts. Kim has a craving for cheesecake while Britney wants chocolate. And loads of it. Liz holds the knife in Billy's back and asks them to throw in some Choco-mint ice cream for her. Then she grabs a bottle of drain cleaner. They tell Billy to take out his wallet and pay for everything.

"If you as much as whimper, I will split you open," Liz whispers, as they come closer to the cashier. "I'll make it look like you attacked me. Who do you think they'll believe, huh? A surfer dude or a decorated war-veteran? A female one on top of it."

After he pays, they open a bottle of gin and take turns drinking from it while they drive, screaming and cheering, back to Cocoa Beach where they park in front of Ron Jon's surf-shop, which is also open 24/7. Yelling and visibly intoxicated, they storm inside with

Billy and take the elevator to the second floor. They run through the aisles of bikinis and pull down one after another.

"I always wanted a yellow one," Kim yells.

"I'm going red this time," Britney says. "Wouldn't this look cute on me?"

"Grab me one of the striped ones over there," Liz says. "Size medium."

Kim giggles cheerfully then grabs one. They don't bother to try them on. There is no time for that. Kim also grabs a couple of nice shirts from Billabong, and then some shorts from Roxy for Liz.

"Oh," Britney says and points at the surfboards on the other side of the store. She looks to the others. "I always wanted a surfboard!"

"Me too," Jamie exclaims. "Let's find one!"

"I…I can't afford that," Billy whimpers. "Aren't they like four hundred dollars?"

"This one is five hundred dollars," Jamie says, and looks at a seven-foot fun-shape. "Doesn't it look GREAT on me?"

"Adorable," Liz says and laughs.

"I can't afford this," Billy whimpers over and over when they pull the boards out.

"Grab one for me too," Liz says, ignoring his complaints. She presses the knife into his back, puts her arm around his neck, then kisses his cheek, making it look like they are a couple.

"You'll have to," she whispers. "I'll make a scene. Make it look like you tried to rape me."

"Okay, okay," he says with a moan. "Just don't hurt me, okay? Just let me go after this, alright?"

She doesn't make any promises. That's not how Liz rolls.

They charge everything to one of Billy's credit cards, then run out of the store carrying surfboards and plastic bags with bikinis, hollering and laughing. They throw everything in the car and strap the boards onto the roof before driving to the International Palms Resort a few blocks further down A1A, where they book a suite for all of them, charging it on his credit card again.

"Please don't make me pay for any more," he says in the elevator.

They ignore his complaints, and then storm into the room. It is huge and has great views of the ocean. Liz lets go of Billy, then throws him on the white couch. Jamie grabs one of the bottles of Vodka and places it to her lips. She drinks it like it is water. Liz laughs and pulls the bottle from Jamie's hand. She places it to her lips and closes her eyes while it burns its way down her throat.

"Hey, leave some for the rest of us," Kim yells, and grabs the bottle out of Liz's hand.

The vodka spills on Liz's white shirt. Liz looks angrily at Kim. "What the hell…?"

Kim laughs, then drinks from the bottle. Liz clenches her fist before she slams it into Kim's face as soon as she lets go of the bottle again. Kim falls backwards, then stares, confused, at Liz.

"What…what happened?" she asks.

Liz grabs the bottle out of her hand forcefully. Jamie and Britney remain quiet. They dare not make a sound. The feeling of power intoxicates Liz. Liz looks at Billy the Kid, who is squirming on the couch while staring at them with terror in his eyes.

Liz approaches him. He squirms again. Liz leans over and kisses him forcefully. He tries to push her away, but two of the other girls grab his arms and hold him down while Liz has her way with him. She pulls off his pants and then she laughs.

"Is that all? Is that the anaconda you wanted me to ride?"

"Please, just let me go," Billy says, crying in humiliation "I've done everything you wanted me to. I've paid for everything. Please, just let me go."

"Now he wants to leave. You finally have the chance to get laid and now you want to leave? No no, Billy, tsk tsk. That's not what a woman wants to hear, is it, girls?"

The three others shake their heads.

Liz puts her hand on his penis and starts to rub. Soon, his anaconda grows sizably and he starts moaning.

"Please…please…"

She puts her lips on it and makes him hard, then sits on top of him and rides him. The other girls are screaming with joy. Liz rides him forcefully, and soon they both come with deep moans.

Liz smiles when Billy arches in spasms and she feels his semen inside of her, then leans over and kisses his forehead.

"If you tell the police what we did tonight, I'll tell them you raped me," she whispers. "That you were holding a gun to my head and you raped me. Boy, I do believe I even have three witnesses. Three VERY reliable witnesses."

Liz finishes with a laugh, then climbs off Billy. "Come on girls," she says. "Let's get *really* drunk."

She grabs a bottle and drinks from it. It is strange how it feels like she can't get drunk anymore. Not like *really* drunk. Not like in the old days. Liz likes being really drunk. It makes her forget. It is the only thing that can make her forget.

The girls throw themselves at the chips and candy they bought at Wal-Mart. Liz looks at them with contempt. They have no self-control, these girls. Kim buries her hands in the cheesecake and eats it, licking her fingers. Jamie stuffs her face with donuts and has sugar all over her mouth.

Liz sighs.

"You want some ice cream?" Jamie asks.

"I don't want some stupid ice cream," Liz says, mocking Jamie. "I'm bored." She looks at Billy, who doesn't dare to move on the couch. "He bores me."

"What do you want to do?" Kim asks.

"Yeah, do you want to have another go?" Jamie asks.

Liz throws the bottle in her hand against the wall. It breaks and leaves a huge mark that Billy is probably going to pay for. Liz growls and kicks the ice cream bucket.

"I'm sick of the prick. He's no fun to play with."

Liz grabs the drain cleaner and walks towards Billy with firm steps. The girls all look at her. Serious eyes follow her every step. The atmosphere in the room immediately changes. No one is laughing anymore. No one is eating.

"What are you doing with that, babe?" Jamie asks.

"Don't do it," Kim yells.

But Liz doesn't listen. She opens the lid and grabs Billy's jaw. She forces it open. Billy is squirming too much and she can't do it on her own.

"Help me, dammit," she yells.

The girls hesitate, but don't dare not to do as they're told. Who knows what Liz might do next? Who will be next? They have seen too much to be able to say no.

Britney is first to grab Billy's right arm and hold it down. Jamie then grabs the left one. Kim holds his head still, while Liz pours the liquid drain cleaner into his mouth and down his throat. The three girls stare at her while she empties the bottle completely. They dare not even to speak. Billy's screams pierce through their bones. No one dares to move.

Liz throws the empty bottle on the ground, then looks at her friends. "Let's get out of here," she yells.

Her words are almost drowned out by Billy's scream.

9

September 2015

I LAND at Orlando airport around noon the next day. Salter and Snowflake are both with me. We have packed two big suitcases, not knowing how long we are going to stay. My dad tried to convince me there is no need for me to come down, but I didn't listen. I need to be there. I need to help my brother.

"What about my school?" Salter says, as we walk to the rental car.

"I called them and told them it's a family emergency," I say. "They told me you have to be back in ten days or your spot goes to someone else. They mean business, that school."

It is one of the best schools in New York and one of the most expensive ones too. I haven't decided if I like it or not. The uniforms I can do without, but that kind of comes with the territory. It is mostly the way they shape them into small soldiers there, always running all these tests, making them stand straight, and never having time to play. It is all Salter knows, so to him, it is fine. But there is something about the school that I don't like. I find it hard to enjoy that my child is going to a school like this. Joey and I are both surfers and free spirits. This school is not us at all. Yet, we signed Salter up for it as soon as we moved to New York.

We moved because of my job, but unfortunately it turned out to be the end of our little family. Joey had nothing to do up there, since no one would hire him, and soon we grew apart. Staying at home and not having anything to do wore on him. He never felt like he accomplished anything or that he was supporting his family, and that is important to him. He started to feel lonely and sought comfort in the arms of a young girl who worked at a small coffee house on our street. He would go there every day to drink his coffee and write. He wants to be an author and has written several books, but no publisher will touch them. I think they are beautiful and inspiring, but I guess I am biased. I love Joey. I still do. But when he told me he had slept with the girl at the coffee house several times a week for at least a year, I threw him out. Well, not right away. First, I gave him a second chance and we tried to make it work for a couple of weeks, for Salter's sake, but I couldn't stand thinking about it all day, whether he'd been with her again. It tore me apart. I have never been a jealous person, but this I couldn't handle. I tried hard to, but realized I wasn't as forgiving as I thought I could be. I didn't have it in me and I felt like I could never trust him again. So, I finally asked him to move out.

"Where do you want me to go?" he asked.

I shrugged. "Go live with that coffee house girl. I don't know."

He decided to go back to Cocoa Beach where we grew up together. That was four months ago now. I miss him every day. But I can't forget what he did. What hurts the most is the betrayal, the deceit. I don't know how to move past it. I don't know if I ever can.

He calls as often as he can and talks to Salter. It's been hard on our son. He loves his dad and needs him in his life, needs a male role model. Salter went to visit him during summer break, and it is the plan that he will be going down for Thanksgiving as well.

"You think I can call Dad now?" Salter asks, as soon as we are in the car and hit the beach line.

I sigh. It is such a big blow to Salter that his dad moved this far away. I know he is excited to see him again. I hate to see that look in his eyes. He doesn't know his dad cheated on me. He only knows that he left, and that is enough. I know he feels guilt and questions if he had something to do with it. I try to tell him it wasn't because of him, that sometimes grown-ups grow apart, that they can't make it work anymore. I am not sure he is convinced.

"Sure," I say.

Salter smiles and grabs my phone and finds his dad's number. While driving towards the beach and listening to him talk to his father, I feel a chill go through my body. I watch the big signs for Ron Jon's surf shop go by and realize my hands are shivering. Everything about this place gives me the creeps. I haven't been back in almost twenty years. Not since I left for college.

Blake was three years old back then. Joey and I have lived all over since. He worked with whatever he could get his hands on, mostly as a carpenter. I spent five years working for CNN in Atlanta, which became my biggest career jump. Before that I held a position with *USA Today* in Virginia. I started my career as a journalist at *Miami Herald* and we lived for a while in Ft. Lauderdale before my job took us out of the state, something I had dreamed of as long as I could remember. To get away.

Salter puts the phone down.

"So, what did he have to say?" I ask, as we approach the bridges that will take us to the Barrier Islands. In the distance, I can see the cruise ships. A sign tells me I can go on a casino cruise for free. Gosh, how I hate this place...with all its tourists and tiki bars.

"He can't wait to see me," Salter says.

I turn onto A1A, where all the condominiums and hotels are lined up like pearls on a string.

"At least you'll have fun seeing your dad," I say, while wondering what is waiting for me once I arrive at my childhood home. What is it going to be like to see my dad again? What about Blake? I haven't seen him in several years. He visited me in New York five years ago, but other than that, we have mainly spoken over the phone or on Facebook. We aren't very close, but he is still the only one in my family I like. He is all the family I have, and I will do anything to help him out.

Anything.

10

April 1977

Penelope and Peter take the baby home to their new house a few days after the birth. In the months to follow, they try everything they can to become a family. But the sleep deprivation is hard on them. Especially on Penelope. She gets up four or sometimes five times a night to breastfeed, and all day long she feels sick from the lack of sleep.

Only a few weeks after the baby arrived Peter gets a new case. It is a big deal, he explains to Penelope, one of those cases that can make or break a career. And Peter is determined to make it.

But that means long days at the office, and Penelope is soon alone for many hours at the house. Sometimes, he even stays away the entire night just to work, and when he finally comes home, he is too worn out to even speak to his wife.

Penelope, on the other hand, longs to speak with an adult and can hardly stop talking to him and asking him questions.

"How was your day? What's the latest on the case? Do you think you'll be done in time?"

Peter answers with a growl and tries to avoid her. As soon as he comes home, he storms to the restroom and stays in there for at least an hour, reading a magazine or the newspaper just to get a little peace and quiet.

The first weeks, Penelope waits outside the door and attacks him with more questions or demands as soon as he pokes his head out again.

"The garage door is acting up again. Could you fix it or call someone who could? We need to start thinking about preschool. I've looked over a few of them, but I need your help to choose the right one. What do you think? I was thinking about painting the living room another color. A light blue, maybe?"

One day he comes home at nine in the evening after a very stressful day and all he dreams of is throwing himself on the couch, putting his feet up, and reading the newspaper, enjoying a nice quiet evening. When he enters the house, Penelope comes down from upstairs holding the baby in her arms with a deep sigh. The look in her eyes is of complete desperation.

"Where have you been?"

He sighs and closes the front door behind him. He doesn't have the energy to explain to her what's been going on at the office.

"A long story," he says, and puts his briefcase down.

The baby wails. Penelope looks at her with concern. "No. No. Not again. Please don't start again." She looks at Peter. "She's been like this all day, Peter. I don't know what to do. I don't know anymore. I just really, really need time…just an hour of sleep. I'm so tired."

Peter looks at her. Is she kidding him?

"We're both tired," he says.

"No. No. It's more than that, Peter. She's driving me nuts. It's like torture. I can't eat. I can't think. I can't…"

"Could you shut up for just one second?"

Penelope stares at her husband. "Excuse me?"

"Do you have ANY idea what kind of day I've had? Do you have ANY idea what I am going through these days? I think you can manage a little crying baby, all right? I would give anything to be in your shoes and not have to deal with this case."

Peter snorts, then walks past her into the living room, where he closes the door. Penelope has a lump in her throat. She feels so helpless. So alone and so so incredibly tired. She looks at the baby, who is still crying.

"Why are you crying little baby, huh? Why are you crying so much?"

She puts her lips on the baby's forehead to kiss her, but the kiss makes her realize something. Something she should have noticed a long time ago. The baby isn't just fussing.

She is burning up with a fever.

11

September 2015

I DRIVE into the driveway at 701 S Atlantic Avenue and park in front of the garage. I turn off the engine with a deep sigh. Everything looks the same from the outside. Same brown garage doors, even though the painting needs to be redone, same lawn in front and same old palm tree, even though it is a lot taller. The bushes to the right have been removed and new flowers have been planted. I know nothing about plants or flowers, but these are orange and look stunning.

"How come we have never visited granddad before?" my son asks.

I look at him. I knew the question had to come at some point. But I am not ready to provide the answer.

"Let's go in," I say.

We grab our suitcases and drag them across the bricks towards the entrance to my dad's beach house, my childhood home. I can smell the ocean from behind the house. I close my eyes and breathe it in. So many memories, good and bad, are combined with this smell. I love the ocean. I still do. Joey and I both love it and spent so many hours surfing together while growing up.

But there is also all the bad stuff. The stuff I haven't talked about since I left town for college at age eighteen. The stuff I had hoped I never would have to talk about again. Ever.

Just before we reach the front door, I turn my head and look down at 7th Street behind me, on the other side of Atlantic Avenue or A1A as we call it. 7th street continues all the way down to the Intracoastal Waters, or Banana River, and in most of those houses had lived kids. I had known all of them. We used to be a tight bunch of seven children. All of us went to Roosevelt Elementary and later Cocoa Beach High School. We used to bicycle to school together and after school we would rush back to check out the surf from the crosswalk on 7th, then grab our boards if the waves were good and surf for hours. We used to call ourselves *The 7th Street Crew*. I was the rich kid among them, with the biggest house on the ocean with a pool and guesthouse. But I was never the happiest.

"Mary!"

The face in the doorway belongs to my dad's girlfriend, Laura. We don't like her. She came into our lives two years before I left home, so I had the privilege of living with her for two very long years before I could finally leave.

"Hi, Laura," I say, forcing a smile.

"Oh…and you brought a dog. How wonderful," she says, staring at Snowflake like he is a vicious monster. Snowflake is anything but that. He is the gentlest dog in the universe, and the fluffiest. He loves children and will run up to anyone simply because he loves people so much. He is white as snow, but has the brownest, deepest puppy-eyes in the world. He is also my best friend in the whole world. He is no guard dog, though. That he cannot do.

"Don't worry," I say. "He doesn't shed. He has poodle in him and they don't shed. He doesn't drool either or bark. He won't be any trouble."

"Well isn't that…nice." Laura speaks through tightened lips. I know she is going to hate having him here, but I couldn't just leave him in the apartment back home. She will have to live with it.

"And this must be Salter," she says with a gasp. "My gosh, how much you look like your granddad."

"Speaking of…where is the old man?" I ask, feeling uncomfortable already.

"He's in his study. Come in. Come in." Laura makes room for us to enter. Salter goes first.

"Whoa!" he exclaims. "This house is huge." He looks at me like he expects me to have told him about this sooner.

"I put you two in one of the rooms upstairs," Laura says.

"I think we could fit our entire apartment just in this hallway," Salter continues. "Don't you think, Mom?"

"Probably. Now let's get our suitcases to our room, Salter, and then find your granddad."

"I'll let him know you're here," she says. "He hasn't really been himself since…well since Blake…you know."

"He got arrested, Laura. You can say the words. It's not like it's a secret."

"I just didn't want to…in front of the b-o-y."

"He's nine, Laura. He knows how to spell boy. Besides, he knows everything. He can take it."

Laura looks at me like I have no idea how to be a parent. She herself has two daughters of her own that had already moved out when she met my dad. They are a little older than me. I met them once at a Thanksgiving dinner right after Laura moved into our house, and that was no success. Since then, I have passed on all invitations to Thanksgiving and Christmas. After a few years, I think they got the message and stopped asking if we would join them.

"Let me show you to your room." Laura goes ahead of me up the stairs. I am surprised that she hasn't placed me in the guesthouse in the back to keep me out of the house as much as possible, like she did when I was a teenager. As soon as she moved in, I was asked to move to the guesthouse in the back. She wanted to turn my old room into a gym. Back then, I didn't understand why she didn't just chose one of the six other bedrooms in the house, but today I do. She wanted me out and maybe my dad did too. I wasn't exactly an easy teenager. I had a lot of anger built up and was constantly taking it out on him. I blamed him for everything that happened with my mother.

I still do.

12

September 2015

"MARY IS HOME!"

Sandra slams the door as she runs inside with Lucky, her brown Chihuahua. Her husband Ryan is sitting by the computer. Usually, they will go out surfing on a day like today where they are both off for once at the same time, but the waves simply aren't good enough. At least not for her.

"I just saw her when I passed her dad's house on my run with Lucky," she says, and takes the leash off the dog. "She parked the car in the driveway."

"And, who is Mary again?" Ryan asks, without looking up from the computer.

A boat passes on the river outside their windows. Ryan wants to go boating later today, but Sandra isn't really in the mood for it. It is so rare she has a Saturday off like this and is home to enjoy it. Usually, she is in California, New York, or Milan. For the first time in years, she has the entire week off and doesn't have to be anywhere until next Monday, when she is going to Germany for a shoot. If they go on the boat, Ryan will take his friend Phillip with them, and then she will feel all left out once they start talking fishing stuff. Still, she wants to be with her husband on this beautiful day.

"Mary is the girl who used to live in the big house at the end of 7th Street. The one on the ocean. She must have come home because of what happened to Blake. I don't think I have seen her in…what is it? Twenty years? Oh, my gosh I'm getting old."

Ryan's eyes leave the screen and he grabs Sandra around the waist and kisses her stomach. "You still look fine to me, babe."

"Are you ever sad that we never had any children?" she asks.

Ryan pauses. "Not really. I never thought much about it. I mean, you're busy with all your modeling and I have my construction business. You travel way too much to have children, and I could never ask you to stop your career. Not as long as you're doing so well for yourself."

"Yeah, but still. My career won't last forever, you know. I might still look great now at thirty-eight, but in a few years, the calls are going to stop coming. I can already feel them slowing down."

"Doesn't Heidi Klum still work? And she's older than you, right?"

"Well, I'm hardly a Heidi Klum."

"Well then, Claudia Schiffer and what's the name of that other one? The one with the mole…"

"Cindy Crawford."

"That's right. I see her everywhere on TV."

"She has this whole furniture business going. It's different with her."

"No, it's not. You could do that. Or something else just as cool. The world is your oyster, baby."

Sandra kisses her husband gently, even though she is sweaty and nasty from her run in the heat.

"Plus, you still make more money in a month than most do in a year," Ryan continues. "I say, you work as long as it's still fun, and then we see what happens. If you want children, we'll have children."

Sandra laughs. "Except I might be too old to have them. The clock is ticking. I can't have children forever."

"Then we'll adopt." He grabs her waist again and pulls her onto his lap. "As long as my baby is happy."

"You're sweet," she says and kisses him again.

"Now, go grab a shower. You're sweating on me," he says with a grin. "And you're hurting me. You're heavy."

Sandra pushes him lovingly, then jumps down. She has gained a little weight lately, which is a big no-go for a woman in her position. She has already got a few lines around her eyes that the magazines Photoshop out, if she is getting chubby as well, it will be the end of it.

"You should go talk to her," Ryan yells after her as she enters the bathroom.

Sandra peeks out. "Who?"

"That Mary person. Catch up on old times."

Sandra's heart drops. "I don't know about that," she says. "I don't think she would want to see me."

13

September 2015

I HAVE my heart in my throat as I walk the long walk through the hallway downstairs to my dad's study. Laura has told my dad I have arrived and tells me I can just walk in. I don't feel good being in the house again. The walls seem to be closing in on me. I can hear my mother's voice calling for me and imagine myself running down the stairs, my mother telling me not to run on the stairs, afraid I will slip and fall.

Once again, I feel a shiver run through my body at the thought of her.

Why mom. Why?

I knock on the door to my dad's study and wait for his response.

There he is. My old man. Sitting in one of the leather chairs in the room that I as a child was only allowed into when I had to be scolded. He looks tired and old.

My dad looks up at me. If he is happy to see me, he hides it well.

"Mary," he says.

"This is Salter," I say, and urge my son forward. I feel bad using my son as an icebreaker, but what can you do?

Finally, my dad smiles. "So, this is Salter, huh? Come here boy and give your granddad a hug."

Salter looks up at me, as if he is asking for my permission. I nod him along. "Go ahead."

Salter hugs my dad a little reluctantly. My dad closes his eyes and holds him for a little while, then grabs him by his shoulders.

"Let me look at you, boy. Hm. You have your mother's eyes and your father's nose."

"I've been told that I look a lot like you," Salter says.

My dad bursts into laughter that soon turns into a cough. My dad has been a smoker all of his adult life. It is a miracle he is still alive at the age of seventy-five. I know Laura doesn't let him smoke inside, but I also know that won't stop him.

"Well, they're right," he says. "And that's not such a bad thing."

Salter laughs. My dad coughs badly again and lets go of Salter's shoulders. The boy comes back to me and grabs my hand in his. He looks up at me with worried eyes.

"Is he sick?" he asks.

"I'm just old, boy," my dad says between coughs.

Salter chuckles. My dad catches his breath then looks at me seriously. "You didn't have to come. There really was no need for it."

"Salter," I say, addressed to my son. "Why don't you go upstairs and find your iPad. Granddad and I need to talk for a little while. Grownup stuff."

"He doesn't need an iPad," my dad intervenes. "He's a kid. Let him run down to the beach or go in the pool. He needs some fresh air. And some sun. Look at those pale cheeks."

"Can I, Mom? Can I go in the pool?"

"He's not a very strong swimmer," I say. "Someone needs to watch him."

"A boy of his age? That's ridiculous," my dad says. "Kids around here swim like fish in the ocean by the time they're two. You used to live your life more under the water than above it."

"This is Florida, Dad. It's different. There's water everywhere. Plus, it's warm all year around. Where we come from, kids don't go swimming every day like we did."

"No, they go on iPads," my dad says.

I sigh deeply. I am already regretting coming here.

14

September 2015

We compromise. Salter is allowed to take the iPad to the beach and sit in one of my dad's chairs and play a game until I am done. I promise I will take him swimming in the ocean when I am done talking to my dad. I am dying to get out in the waves myself anyway. That is the one thing I have missed about this town. The one thing I am sad that Salter doesn't have in his life growing up.

"So, what's the deal, Dad?" I ask, when Salter has left. "What's going on with Blake?"

"They arrested him at his place yesterday," my dad says. "They're charging him with murder."

"Murder? Blake?" I laugh mockingly at the idea. It's ridiculous. "Blake is many things. He is lazy, he is…well, he's never done a day's work in his life…"

"He's a spoiled brat," my dad interrupts me. "You can say it the way it is."

"But, a murderer? That he is not."

I look at my dad. It is scary how much we look alike. I see it every time I look in my mirror. Every day, I am reminded of where I have come from, even though I try so hard to forget.

"I'm guessing you have put your army of lawyers on the case?" I ask. "Has bail been set?"

"No," he says, shaking his head. "There's a hearing today. But there is no way a judge will give him bail for murder."

"But…but we've got to get him out of there," I say.

"I got him a good lawyer; that's all I can do. But the charges are severe. He risks prison for life. They have an eye witness that claims to have seen Blake kill the woman."

"What?"

My dad draws in a deep sigh. This entire affair is wearing on him. Blake has always been his favorite; there is no doubt about it. He is sort of his second chance to make things better, but it hurts him that he has turned out to be the way he is.

"They claim he met the two girls in a bar and brought them back to his studio, where he had some kind of weird sex game with them and stabbed the one to death while the other managed to escape. They found a bloody stone-carving chisel in his studio when searching it after his arrest."

"A chisel? Stone carving? But Blake is a painter. He doesn't use chisels," I say, confused.

"Well, he's been experimenting a lot lately with his work. He's been doing everything from coffee tables to decorative water-fountains to cutting tiki bars for people's yards. He had to expand a little if he wanted to make money, you know. I couldn't keep supporting him. Laura wouldn't have it."

Of course she wouldn't. Just like she never wanted me in their life either.

"Well, we have to help him the best we can," I say. "I mean, you do believe in his innocence, right?"

My dad hesitates just long enough for me to know. He doesn't. It makes me furious. I try to hold it back.

"You're kidding me. This is your son. It's Blake. He's a good kid, Dad. Confused, yes. Spoiled, yes. Lazy, heck yes. But no killer, and you know it. Deep down, you know it. Don't tell me you believe he could have done this."

"I still have a hope that he didn't do it, but Laura feels differently. She believes he got himself into the mess and that he doesn't deserve our help. She's got a point, you know. I can't keep cleaning up his messes."

I freeze. "You're not going to pay for his lawyer, are you? You're going to let him take care of it himself, even though he has no money? Just because of *her*?"

"It's his mess, Mary."

I stare at my old man sitting in his chair. He is even more pathetic than I remember him. I can't believe a man like him, with the esteem he has in this community, with all the power he has, that he can be such a wimp. My dad is among the most influential people in Brevard County. If he says jump, they all do, simultaneously. But when it comes to making decisions concerning his own family, he is such a coward. It is one of the things that make me loathe being his daughter.

"All right," I say and walk to the door. "I'll take care of it. Like always, I'll take care of everything."

"You're wasting your time." My dad stops me as I am about to leave. "Oh, and about that dog of yours. Try to keep it in your room, would you? Laura isn't much of a dog person."

15

September 2015

Blake feels sick to his stomach when they come for him. The hearing ended less than an hour ago and he has been put back in his cell. He is shaken. Constantly on the verge of crying. But he tries to hold it back, tries to be tough. A guy like him has no place in jail. He isn't going to last a week.

Blake looked for Olivia during the hearing, but didn't see her. He saw his older sister Mary and their eyes met briefly while his lawyer pleaded with the judge for bail. As expected, he didn't get it.

It made him feel a little comforted to see his sister's face in the crowd. He doesn't know her very well, but they write messages on Facebook and sometimes talk on the phone. She never comes to visit. But, still, he knows she will always be there for him when he needs it.

Mary is the closest he will ever come to having a mother. Growing up with Laura was no party.

They sent him away to a boarding school in Jacksonville for a few years once he reached school age, but he was caught smoking weed on the school grounds in seventh grade and sent home. After that, he lived at the house with them, but tried hard to stay out of

Laura's way. He believes his dad feels sorry for him, and because he knows that Laura doesn't like him, he spoils him with a new car every year, his own boat, and basically gives him everything he wants. Either that or he just gives him everything to get him to leave him alone.

"You have a visitor," the prison guard tells him.

Blake feels a sting in his heart. He hopes it is Olivia. He doesn't know what they did to her afterwards, after they dragged him away. He just hopes that he didn't get her in trouble with the general.

He is taken to a small room where his sister is waiting. Blake tears up when he sees her again. He is disappointed that it isn't Olivia, but at the same time happy that she is here.

"Blake," she says and stands up when he enters.

He can tell the sight of his orange uniform and chained feet and hands horrifies her. He sits down.

"It's good to see you, Mary," he says with a sniffle. "What has it been since I was up to visit you? Three years?"

"Five, Blake," she says with tears in her eyes. "It's been five years. How are you?"

He scoffs and answers with sarcasm. "Great!"

"Blake, be serious. How are you holding up in here?"

He looks into her eyes and feels tears pile up. He has tried to act so tough ever since the arrest, but the reality is that he is devastated. Completely. It is a nightmare. He doesn't know what to do. He has been questioned for hours and hours, and still they keep asking him the exact same questions. No, he didn't kill that woman. No, he doesn't know who she is. How could he have stabbed her in his studio if he has never seen her before in his life?

"I'm trying my best," he says.

"It's awful," she says. "I can't believe anyone would think you could have killed that woman."

Blake smiles through his tears. Finally, someone believes in him. Finally. "Where is Dad?" he asks. "I didn't see him at the hearing."

Mary hesitates before she gives him her answer. "It's just me for now."

"He's not coming, huh?" Blake bites his lip. It is dry and sore.

"Maybe later," Mary says, but he knows she is lying. "You know how he is, Blake. Let's not focus on him. Let's focus on you. You have to tell me everything. From the beginning."

16

September 2015

"There really isn't much I can tell you," Blake says.

I am trying hard to keep myself collected in the small room with the guards listening in on our every word. I know if Blake says anything about the case that he hasn't mentioned before they can use it against him. But I have to know more. I have to hear it from his own lips. I just have to make sure he doesn't say anything to make it worse on himself.

I can't stand watching my younger brother in distress like this. He is so pale and the look in his eyes so terrified it makes my stomach turn. I feel so bad for him. Especially since I can tell he is trying to play the tough guy. Blake isn't a tough guy. He is a sweet little boy, an artist. He drinks too much, he parties way too much, and thinks the world revolves around him, but he could never hurt a fly. I just know he couldn't. Prison is going to kill him. He is way too soft and sensitive. That was his problem at the boarding school my dad sent him to. My dad wanted to toughen the boy up, but he came back an even bigger mess than he left. He isn't cut out for this world and all it's harshness.

"I've never seen the girl in my life," he says. "I swear I haven't."

"What about her friend? The one that testified against you? Do you know who she is?"

Blake shakes his head. "I have no idea."

"Could you have met them while drunk in a bar or something? It's no secret you like to go out and drink every now and then."

Blake shrugs. "I…I mean, it is possible, but I don't remember it. She's not even my type. I don't like blondes."

"Hardly an argument that will stand in court."

I look into the eyes of my baby brother. He still has the innocence of youth in them. I always thought he would be one of those people that simply never grew up, the ones that hustle through life, but always seem to make it even if they don't take life as seriously as the rest of us.

But now I see something else in those eyes of his. Something I have never seen in them before. He is afraid. He is shaken to his core.

"I spoke to your lawyer earlier today, and he told me the witness was capable of describing your body in detail, and could even remember the mole on the lower part of your back. How could she know this stuff if you've never met her before?"

"I…I…I don't know, Mary. You have to believe me. I really don't know. I didn't kill this woman. I didn't."

"They found the bloody chisel in your kitchen, under the sink," I say, quoting the lawyer's information. "It was thrown into a bucket like someone had to hide it fast, and then a dishtowel had been thrown on top of it to cover it. Now, they haven't matched the blood on the chisel with hers yet, so that part is still open. Besides, there was no bloodstain evidence found in your studio, which speaks well for your case. The state attorney will argue that you could have cleaned the place up, whereas the defense will try and make the case that blood always leaves some kind of evidence behind. Even when the scene has been wiped clean, there are still ways for forensic investigators to detect washed away blood, like using a reagent called Luminol, which reacts with iron found in hemoglobin. And, as far as we know, the forensics haven't been able to locate anything, but they're still working your apartment for evidence, so we'll have to see about that."

"I'm not getting out, am I?" he asks.

"Don't say that, Blake. We don't know anything yet."

Blake is suddenly short of breath. He starts hyperventilating.

"Calm down, Blake. You've got to calm down."

"I'm going to be one of those cases, one of those that are convicted of a crime they didn't commit. Oh, my God, like those you hear about that are put away for life even though they're innocent."

"Not if I have any say in this," I say.

I have a lump in my throat from watching my baby brother lose it like this. He is panicking. It is the worst thing he can do in this situation.

"But, you don't, do you?" Blake pauses and leans back in his chair. "It doesn't matter what we do. It doesn't matter that I didn't do it. They told me I could get a shorter sentence if I pleaded guilty..."

"Don't you even think about that!"

Blake's eyes widen. He tries to speak, but is choked up.

"He's not going to help me, is he?"

"Who?"

"Dad. He's not coming because he thinks I'm guilty. He's not going to pay for that lawyer he sent me, is he?"

I sigh. I have to be honest. "No. He has paid the bills so far, to make sure you have a chance. But he is not going to pay anymore."

Blake lets out a sound of despair. "How am I going to pay for it then? Boy, am I screwed."

"You will have an attorney appointed to you by the court," I say, knowing very well that it is far from the same. Right now, all Blake needs is the best lawyer money can buy. The same kind that got O.J. Simpson acquitted.

17

April 1977

PETER TURNS pale when he feels how warm the baby is.

"We have to get her to the doctor immediately," he says. "Oh, the poor thing. No wonder she's been crying all day."

He helps Penelope get into the car with the baby and they drive fast to the emergency room, where a doctor attends to them immediately. Penelope feels a huge sensation of relief when the baby is finally in the hands of the doctors and nurses. It is like the responsibility is no longer hers and she isn't alone anymore.

Peter has a complete change of attitude towards her and puts his arm around her. He holds her tight while the doctor takes care of the baby. Penelope closes her eyes and enjoys his embrace once again. How badly she has missed it, has missed being close to him, has missed being his one and only. A tear escapes the corner of her eye and rolls down her cheek. Peter sees it and wipes it away.

"Shhh, she'll be alright. Don't worry. Our baby is in good hands now. She's safe here."

Penelope opens her eyes and looks at him. Yes, her baby is in good hands now, and so is she. Standing in the waiting room with her husband's arms around her again, Penelope feels something she hasn't felt since the baby came into their world. She feels safe. She feels loved.

"Your baby is going to be just fine." The doctor approaches them carrying the good news.

"See, I told you, Penelope," Peter says joyfully. "So, what is wrong with her, Doctor?"

"An ear infection. It's very common at her age. But it can give a nasty fever if not treated. It's amazing what that small size can cope with, right? I mean, a fever this high would kill most adults, but babies, they have them from time to time and still they're fine. Nevertheless, I have prescribed some eardrops for her and something for her rash as well. She has a little diaper rash, which is very normal. You can take her home right away if you like."

"Home?" Penelope asks, concerned. "Wouldn't it be better if she stayed the night? For observation? She might get worse."

"If you treat her with the eardrops, she'll be fine very soon," the doctor says. "Like I said, it's very common and highly treatable."

"But, I'm no doctor," Penelope says.

Peter chuckles. "I think you might be able to handle a few eardrops, right?"

"It's not that hard. Just hold her head still, then let the drops land inside the ear. Three times a day. The infection should be gone in a few days."

"But, what if it doesn't go away?" she asks, feeling very uncomfortable with having to take the baby home right now when she is still sick. She doesn't feel safe alone with her at the house when she isn't well. This time, she hadn't even known that she was sick. Will she know the next time? Will she be able to make the right decision? She doesn't want to be alone with her again.

"Tsk, of course it will go away if the doctor says so," Peter says. "It's nothing serious. Why are you so worried all of a sudden?"

"I...I just don't feel like...I mean what if I don't...what if..."

The doctor places a hand on her shoulder. He looks into her eyes. There is something about him that makes her feel safe.

"It's only natural to feel insecure as a young mother. It's a big responsibility. How about you go home now, and then I'll call you in the morning and make sure everything is all right. Let me know if there is anything, and I do mean *anything*, that is wrong, and I'll have you come in and we'll look at it. I believe you can do this."

Peter puts his arm around her waist. Penelope relaxes.

"I'll be there too, remember? You're not alone."

18

September 2015

I CRY in the car on my way back to the beach. I can't believe what a mess my little brother has gotten himself into. I feel so terrible for him and want to do everything I can to help him. I decide I am going to use whatever little money I have saved to pay for his lawyer. He needs the best there is. But I don't have much to offer, and it won't last long. Still, it is a start. I call the lawyer, James Holland, and tell him to continue his work.

"I'll go as far as I can for you, Mary," he says. "Me and your dad go back many years, but I still can't work without getting paid. I hope you realize that."

"I'll pay you. I'll find the money; don't worry."

"That's good to hear, Mary. I'll get to work, then."

I draw in a sigh of relief and turn the car in front of the driveway to my dad's house. I am about to drive in when I spot a face from my past. She is standing on the pavement in front of the fence, with a dog on a leash. I roll down the window. She doesn't seem surprised to see me.

"Sandra?" I ask. "Is that really you?"

She smiles and nods. "I heard you were home. I wanted to stop by and say hello."

Sandra. Sandra was probably my best friend growing up. The best surfer on the block, and by far the most gorgeous one of us. She used to be so good she was invited to join the pro-tour for women once, back when she was eighteen and everyone wanted a piece of her. She was so beautiful and cool that all the brands and magazines wanted her as a model, and soon after the modeling took over more and more. Since she is also tall, she soon became a fashion model who travelled all over the world and did fashion shows for the big names and became friends with Naomi Campbell and Helena Christensen. For years, we all envied her the life she had.

She still looks great. Unbearably great.

Looking at her now at the age of thirty-eight, she still takes the prize for best looking. She is stunning. And slim. Looking at her makes me feel fat. Ever since we hit the teenage years, I became the chubby one between us, and the years have not been kind to me in that direction. I guess I just like food a little too much. Apparently, she doesn't.

"How have you been?" I ask.

"Good. I'm good. Married," she says, and shows me her ring finger.

"That's right. To Ryan, right? He was a senior when we started high school, as far as I remember. Who would have known it was going to be you two?"

Sandra chuckles. "Not me."

"So, you're back here?" I ask. "Last thing I heard you were living in Italy?"

"I was. For many years I lived in Milan. But then my mother got sick and I came back and ran into Ryan. He had just started his own construction company. A year later, we got married and when my dad died two years after my mom, I inherited their old house right down there by the end of 7th Street. We rebuilt it, so you can probably hardly recognize it."

"So, you're still in that old house? That's amazing," I say. "You still work?"

"A little here and there," she says.

I can tell she is being modest.

"I bet you've made enough to last you a lifetime, huh?"

She shrugs. "I guess. It's not all it's cracked up to be, though. I mean it was fun when I was younger, but the pressure…I'm feeling it now that I'm getting older. I try to say yes to anything they give me. I still travel a lot."

"Any kids?"

She looks at me, then shakes her head. "There just hasn't been time, you know?"

I do know what she is talking about. In my career, I have met so many women that believed they were too busy to have a child. I have the impression many of them simply let time pass, thinking there would come a perfect time to have children. But the thing is, it will never come. There is no such thing as the perfect time to have children. My son came to me when I least expected or wanted it. I was at the highlight of my career, rocking it at CNN in Atlanta, so I blamed God for having bad timing. Of course, today, I wouldn't change him for any career in the world. Not even Sandra's.

"So, any of the others from the old crew still live around here?" I ask.

Her face lights up. "Yeah. As a matter of fact, they all do. You know how it is. You go away, but you come back because it's the best place on earth, right?"

To hear Sandra call Cocoa Beach the best place on earth is very strange. Can this really be the same girl I grew up with? She used to go on and on about how she couldn't wait to get out of here and how she dreamt of touring the world as a pro surfer.

"Well, I guess you already know that Joey recently came back," she says.

"I know that, thank you very much," I say with a sigh.

I can tell Sandra wants to go deeper into the subject, but she holds back.

"Well, Marcia has been here since she divorced her husband four years ago. She bought a condo on the beach close to 8th Street. You'll see her around. She had her license revoked because of a DUI, so she rides her bike everywhere. Alex works at the school. He's a teacher at Roosevelt now. Danny has been promoted to captain at the fire department. They just recently got a new big building down by Minutemen, and Chloe…well, you know Chloe… she is who she is. She still lives in her mom's house down the street."

I chuckle. "She still lives there?"

"Yeah. We don't see her much. She is nocturnal. Only up when the sun goes down."

"What does she do? Is she still hacking?" I ask, thinking about how Chloe back then had engaged in a world none of us had any clue about. I always believed she was an overlooked genius.

"Actually, she works in cyber-security now for some of the biggest companies around here, one of her clients being NASA. But she works from home. Takes care of her mother that way. I think she makes a decent amount of money doing that."

I picture Chloe sitting in her old room, surrounded by chips and sodas, her eyes fixated on a screen and her fingers dancing across the keyboard. She was never among the best surfers around here, but she used to go out with us anyway. I wonder if she still surfs.

"So, I take it you're back because of what happened to Blake?" Sandra asks after a long pause, where I sense she was working up the courage to ask me.

"Yes. To be frank, I really don't know how to deal with it right now."

"And your old man?"

"Washing his hands, as always," I say. "He believes Blake needs to get himself out of it. He doesn't really care."

"He still called you, didn't he?" Sandra asks.

"What do you mean?"

"Well, he called to tell you, so he has to care to some extent, right?"

"I guess you're right," I say and look at my old childhood friend. I realize I have missed her. We used to be able to talk for hours and hours. Now it feels awkward.

"Maybe we should get the old crew together while you're here," she says. "Just for old time's sake."

I freeze completely.

"Unless you don't want to?"

I shake my head. "No. No. I mean, I do. I think I do. There is just so much…I mean we haven't seen each other in a very long time; we haven't hung out since…" I pause and look at her, not knowing what to say. We both know what I am talking about. We have avoided bringing up the subject and we both know everyone will try to avoid it if we are brought together again. It will only be awkward. So extremely awkward.

"You know what?" Sandra says. "Maybe it was a bad idea. It was good to see you again, Mary."

She touches my shoulder briefly and walks past me, nudging her little Chihuahua along as she walks across A1A towards her own house by the end of 7th Street. I watch her walk away, her perfect little behind moving beautifully in her tight shorts, then curse Blake for getting himself—and thereby me—into this awful mess. I was doing so well up there in New York, minding my own business, slowly forgetting my past. Now it has all come back to laugh in my face.

19

September 2015

Jean Schmidt closes the window of her small house. She feels a chill of happiness rush through her body while looking out on the canal where the sun is about to set in the distance. She can't believe they have finally moved into the house of their dreams. She has dreamt of living canal-front ever since she was just a young child growing up in Cocoa Beach. She remembers sitting on the school bus, driving around town picking up kids, her nose pressed against the window, dreaming about living in one of the houses that has a view of the water and a dock and maybe a boat in the back. And for years, she worked to save enough to buy it. Neither she nor her husband, Danny, make much money, so for years they lived in a small townhouse by Fifth Street. But three months ago, Danny was made captain at the fire station, and with his raise, the bank finally agreed to give them the loan for the house of their dreams. They had saved just enough for the down payment.

They bought a beautiful two-story house with a dock big enough for them to have a table and six chairs and a tiki bar on it, and it even has a boat ramp. That is their next goal, Danny says. To get a boat. Jean doesn't care about sailing. She just wants to have it so the neighbors can see it docked by her house.

"I'm going to my room to watch TV," Daniel Junior says, as he enters the kitchen where Jean is standing admiring the view and the sunset over the Thousand Islands. It is gorgeous. There is nothing like a Florida sunset.

Jean turns her head and nods. "Sure."

Junior grabs a soda from the fridge. Jean gives him a look. "Soda right before bed? Is that a good choice, do you think?"

Junior growls. At the age of eighteen, she can rarely still tell him what to do and what not to. Junior puts the soda can back and grabs a water bottle instead.

"Is Dad at the station?" he asks.

Jean nods. "Last night of his 48-hour shift. He'll be home in the morning. He talked about taking you fishing if you like?"

Junior nods. "Sure. I mean whatever. If he wants."

"Great. I'll tell him. Once he has slept, he'll take you out on Alex's boat."

Junior shrugs, pretending like he doesn't care, but Jean knows he loves to go fishing with his dad. It just isn't cool to show it.

"Okay. Goodnight."

Junior leaves and Jean returns to look at the sunset. She takes a picture of it with her phone and posts it on Facebook. Not that her friends haven't seen it before. She has posted those pictures every day since they moved in, but she just can't help herself. It is truly spectacular.

Jean pours herself a glass of wine and walks outside to catch a glimpse of the orange sun. She sits in one of her lounge chairs and sips her wine. She has the entire weekend off from the DMV office, but she is tired from having worked all week. Gosh, how she loathes her job. Sitting all day taking care of people that need to renew their driver's licenses, or who have lost them somehow, is so tedious, so mind numbing she sometimes has to swim away in strange fantasies about her piercing their eyes with a pen or using the stapler to make art out of their faces. What would it feel like to put someone's finger inside a stapler, then accidentally press it down? Would she hear the bones crush if she pressed hard enough? Would it bleed? Would the idiot scream? It's those small fantasies that keep her going. Otherwise, she would simply go insane. These people are so stupid, so idiotic, it is mind-blowing. But it pays the bills, and now it had helped Jean get the house of her dreams. Well, that and Danny's promotion.

The sun disappears behind the islands and darkness surrounds her fast. There is no wind and soon the mosquitoes have a feast. Especially the *No See Ums* are terrible at this time of day. Those small bastards will eat you up in seconds and leave small red bumps, but you can never see them, hence the name. They are even small enough to go through your screen. It is so annoying.

Jean tries to ignore the itching and burning sensation that soon covers her legs, but soon it is too overwhelming and she has to go back inside. She didn't know the No See Ums were this bad by the canals, but apparently this is where they live and multiply. They love the murky fresh water in the canals. And when there is no wind to keep them away, like this evening, there is no way to fight them. Jean has tried everything. Candles, different sprays. Nothing works.

Jean takes her wine and sits in the living room and turns on the TV. She watches an episode of *CSI Miami*, but halfway through she has emptied her glass of wine and needs a refill. Junior is quiet upstairs and she figures he has fallen asleep. Jean likes having the house to herself. Danny is a sweet man, but he is incredibly boring. The way he eats is the worst part. She simply loathes eating with him. She always looks forward to when his shift starts. That gives her forty-eight hours on her own to enjoy her life.

Jean sighs and pours more wine into the glass, then throws away the bottle. It has become a habit for her to open a bottle of Cupcake white wine every afternoon and finish it at night. It is the only way she can really get through the day…knowing that a bottle of wine is waiting for her at home.

Jean closes her eyes and sips her wine, standing in the kitchen, when suddenly the wind chime on her back porch starts making an awful lot of noise. Jean opens her eyes. There is nothing but darkness outside of her windows.

That's strange, she thinks to herself. *Has the wind suddenly picked up?*

Are we expecting a storm tonight? There wasn't a cloud in the sky at sunset. Has it come from the ocean side?

The wind chime plays again. The music is haunting. Jean opens the door to the porch and peeks out, but there is nothing there. The wind chime is completely still now. It isn't even moving. Jean looks at the flagpole with the flag they have put up and put a spotlight on. The flag is hanging flat down.

That's odd. There is no wind at all.

Thinking that she is probably just imagining things, Jean decides to go back into the house. Just as she closes the sliding door, the music starts over again. Jean gasps and looks out through the window. She can't see anything.

Maybe it's an animal? Could a bird have flown into it?

Jean shakes her head. She is probably just tired. All those hours of listening to people and all their crap is making her hear things.

She decides it's time for bed and turns off the TV, then the light in the living room. As she walks through the kitchen, she hears the noise again. This time, the wind chime is louder than any of the other times.

What is this?

"That's it," Jean says. "I'm taking that thing down. I won't be able to sleep if it is going to make this loud noise all night."

With determined steps, she walks to the sliding door and opens it out to the porch, where the wind chime is so noisy it drowns out every other sound, even the crickets that are usually very busy at this time of night.

The chime is hanging from a hook under the roof of the porch. Jean turns on the light to better see. She looks in the direction of the chime, then stops.

A woman wearing a surgical mask is standing underneath it. Jean stares at her. She is short, wearing a black coat hiding most of her body.

"Who are you? What are you doing in my yard?" Jean asks.

The woman tilts her head. "Am I pretty?" she asks.

Jean stares at her. "I can't see your face because of the mask, but

I am sure you're very pretty. Now get out of my yard before I call the police."

The woman tilts her head to the side a few times, then asks again. "Am I pretty?"

"What does that have to do with anything?" Jean asks. "I really have to..."

"Am I PRETTY??"

The yelling startles Jean. She feels all of a sudden very uncomfortable in the presence of this strange woman.

"You do know we are pro-gun in this house, right? There's a sign by the driveway."

The woman doesn't seem to react. Something about her eyes seems familiar to Jean. Is she one of the weirdoes that she has met at the DMV office? Jean sees so many faces every day. It is hard to tell them apart.

"Am...I...Pretty?" she asks again. This time much calmer.

Jean sighs. The woman is probably drunk or stoned. She rolls her eyes at her. "Well, if you have to know, then yes, you're very pretty."

That seems to help. The woman's face lights up. She grabs the surgical mask and pulls it off. The sight that meets her makes Jean gasp, horrified, and clasp her mouth.

"How about now?" the woman asks.

20

February 1992

Ally Meyer starts at Cocoa Beach High in the middle of ninth grade. She has just moved to town because her mother is starting a new job at Kennedy Space Center. Ally is angry with her mother for pulling her away from her comfortable surroundings once again, and even before she has given it a chance, she hates the new place more than all the others she has moved to over the years.

On her first day, she keeps to herself. Or at least she tries to. Decisive that she doesn't want to make friends, she doesn't want to be happy here, she avoids talking to anyone or sitting with anyone at lunch.

Still, she can't be left alone. Two of the girls from her class come up to her during lunch break and sit with her. Mary and Sandra are their names. They both live on 7th Street, they tell her.

"We all surf. Do you surf?" Mary asks.

She is the chubby one. The other, Sandra, is so beautiful Ally feels intimidated by her. And on top of it, she is also sweet. It is too much. Almost nauseating.

"N-no. I don't," she says, shaking her head.

Ally isn't very athletic. Never has been. When all the other kids on the street ride their bikes or jump rope, Ally stays inside listening to music on her Walkman. Sports just aren't her thing.

"Maybe we can teach you," Sandra says.

"Yeah," Mary says. "Sandra here is the best. You should see her turn off the lip. Slam! She's like Kelly, dude."

"Who's Kelly?" Ally asks.

"Kelly Slater!" Mary exclaims. "Only like the best surfer ever."

"Well, Mary thinks he is," Sandra says.

"Oh, he's gonna be. Just you wait and see. Used to go to this high school, you know. He's only like five years older than us. He won Rookie of the Year last year on the pro tour and he is in the lead to win the world title this year. Isn't it crazy? I even heard rumors that he is going to appear on an episode of *Baywatch* this year."

"You're kidding me, right?" Sandra says.

Ally stares at the two girls, not knowing what to say to them. She has no clue who this Kelly-character is, and she certainly doesn't like to watch *Baywatch*. She has a pretty good idea that surfing probably isn't her thing either. She has no desire to show herself in a bikini.

"I-I have to go," she says and grabs her things, then leaves the table. Ally feels a huge relief as she walks away. There is no way she is going to make friends here at this school. None of them are like her.

At least she doesn't think they are, until another girl approaches her as she reaches her locker. Ally is fighting with the lock on it. Ally doesn't notice the girl until after she slams her fist into the locker in anger because it won't open.

"Nice punch," the girl says.

She is flanked by two other girls. They are all wearing black makeup around their eyes and the girl in front even has a green Mohawk. Ally thinks she looks so cool. She has at least four or five earrings in each ear and one in her nose as well. She is like a rock star.

"Thanks," Ally says, feeling even more intimidated than earlier.

"Say, I saw you with the surfers earlier," the girl says. "Are you one of them?"

"I-I-I don't know them. They just came up to me and started talking about surfing and some guy..."

The girl chuckles. "Yeah, they're all about that. Always talking about Kelly Slater and surfing and the waves and crap like that. There are a lot of those in this school. Surfers are all over. The question is, will you be one of them or are you with us?"

She is very upfront. Ally likes that. She stares at the girl, who now slams her fist into the lock and smashes it, then pulls the door to Ally's locker open. "You might need a new lock for that," she says.

"Thanks. I'm Ally." Ally holds out her hand.

The girl looks at the hand, then laughs. "Welcome to our school, Ally," she says, and walks away.

"Hey, how will I know your name?"

The girl turns and smiles.

"People around here call me AK," she yells back. "Like the rifle."

21

September 2015

I FINALLY HAVE some time to spend at the beach with Salter. The next morning, we grab two of my old surfboards and paddle out together. Salter has surfed a bit this past summer when visiting his dad, so he is eager to show me how good he has become. I feel nervous because he is not a very strong swimmer.

It is a gorgeous day out. Not a cloud in the sky and the ocean is glassy. The waves are really good. There is a storm in the Atlantic. Hurricane Joaquin is roaring somewhere far out and creates some good and decent ground swell for us, and soon we both ride one wave after the other. I am impressed with how good my son has become. He seems to have no trouble anymore, not even with the swimming. I realize I was mistaken about him.

I am a little rusty, but surfing is kind of like riding a bike. You never forget completely. In the beginning, when we moved to Manhattan, Joey and I would go up to Montauk and surf, but as the years passed we did it less and less. Just like all the other things we never did anymore. It wasn't something that happened all of a sudden. It kind of snuck up on us.

While waiting for a wave, I wonder if things would be different today if I had been better at taking care of my marriage, if I had prioritized it more. As soon as Salter came into our lives, Joey moved down to like number three on my list of priorities. I kept Salter and my career ahead of him. That can never be a great cocktail. Looking back, it is pretty obvious. It just isn't when you are in the middle of it. I somehow kept telling myself things were going to change soon, as soon as I was done with this assignment or that project, as soon as Salter grew a little older, or as soon as Joey got a job. But things never improved. Not when I didn't do anything about them. I let this happen. I was as much at fault as he was.

And now there is no going back.

After about half an hour in the water, the line-up is beginning to get crowded. It is Sunday and the waves are good, a very rare combination. They are usually always perfect Monday morning when everyone has to work or go to school. I must have skipped the first two hours of school a hundred times because the waves were good on a Monday morning.

"Hi there. I thought I might find you here."

"Daaad!"

Salter almost falls off his board while trying to greet his father. Joey paddles up and stays close to him so they can hug. Seeing them together makes me happy and sad at the same time. Why did I ruin this? Why did he?

"Hi," he says when our eyes meet. "I hope it's all right with you that I join you?"

I smile. "Of course. Just don't drop in on me."

Joey laughs. It seems a little forced. "What happened to *sharing is caring*?"

Sharing is caring is something we used to say when the 7th Street Crew surfed together. We made it a deal to never get angry if someone dropped in on your wave. Between us, we knew how to share a good wave and sometimes it made it even more fun.

I feel a pinch in my heart, remembering all the Sundays we used to spend out here on the ocean, cheering each other on when someone had a good wave, laughing at Marcia when she wiped out, which she always did. Or cheering on Danny when he finally made it to the nose of his humongous long board.

As I sit on my board remembering all this, I spot Sandra paddling out on her short board. Alex, who has the same big smile on his face as he always used to when paddling out, follows her.

"Yeah! The 7th Street Crew breaks rules," he exclaims with a loud cheer.

I can't help smiling. Even if it is not all of us, it suddenly feels a little like the old days. It fills me with both joy and sadness as well. I say hello to Alex as he comes out and sits on his board. He hasn't changed much. Still small and chubby like me. Well, he has gotten a little chubbier, but he still has great hair and the sweetest smile. I have always loved hanging out with Alex. He is such a happy guy. Easy to please.

I look at Joey, who instructs Salter to start paddling for a wave.

"It's your wave, go get it, go, go. Now get up. Get up fast!"

And there he goes. I have never been more proud of my son than in this moment when he catches the wave and I see the smile on his face as he rides it in.

"That's it, Salter. Take it all the way to the beach."

Joey laughs. Meanwhile, Sandra catches a wave and shreds it completely.

"Almost like the good old times, huh?" Alex says. "I should bring my kid out here next time. He's about your kid's age. We could all hang out together."

"We're only staying a few days," I say.

I like the thought of the kids hanging out together like we used to, but it also reminds me of something I was trying to forget. I can't have Salter making friends here. He can't get attached to the town. We won't stay here.

"There is someone on the beach who wants to talk to you," Salter says, addressed to Joey when he comes back out. "She told me to tell you."

We all look to the beach and spot another of our old friends, Marcia. She is standing with her arms over her head, waving at us to come back in. She is using the old sign with her arms that we used to for letting someone know to come back in.

I shrug. "I guess it's time for lunch anyway," I say, addressed to Salter.

"Let's all go in and see what she wants," Alex says. "Here's a wave. Wanna share it?"

22

September 2015

We all grab the same wave and ride it into the beach. It is the party-wave of a lifetime for me. I can't believe I am riding it with my son. I feel so happy when we hit the beach and I run to give him a high-five. Sandra is, of course, shredding the wave to pieces ending on a floater, while Alex nosedives and Joey rides it old school and cool on his long board.

"That was a good one," he yells at me once we get up on the beach. He looks so handsome coming out of the water with his well-built torso and long curly hair. I always picture him being played by Chris Hemsworth if they ever make a movie about our lives. Okay, so Joey isn't quite as handsome as the Thor-actor, but he is up there. At least in my opinion.

"What's going on, Marcia?" Sandra asks when we approach her.

Marcia looks very upset. She has gotten old, I am surprised to see. She used to have a very pretty face with deep brown eyes, but age hasn't been good to her. She has gained a lot of weight, but we all have, except for Sandra, of course. Marcia's skin is damaged. Lots of age-spots from too much sun, and visible veins on her nose bear witness of too much alcohol.

"I-i-it's Danny. I-I-I can't believe it…"

"What happened, Marcia?" Joey asks.

We are all beginning to feel uncomfortable. The look in Marcia's eyes tells us something is terribly wrong.

"It's Jean…Danny…he came home…police…Junior…"

She is making no sense at all.

"What happened to Danny, Marcia?" Sandra asks, putting her hand on Marcia's shoulder to calm her down.

"It's Jean. He came home around ten-thirty. Danny came home from his shift this morning. He found her on the porch. Stabbed in the throat. The scissors were still there. Sitting in her throat. She was in a huge pool of blood. The police are there."

"Oh, my God," Sandra gasps, cupping her mouth.

None of us can believe what we hear. A million thoughts run through my mind. I have known Jean since we were in Kindergarten. She is one of the local girls. I know her pretty well, even though I have never been particularly close to her.

"Is she dead?" Alex asks.

"Yes. I saw the body be moved on the stretcher in a closed bag. I've seen enough *CSI* to know what that means."

Sandra lets out a moan of terror. Alex hugs her. She cries. I feel like crying too, but hold it back.

"Poor Danny," Sandra says.

"How did this happen?" Joey asks. "Who?"

Marcia shrugs. "I just spoke shortly with one of the neighbors, then thought I would bike down here and tell you guys. Danny needs us now."

"Maybe we should go there and see if there is anything we can do," I say.

The entire flock turns and looks at me. Marcia hasn't noticed me until now.

"Mary? You're home?" she says very loudly, then throws herself in my arms. She reeks of alcohol.

"Yes, I'm home. Just for a few days, though," I say, and give her a quick hug. "Got a few things to take care of."

"Ah, don't pretend like we don't know about your brother," Marcia says with a sniffle. "Everyone here knows what happened, and everyone here believes he is innocent. Don't you ever doubt that. We're behind Blake in all of this. Right guys?"

They all nod, to my surprise.

"Yeah, we know Blake," Alex says. "He is many things, but not a killer."

"Thank you," I exclaim, maybe a little too loud. I am just so happy to hear it from someone else. "That's what I keep telling people."

We leave our boards on the beach and walk up to the crosswalk and down 7th Street. The sun is baking from the clear sky, the moisture in the air making it feel hotter than it really is. I know the others don't feel it as much as I do, since they are used to it. But it has been a long time since I was last in Florida's humid climate, and even though I am wearing nothing but a bikini bottom and a rash guard, I am sweating heavily by the time we arrive at Danny's house in Snug Harbor after a fifteen-minute walk.

A crowd has gathered in front of the police tape. Some are crying, others just staring at the scenery, shaking their heads in disbelief. I know what they are thinking. This is a quiet neighborhood. Nothing like this happens around here.

The ambulance is still at the scene, and we spot Danny, who is speaking to an officer. He is sitting on the bumper of the ambulance, shaking his head, his son sitting next to him, crying his eyes out, the poor thing. Danny is shaking his head, then pointing at the house like he is explaining. The officer takes notes. Danny looks devastated. The officer leaves him and he is just sitting there, staring at his house and the people coming in and out of it, wearing gloves and body suits.

"Danny!"

Joey yells. That is so typically Joey. The entire crowd turns their heads and lets him go through. Joey walks up to the police tape. Danny spots him, then gets up and walks closer. An officer stops Joey from going under the tape. We are all right behind him. Danny approaches us, his eyes bloodshot and disoriented.

"Oh, man," Joey says. His voice is breaking.

Danny was probably his best friend growing up. Joey reaches in over the tape and hugs his buddy. Danny hides his face in Joey's shoulder and sobs, his upper body jerking back and forth.

"I'm so sorry, man," Joey says, then repeats it over and over again. "I'm so sorry."

"She's gone, Joey. She's really gone. I can't believe it," Danny says. "How am I going to do this? How am I going to get through this?"

"One step at a time, man," Joey says.

"Yeah, one step at a time," Marcia says, and puts her arms around him as well.

"We're all here for you," Sandra says, and joins in.

Alex nods and wipes away a tear, then he leans in on me, and not knowing what else to do, I try to comfort him. That is when I spot someone in the crowd. She is kind of hiding behind a bigger guy, but I can always spot Chloe from a distance.

"Chloe," I say and wave. "Chloe!"

She approaches me with her arms crossed in front of her chest. "What the heck is going on?" she asks and gives me a quick hug.

I can't believe how much she has changed. It is quite a surprise to me. She looks nothing like the old Chloe from twenty years earlier. Gone are the many piercings. Gone are the military boots and the black hair. Now she is wearing sporty shorts and a T-shirt and a baseball cap, making her look like any of the other soccer moms around here. But in her eyes, behind the glasses, I still spot the defiance I always loved so much about her.

"Something happened to Danny?" she asks.

I shake my head. "Jean is dead," I say. "She was found killed this morning."

Chloe looks at me. "Jean is dead?" she whispers back. "Killed here in this neighborhood?"

I nod.

"I bet he did it," she says, looking in Danny's direction.

"Chloe!"

"I know. I know. Danny could never have done it. But I wouldn't blame him if he had," she says. "That woman treated Danny like he was garbage. Nothing was ever good enough for her."

"That's hardly a reason to kill her," I say.

I know she is right about one thing, though. Jean has made a lot of enemies over the years. She wasn't a very nice person, at least not back in high school, and I never understood what Danny saw in her. But, still, I can't imagine why anyone would want to kill her.

"He loved her," I say. "Danny loved her."

23

May 1977

THE EAR INFECTION is gone quickly, and soon everything goes back to normal. Penelope stays at home with the baby while Peter goes to the office and spends long hours working on his case. Long afternoons turn into evenings, and soon he doesn't even come home at night.

At the house, Penelope tries to make everything work. The baby doesn't cry as much as when she was sick, but it is still enough to drive Penelope crazy. She feels so claustrophobic in the house. It is like the walls are closing in on her, like the house is getting ready to suffocate her.

Penelope tries to make the best of it. She takes long walks on the beach with the stroller or drives to Lori Wilson Park and sits at the playground while the baby sleeps. She looks at all the small children playing, running, screaming, and thinks that this is soon going to be her life. Worried mothers are chasing the youngest among them around, making sure they don't fall and hurt themselves or put dirt in their mouths.

Is she looking forward to this? She isn't sure. She loves her little girl and is looking forward to seeing her grow up, but she is just so insecure of her own abilities as a mother. Is she good enough?

There is so much that can go wrong, especially when they start walking and running around. Penelope doesn't feel certain she will be able to be there constantly, watching over the baby every minute of her life. What if something happens?

One day, when Penelope is watching the kids on the playground, one of them picks up a small piece of metal and puts it in his mouth. The mother doesn't see anything and soon it is stuck in his throat. The kid starts to cough and turns blue before the mother discovers it and completely panics. Minutes later, the kid is taken to the hospital.

Penelope watches the scene with terror, thinking anything could happen at any moment if you aren't careful.

That same night, she prepares dinner for her husband at six, as usual, and sits down and waits for him to come home. At seven, when the lamb has turned cold and grey, she decides to clean it all up again. Peter isn't coming home for dinner tonight either. While cleaning up, she wonders where he is and what he is doing. She knows he is done with the case he worked on before, but apparently he has a new one now that takes up all of his time. She doesn't understand how he has to work this much constantly. Isn't there any time for a break? Any time for his family?

She grabs the phone and calls the office to hear how he is doing. It isn't something she has ever done before, because Peter told her not to unless it is an emergency, but today she is tired of waiting. She is sick and tired of sitting alone in this big, empty house talking to a baby all day. She wants to be with the man she loves; she wants him to be with her, to notice her, to love her like he used to. In the days after the ear infection, he was like in the old days. He stayed at home when they came home from the hospital. He was with her and the baby and looked at her like he used to back in the days when their love for one another was still new and warm. But as soon as the ear infection was healed, he stopped paying attention to her again. He went back to his old self, his old overworking, and serious self, telling her she can handle the home and the baby perfectly fine and that she doesn't need him around now that the baby is well.

"Hello, Penelope? What's wrong?" he says when he answers. "Is the baby sick again?"

Penelope looks at the sleeping baby in the crib. Then she starts to cry.

"Penelope. Is everything all right? Why are you crying?"

"The baby is sick again, Peter. You'd better come home."

24

September 2015

I TAKE Salter back to my dad's house and take a shower while Salter walks Snowflake. Dogs aren't allowed on the beach, so he has to walk him on the street. Meanwhile, I get all the salt and sand washed off of me while wondering about Jean. I remember her vividly from my high school days.

She belonged to a flock of girls that I hadn't socialized a lot with. They were sort of the outsiders at the school. When the rest of us went surfing or skateboarding, they liked to just hang out and drink at the beach. Often they would stay there after dark. They would steal chairs from people's yards or old wood, or even break down part of people's fences to have wood for their bonfires. Then they would get drunk and be very loud all night. Our neighbors often called the police on them, especially when they had fires on the beach during turtle season. When the police came, they would confiscate the girls' beers and send them home. But the next weekend, they would be down there again. They always chose 7th Street as their location, and always right in front of our house. Sometimes, they would have boys down there with them and could be very loud. My dad never called the cops on them, yet they still had it in for us. One morning, when I came down to the beach to clean up after them as usual on Saturday mornings, they had written something, a message using the empty beer cans. It said:

BURN IN HELL MILLS

I felt extremely uneasy reading the message. Coming back to the house, I told my father about it, but he told me to leave it alone. They were just *drunk and fooling around*. Meanwhile, I was terrified of these girls and avoided them the best I could in school. But their dirty looks were always on me when I walked the hallways or in class.

I shiver thinking about them again and turn off the shower. I grab a towel and get out. I can't help but wonder if Jean had changed since those days. We were, after all, very young…just teenagers. I can't believe that our sweet Danny would marry her if she hadn't changed.

I get dressed and brush my hair. I am about to put on make-up, but decide not to. I am not going to impress anyone anyway. It is a very liberating feeling to not wear make-up for once. I leave the room feeling ten pounds lighter. Today, I am just going to wear a light summer dress and no makeup.

This is me. Nothing but just me.

Salter has apparently decided to take a longer walk, so I have nothing much to do while I wait. I decide to go down to the kitchen and prepare some lunch for the entire family. I know Laura won't make anything; she probably doesn't even eat lunch while on her paleo-gluten-free non-fat, no-sugar diet. Does she eat at all? I wonder. She doesn't look like it.

I walk down the stairs and into the hallway. When I am supposed to turn right to go to the kitchen, I stop instead and look down the hallway to the left. I don't know what comes over me at that moment, but my heart suddenly starts racing. I have a hard time breathing, and I feel an enormous pressure on my chest. I gasp for air as I look down the hallway to the rooms at this part of the house that no one ever uses except for Laura. I hear a voice in my head, a small childlike voice.

Please! No, no, please, please don't.

I grasp the railing of the stairwell so I won't fall. I am panting for air as the many pictures run through my mind. Usually, I can block them out, but these won't go away. I see my mother, my beautiful, stoic mother on the stairs. She is smiling, smiling at me.

Please don't! Please stop!

The screams get louder, then are replaced by a child crying. I see myself. I am not a child, though. I am a young teenager. I am crying. I can't stop. I feel so helpless. Then the screams are back. Squeals of pain. I close my eyes and try to focus on my breathing.

Think about something good. Think about Salter. Salter and Snowflake. The two things in your life that are good, that make it all worth it.

My heart is finally calmed down and I can open my eyes again. At the top of the stairs, I spot my dad. He is looking down at me. I can tell he has been there for a long time. He watches me for a few seconds, then turns and walks away.

I want to yell after him, tell him to come back, to face me and my pain, but I don't.

25

September 2015

Liz can't find rest. She goes for a run at the track on base. The sweat is springing from her forehead. She is alone on the track. No one in their right mind would run in the middle of the day in the baking sun in Florida.

Liz doesn't care. She wants it to be hard. She wants to sweat and exhaust herself, she wants to get some of all that anger inside of her out.

So far, there has been nothing in the local media about Billy the Kid or anyone talking about what happened to him at the resort. Liz smiles to herself when thinking about how much pain she inflicted on the guy. It fills her with so much pleasure, she has goose bumps in eighty-six degrees.

The sucker. Thought that he could get lucky, huh? I guess I showed him. Oh, I showed him good.

The other girls were scared when they were driving back to base.

"What if he tells the police?" Kim asked.

"What if he is found by a cleaning lady or something?" Jamie asked. "And she calls the police?"

But they were wrong for worrying. Liz always knows what she is doing. She knows a guy like Billy will never admit to anyone that a bunch of girls humiliated and degraded him like that. It is just like back in the schoolyard. Boys never tell if a girl beats them up. They know they will never hear the end of it from the other kids if they do.

"Take it easy, guys," Liz had told them. "It's me, remember? I've got this. Anyone who wants out can simply say so."

That quieted them down. They all knew what happened to the last girl who had tried to leave the group.

Liz has no idea what happened to Billy the Kid after they left him. Maybe he died? Nah, then she would have heard about it. It would have been on TV, and there was nothing the next morning or today. Part of her wants the media to tell about what she did. She likes it when they shiver in fear of what she can do. It isn't like they would ever know it was her. She is very good at covering her tracks. It is easy for her. Almost too easy.

She likes being in control. She likes having all the power. It almost went wrong once, but she always lands on top. She is that good at what she does. It is almost a sport for her.

In this moment, while running the track in the burning heat, Liz is feeling a great thrill go through her body. She saw the girl. Early in the morning, Liz took a drive up the coast, burning some rubber, speeding across A1A like she loves to do when she is not on duty, and right there, she saw her. She saw her walking across the street along with all the other idiots from back then.

Mary. Mary Mills.

Seeing her, Liz sped up with the intention of killing her right there on the spot, simply run her car into her floppy body. Oh how much she desired to do it, to finally finish her off, but in the last moment she had decided not to.

Not like this. Not yet. When she goes, it has to be spectacular. Your best work to date.

She isn't surprised that Mary Mills is back. Of course she came. Liz was waiting for it. Of course she came down to help that stupid brother of hers. Of course she is here.

Miss Mary Mack, Mack, Mack,

All dressed in black, black, black,

Liz laughs out loud while running and pretending to be punching someone.

I'll grab you hard, hard, hard

And give you smack, smack, smack

Liz speeds up and storms towards the finish line, pressing herself to the utmost, her heart pounding in her chest, threatening to burst. She throws herself on the grass, panting for her breath, then looks at her watch. She has beaten her personal best. She is in even better shape than when she was in her twenties and travelled all over the world as a soldier. She feels invincible, unbeatable. She is a freaking goddess. *The goddess of revenge.*

And she is ready to settle the score.

26

September 2015

"Could you please keep the dog in your room?"

My dad is standing in the entrance to the kitchen. Salter and I are sitting at the kitchen table, eating the salad I have created from what little I could find in the kitchen. I am not much of a salad eater, so I have poured a lot of cheese on it and found some pieces of chicken that I prepared and put in. I am planning on going grocery shopping afterwards to get us some real food.

I look down at Snowflake, who is sleeping under my feet. Salter walked him for a long time, so he is exhausted.

"He's not really bothering anyone, Dad."

"Laura doesn't like him being in here," he says.

Of course. Laura. She came in here briefly and gave us one short look, then ran to tell. Tattletale.

"I know, but he needed to get some water and food as well, and I thought it was better to keep his bowls down here instead of on the white carpet upstairs, where he will only spill and stain."

My dad sighs and rubs his forehead. "Alright. Just take him to your room when he has eaten and you're done. I'll take care of Laura. Could you please remove the surfboards from the yard as well?"

"Oh, those. Well, I kind of told Joey he could keep his board here, since he wants to go surfing with Salter tomorrow morning, and then Alex and Sandra asked if they could leave theirs as well. It's just till tomorrow."

"Well, we can't have them all over the yard, Mary," my dad says. Again, I can hear this isn't coming from him. He never used to care when people left their boards in our yard, so they didn't have to carry them so far. But, of course, Laura has changed that as well.

"It looks terrible. All the neighbors can see them."

"Come on, Dad! One of our friends just lost his wife this morning in a terrible tragedy. We're all pretty shaken up here. Can't it wait till tomorrow? They plan on stopping by and surfing early anyway before work, and I'll tell them to take their boards home afterwards, all right? I think we have more important things on our minds right now. Like your son. Remember Blake?"

My dad stares at me, then turns on his heel and leaves with an angry grunt. Salter looks at me.

"Eat your food," I say. "After this, we're going to Publix to buy some real food for this house. I can't survive on salad alone. I am a woman in my growing age. I need calories and so do you."

Salter laughs, then finishes his salad. I drink my carrot juice, holding my nose so I won't taste it.

"Maybe I could spend the day with Dad instead?" Salter asks cautiously.

"You mean to tell me you'd rather be with your father, whom you never see, than spend the next couple of hours with your mother whom you *always* see, buying groceries?" I ask with a smile.

I mess up his hair. He hates when I do that. I think it's a little early for him to be vain, so that's why I keep doing it. He has just recently gotten a new haircut and a lock of hair keeps falling into his face, making him look cool. I like it, but I don't like that he is getting so teenage-like. It is too early. I, for one, am not ready.

"All right, kid. I'll call your father and drop you off on the way there. You'll miss out on the samples, though. They have some good ones down here. And you won't be able to pick what we eat for dinner either."

"I think I'll live," he says.

I chuckle, yet feel a pinch of sadness. Grocery shopping is our thing to do usually on Saturdays. We love it. Eating all the samples that the nice ladies hand us, buying a delicious dinner and ice cream for dessert, then killing a bag of chips while chasing the aisles for the things that are actually on our list.

I enjoy having him as my life companion, and I'm not ready to let him go. At least, not yet. It is my greatest fear that he will ask me if he can move in with Joey. It would simply kill me.

"Mom, call him," he says, and pushes my phone closer to me.

"All right, all right. Hold your horses, cowboy."

27

May 1977

When Peter comes home, Penelope is holding the baby in her arms while she throws up violently. Peter is startled to learn that their baby is sick once again.

"What happened?" he asks.

Penelope looks at him. "I don't know. She just started to throw up all of a sudden. And I think she has a fever."

"We better take her to the emergency room again," Peter says. "She looks all pale."

Penelope nods and shows him she has packed a bag with diapers and extra clothes, in case they have to stay the night.

"We're not going to need that, Penelope," he says. "It's probably nothing. I think it needs to be really bad for them to want to keep her overnight."

But Penelope insists on bringing the bag, and soon they rush out to the car, and just as they get in, the baby vomits once again, all over the car seat.

Penelope immediately tries to wipe it off, but Peter stops her. "It doesn't matter. We need to go. Nothing is more important than our baby right now."

Penelope looks into the eyes of her beloved husband and nods. "Of course not."

When they arrive at the hospital, a doctor and a nurse take care of the baby after only a short waiting period, during which the baby throws up once again. Penelope feels such a relief when they examine her. Peter puts his arm around her while the nurses take her temperature.

"She'll be fine," he whispers. "Don't worry."

"What about your case?" Penelope says.

"Well, the hearing is tomorrow," he says. "I put Greg and Mark on it. They can gather the things we need."

"Don't you want to go and call the office and hear how they're doing?" she asks, hoping he won't. "There was a payphone down the hall. I can stay here and hear what they say."

"No. They'll be fine. This is more important."

Penelope sighs deeply. Yes, the baby was the most important thing now. She is so relieved he also feels that way.

"I can't seem to find anything wrong with your baby," the doctor says, when he is done listening to her heart, checking her ears and throat. "She has a little fever and she is a little dehydrated. I would like to, however, keep her for the night. Just for observation and to make sure she keeps hydrated."

Penelope looks at Peter, who seems baffled. "Keep her overnight?"

"I assure you, it's nothing but a precaution," the doctor says. "If she continues to throw up all night, she will need lots of hydration. She is, after all, still only a very young baby. We can't be too careful."

"Of course not, Doctor," Penelope says. "See, I told you we were going to need that bag. I even packed some clothes for you as well."

Both parents sleep in chairs in the baby's room at the hospital. The baby vomits another time violently before she finally finds rest. Penelope and Peter stay by her side and hardly sleep all night. Every time the baby makes the smallest sound, Penelope calls the nurses and asks for the doctor to come and see her. Peter tells her she is just too worried and the doctors assure her the baby is in good hands. Penelope listens to everything they tell her, and even writes little notes in her notebook afterwards. She is determined to know everything there is to know about this to make sure she is prepared.

The next morning, the baby wakes up feeling fine. She is cooing and smiling in her bed. Peter wants to pick her up and hold her in his arms, but Penelope stops him.

"No. Not until the doctor says it's alright," she says.

Peter looks at her like she has lost it. Still, he decides to wait.

A nurse enters the room and looks at the baby. "Aw, she is such a cutie. How is she doing this morning?"

"She still seems very pale," Penelope says. "I hope she's not going to vomit again."

"The poor thing. Does your tummy hurt, little baby? I feel bad for her," the nurse says, taking her temperature with a thermometer. "I hate it when they're this young. Being in a hospital bed when you're this young is no fun, is it? No, it isn't. You should be at home in your own comfortable bed with your mommy and not all these tubes and machines everywhere that go beep-beep-beep." The nurse tickled the baby on her tummy. The baby responds with a huge grin.

"I know," Penelope says. "It's tough. But it's for the best. She was really sick yesterday. I'm not sure she'll be better today. I fear the worst. She threw up a lot. It was bad, right Peter?"

Peter nods. "It was pretty bad."

The nurse looks at Penelope. "How are you holding up?"

"Me? Ah. I'm fine. Don't worry about me." Penelope let out a light laugh. "This is not about me."

"I bet neither of you got much sleep last night, huh?"

Penelope shakes her head. "No, you're right. It's hard when your little one is sick."

"It's the worst. I tell you that," the nurse says. "My oldest has leukemia. He is home now, but you never know when you're going to spend a night like this holding his hand, you know? And all the medicine he has to take constantly. Argh. I tell you. It's tough on a mother. I feel for you. I really do. Sometimes I think we mothers feel the pain as much as the child."

The nurse put her hand on Penelope's shoulder and she feels suddenly a lot more relaxed, like the anxiety that is constantly eating at her suddenly is drowned out for a little while. It feels good. Penelope feels calm. She can't remember feeling like this ever since the baby came into her life.

"It hasn't been easy," she says.

"Oh. I know," the nurse says. "No one ever notices the mother when the child is sick, but she is suffering as well, you know."

"So true."

"Anyway. I sure hope your baby will be better," the nurse says and waves at the girl who gives her a big toothless grin. "She seems to be doing very well this morning." The nurse looks at the thermometer in her hand. "There is no fever. That's a good sign. The doctor will be with you shortly on his rounds. I'm sure she is ready to go home."

Home? Now? But...but what if she gets sick again?

Penelope looks at the baby in the bed, feeling all of a sudden terrified once again. The thought of having all the responsibility on her shoulders, alone, is weighing her down. She doesn't know how to do it. She really doesn't.

Peter comes up behind her. "Did you hear that? She said the baby seems better. That's great news, huh honey?"

Penelope swallows hard. "Yes, dear. That is wonderful news. Wonderful indeed."

28

September 2015

I DRIVE up in front of the complex where Joey has rented a small townhouse. I kill the engine, then look at Salter. His cheeks and nose are red from the exposure to the sun this morning. Surfing does that to you. Even if we slap on a lot of sunscreen before we go out. Our skin hasn't been in this much direct sunlight for a very long time. I wonder how I all of a sudden have become this indoor person when I have always been the opposite. But the past many months, after Joey left us, I didn't want to go outside. I wanted to hide from the world. I wanted to stay in with Salter and Snowflake and eat chips on the couch and feel sorry for myself. I still want that. Being fired hasn't helped.

"Aren't you coming in to say hello?" Salter asks.

Joey has heard us drive up and is in the doorway waiting for us. He is wearing a T-shirt and he is still in his board shorts. That is Sundays for you in Florida. I remember wearing nothing but my swimsuit all weekend. You might as well. It is so extremely hot, and either you are in the ocean or you are in the pool. There isn't much time you spend dry on land in this place.

Joey looks devilishly handsome.

I bite my lip while staring at him from inside the car. I really don't want to come in. I have so much to do.

"I just saw him earlier," I say. "I don't think…"

I have barely finished the sentence before Joey opens the door to my rented car and peeks in. "Are you coming, or what?" he asks Salter.

Salter jumps out. Joey looks at me. "Do you want to come in for a beer or something?"

I shake my head. "No. I was just…"

And there it is. The look in Joey's eyes that I simply can't resist. I miss him. I miss talking to him.

You can't have a beer with him! He was a bastard, remember? He cheated on you!

"I- I-I have to go buy some groceries…"

Joey looks disappointed. "Oh. Okay. See you later then."

I stare at him. Stare at those deep-set blue eyes. He doesn't leave. It's like he knows I am fighting within.

"Ah, what the heck. Just one beer can't hurt anything. Lord knows I could use something after the morning we had," I finally say and get out.

You have the spine of a worm!

It is true. I have no backbone. Not when it comes to Joey.

"Let me give you a tour of the palace," he says, when I walk inside. The townhouse is a lot bigger than it appears from the outside. It has two nice bedrooms upstairs and a living room downstairs with a nice new kitchen. It is astonishing to me how much you can get for your money down here, compared to The Big Apple.

When he opens the door to the bedroom, a big black lab comes jumping out. It jumps up at me and I squeal in surprise. Behind it tags a small brown pig. I stare at Joey.

"Really?"

"They kind of came together," he says.

"Like a package deal?"

"Yeah. Kind of. They grew up together at a farm in Fellsmere. A friend of mine had them, actually he used to live right next door, but he had to move to California. He was a drummer in a band and they had a breakthrough so he had to leave. He couldn't take Bonnie and Clyde, so I said I would take them till he came back. If he ever comes back. Who knows."

"Bonnie and Clyde?"

"Yes. One can't live without the other. They need to stay together. What can I say? They keep me company when I get lonely down here. Besides, Salter loves them."

I look at my son, who pets the pig on her head and kisses her. Bonnie returns the gesture with a series of grunts. Salter laughs. I don't know what to think of this entire set-up. It is very far from the life we lived in Manhattan. But I can tell Joey enjoys it. He likes being back. It is like he is suddenly that same old Joey that I have known most of my life, the same Joey I fell in love with in high school.

He smiles. His white teeth light up his tanned face. He is in a lot better shape than before he left me. Probably all that surfing.

"So, how about that beer?" he says. "We can bring Bonnie and Clyde out with us in the backyard. They need some fresh air."

29

September 2015

Salter plays with the animals, throwing a ball around in the grass, and for the most part it is Bonnie who picks it up. I wonder if it is like in the movie *Ice Age* where the mammoth thinks she's a possum and acts like one. Maybe Bonnie thinks she is a dog like Clyde. She sure acts like one.

"So, some day, huh?" Joey asks. "I can't believe what happened to Jean. I keep thinking about it."

I sip my beer. I grabbed a light one since I am driving after this. It feels good to be with Joey again, back in our old *hood*. Even though I still hate this place, it is kind of beginning to grow on me a little. If only it wasn't combined with so much pain for me.

"I know. It's crazy."

"It's all over the local news. They say she was stabbed in the throat with a pair of scissors, then bled to death. Can you imagine coming home and finding your wife like that? I would be devastated. I don't know how I would be able to keep on living."

Being still his wife, even if we are separated, it makes me feel flattered.

"He seemed pretty shaken. Have you heard from any of the others?"

"Alex called just before you got here. Danny is still at the police station for questioning. I can't believe they can't let a man grieve in peace. I mean, he just lost his wife. Give him a break."

"But, they know Danny, right? He is, after all, captain at the fire station next door to them."

"I know. They work pretty close together. They won't give him a hard time, but still it must be so hard for him to have to go through the interrogation right away."

"I'm guessing they need to. Because of the investigation," I say, drawing on my experience from writing crime stories as a reporter. "It all needs to be fresh in his memory. Any little detail might help in finding whoever did this."

Joey shrugs. "I guess. I still think it's inhuman."

"I'm guessing there isn't much we can do right now, is there?" I ask.

"Just be there for him," he says. "Alex told me he had picked up Junior and that the boy was at Alex's house now. He is going to pick up Danny as soon as he's done at the station. Then I figure we all should go there."

"Sounds like a good idea. I thought I might cook for them. I can throw something together for all of us and fill Alex's freezer, so they have food for some days while Junior and Danny stay with him. It will be a few days, maybe more, before Danny and Junior can go back to their house again. Forensic work takes a long time."

Joey looks at me. "You cook now?"

I put a hand to my side. "And why do you sound so surprised?"

"Maybe because in the fifteen years we were married, you never cooked."

"That's not true!"

"All right, you did cook a few times. A *few* times in fifteen years."

"That was because I was always tired when I came home from work."

Joey's face turns serious. "Oh, yeah. That's right. Your precious work. I remember that." His eyes avoid mine all of a sudden.

My heart drops. I know I took him for granted back then. Since he didn't work much, he had done most of the cooking or we had ordered in. I am not very good with compliments. Growing up in a house where compliments were something you had to work hard to get, it doesn't come natural to me. I want to say something nice to him at this moment, but simply can't get myself to it. I can't get it through my lips. I am still so angry at him for sleeping with that girl, for leaving us. I am not sure he deserves a compliment.

"Well, I brought home the money, didn't I?" I say instead. "I never heard you complain about that. Or maybe you did when you went to the coffee house?"

I immediately regret having said it when the words leave my lips. I sense how Joey almost jumps when I say it.

"Are you saying I didn't work? You were gone all day long, every freaking day. Who picked up Salter? Who changed his diapers when he was a baby? Who took him to the park? Who was there when he took his first step? Who grocery shopped? Who washed and ironed all your little skirts so you could wear them at your fancy office? Huh? Who did all that?"

And there it is. We are right back where we started.

I put the beer bottle down on the patio table. "This was a mistake," I say and get up. "Salter, give Mommy a kiss. I'll be back to pick you up at four."

30

March 1992

Ally is already happier in Cocoa Beach than in any of the seven other places she had lived in. She never shows her parents, though. To them, she is still angry, slamming doors and yelling at them, but she has immediately fallen in. She has found her place hanging out with the girls from school. None of these girls are like any of the others at Cocoa Beach High, Ally soon learns. They aren't the pretty ones; they aren't cheerleaders or surfers or soccer players like the rest. They don't care about good grades or pleasing the teachers. Instead, they skip school together, a lot, and go downtown to hang out on the streets. Their favorite thing to do is to yell mocking words at tourists. That is a lot of fun. If they see a tourist waiting for the light to turn green at a crosswalk, one of them will approach him while the others watch. The dare is to steal his wallet without him noticing it.

They have tried to get Ally to do it too, but so far she has refused. One of the girls, AK, soon starts to nag her about it, telling her that *you can't just be a bystander*. You can't just let all the others do the hard work while you have the fun laughing at it. Not in this group. They all contribute.

"Besides, it's fun," she says, while touching her Mohawk. "It's like a drug. Once you've stolen your first wallet, there is no going back. You'll want to do it again and again to feel the kick."

A few days later, Ally volunteers herself, even though she really doesn't want to. She isn't sure she has it in her, and she is terrified of getting caught.

She walks up to a couple that are clearly tourists (fanny packs, T-shirts that say Ron Jon's, that look in their eyes that tells you they have no idea where they are going). They are standing at the intersection at Minutemen, looking clueless, when the girls nudge Ally along.

Ally smiles kindly. "Are you looking for something?"

The man looks at Ally. "Yes. Yes we are. We want to find a nice place to eat. Do you know any around here?"

"Heidi's just opened on the corner over there. I don't know if it has good food, though," she says, sounding nice and polite.

Meanwhile, the other girls giggle behind her as her hands creep into the woman's purse and pull out a wallet. Ally's hands are sweaty. Her heart is racing. She has never done anything like this before. Her hands are shaking heavily as she pulls it out and places it inside the pocket of her neon windbreaker that she wears backwards like *Kris Kross*. Her forehead is itching underneath her bandana.

"Thank you, dearie," the woman says.

"You're welcome. By the way…"

"Yes?"

"Did anyone ever tell you you're fat?"

The woman looks at the man like she expects him to clarify what she just heard. "Excuse me?"

The girls are giggling loudly behind her now. It makes her feel strong and more self-confident to know they are with her. She wants to show them. She wants to earn their respect and her worth in the group.

"Did you just tell my wife that she is fat?" the man says.

Ally smiles like he has heard her wrong. "No, no, no. That's not what I meant. I meant you're *both* very overweight. You really should consider exercising or maybe lay off the donuts a little, huh?"

Ally pokes the woman's belly, then laughs. "See. It's not supposed to move like that."

The man steps up. He gets threatening. Ally stays in position. It is all about not showing fear now. The man's face turns red.

"Why. You little…"

He swings out his hand with the intention of slapping her face, but Ally ducks and he misses. Instead, she throws a punch as hard as she can and knocks the air out of him. He gasps and bends forward, then falls to his knees. The woman lifts her hands in the air and screams.

"Help! Police! Help!"

Ally stares nervously at the man and realizes what she has done. Then she looks at her girls for approval. They all laugh. Especially AK seems captivated by the situation. She walks up to the man, who is still on all fours, and kicks him in the stomach. The man screams in pain. Ally looks at him, terrified.

What have I done?

"We gotta go now," one of the girls yells. "We're attracting too much attention."

The girls take turns to throw one last punch each into the man's stomach before they flee the place.

While running, Ally is happy to realize she now has the approval of the group. No one will ever question her again. Not only has she convinced the girls that she is capable of almost anything and getting away with it, she has also discovered a new side to herself.

31

September 2015

I COOK ALL AFTERNOON, much to my stepmother's irritation. I am making a mess of the place, and when she peeks in now and then, she does nothing but send an annoyed sigh my way before she leaves, and soon after my dad comes into the kitchen and tells me to remember to clean up after myself.

That little spectacle goes on for a few hours, while I create so many dishes I could open a restaurant. Cooking helps me relax; it makes me forget all the bad emotions, all the frustrations from arguing with Joey again. Even all the sadness from knowing my brother might end up in prison, along with the sorrow from knowing Danny lost his wife in such a brutal manner last night, and the worry that Salter will never want to live with me again. I try not to think about it, but I am certain that he will choose his dad over me, and then what do I do?

There is a lot going on inside of me, to put it mildly. And the cooking takes all that away for a few hours. It makes me clear my mind. It is my yoga, my meditation, if you will.

Around four o'clock, I take the car to pick up Salter. I take both him and Joey with me to Alex's place. We don't speak to one another the entire drive there, only Salter babbles on about how he and his dad went fishing in the river and he almost caught a rainbow trout, but it got away from him, and how he wishes he could do that every day.

"That's great, honey," I say, not really listening. My mind is elsewhere. I am thinking about the argument and the emotions that have once again been ripped up between Joey and me. I am beginning to long for Manhattan and my quiet life up there. Except I don't look forward to facing unemployment with no money in the bank. I am spending the last of my savings on Blake's lawyer, and I don't like to think about what is going to happen after that.

"Could you help me with the food?" I ask both of them, as we park the car in front of Alex's beach house on 7th Street. He can peek over to my dad's house on the other side of A1A. It was a little overkill to drive there, but there is no way I could have carried all this food.

It is amusing that Alex now actually lives on 7th Street. Growing up, we always made fun of Alex because he lived on 6th, whereas the rest of us lived on 7th. We would always tease him—lovingly of course—and call him an outsider, a loser, since he wasn't a real *7th Streeter*. Living on this street now means he is almost a neighbor to Sandra, which to me is a little odd. He and Sandra used to have a thing for each other back in the day. I wonder if they ever think of each other in the same way they used to. I never understood what went wrong with them, why they didn't end up together. They were so perfect for each other, and we all thought they would become a couple, but it never happened.

I am about to ring the doorbell, my hands full of lasagna and burritos, when Joey walks in front of me, grabs the handle, and opens the door.

"Around here, we just walk in," he says. "But I guess you've forgotten about that. Or maybe you're too tired or too busy to care?"

Ouch!

I think long and hard for a comeback, but unfortunately I have never been fast at those things. I can always come up with something a few days later, something real clever and witty, but never in the moment. I often wonder if people will think it weird if I call them a few weeks later and give them the line.

Joey walks inside. Salter and I follow. Everyone is there. Alex, Sandra and her husband Ryan, Marcia and four kids I assume are hers, since they look just like her. Danny and Junior are there too, and even Chloe.

"Mary!" Alex says. "I want you to meet my wife, Maria."

"Nice to meet you," I say and smile at the woman in front of me. She is short and has long black hair that she obviously dyes. She has pretty blue eyes. She seems nice. I guess I could approve of her for Alex, even though I always wanted him to be with Sandra. Alex is a sweet guy. He needs a sweet woman.

"I would shake your hand, but...well, they're both pretty full, as you can see."

"Where are my manners?" Alex says and grabs the food out of my hands.

"I made some for tonight," I say, "and then a lot for the freezer. You know, for Danny and Junior and all of you. To help you out."

"That is very nice of you," Maria says with a smile. "Here, let me take the rest." Maria grabs the dishes Salter is carrying.

I look at all the familiar faces and feel slightly emotional. It has been a long time since the crew was back together. I miss every one of them, but at the same time seeing them again, together like this, overwhelms me with a deep sadness as well. I am not sure I can cope with it. I am suddenly not sure I am ready. The thing is, I am not sure I will ever be.

I spot Danny and walk up to him, drawing in a deep breath. I have to get over myself. This night isn't about me or how I feel. It is about him and his son and being there for them, no matter what. That's the deal with friends, right? They are there for you no matter what.

32

September 2015

"I KNOW you've probably gotten this question a lot," I say as I approach Danny.

He is sitting in a barstool at the breakfast bar, scratching the label on his beer. Meanwhile, it seems that everyone else is somehow moving around him and not talking directly to him. He looks up.

"How are you holding up?" I ask and sit down on a barstool next to him. The expression on his face is rough to take in. Those eyes and the deep sadness in them almost make me cry.

Oh, you're such a crybaby, Mary. Pull yourself together.

"Actually, you're the first one to ask me that since I got here," he answers. "The rest are only asking me if I want something to eat or drink. Apparently, people think food can make pain go away or something."

I blush. "Yeah, well…some people can be so insensitive. Pah. Food. As if that ever made you happier."

"Exactly," he says. "The last thing I want right now is to eat."

Wow. Right to my face, huh? That's okay. I can take it. I'm a big girl.

"Yeah, well. You still didn't answer my question."

He scoffs. "How am I holding up? Right now I'm just trying to stay on this stool, sit still, and hold onto this beer. I want to drink it.

I want to drink all of the beers in Alex's fridge. I want to get so drunk I can't feel anything, but I can't get myself to do it. It feels wrong. I feel like I need to grieve and feel the grief, if you know what I mean? I keep thinking I deserve to feel pain."

He pauses and looks first down at his beer, then back up at me. "You know what it's like," he says. "Like back when..."

Danny pauses. I stare at him, hoping, praying that he won't finish the sentence. Luckily, he doesn't.

"I'm sorry," he says and drinks from his beer.

"That's okay," I say. "I still don't like to talk about it. Maybe I will one day. I don't know."

Awkward silence between us. I sip my beer and throw a glance around the room. Junior is sitting in the corner on a couch while the other kids are storming around. Salter is playing with Marcia's many kids, having a blast, it seems.

"You just wonder, you know?" Danny says.

I look back at him. He is ripping off parts of the label on his beer. "Who would do this to her? You wouldn't believe how much blood there was on the porch. A pair of scissors? I mean, come on. That's brutal!"

"It sure is," I say, trying not to picture Jean lying on the porch in a pool of blood with a pair of scissors in her throat. It is hard not to. "What do the police say?"

"Not much so far. But they don't believe she was a random victim. It wasn't a burglary gone wrong."

"Wow. So brutal murder, huh? Do you have any idea who might have had it in for her? I mean, did she have any enemies or anything? Someone she pissed off? A neighbor or something?"

Danny scoffs. "You knew Jean. Probably half the town had it in for her. People hated her."

I nod and drink again. I am glad he said it so I don't have to. "May I ask what you liked about her?"

He looks at me. I regret the question. Have I gone too far?

Me and my big mouth!

Then he laughs. Waves of relief go through my body.

"She had a great body," he says. "Yes, you heard me. I was that superficial. I took her because she was gorgeous back then. I wanted to have sex with her so bad, and then she got pregnant. It wasn't like I had much of a choice. It was the right thing to marry her."

I throw a glance back at Junior on the couch. It makes sense. The boy is about eighteen now, ready to graduate high school.

"So, do they have any clues?" I ask.

He shrugs. "They say they believe the person can't have been very tall. Something about the angle of the scissors or something. I have to admit, I can't remember. It's all a blur. I just really hope they find whoever did this. Mostly for Junior. To give him closure, you know?"

33

February 1978

By the time she turns one year old, Penelope has had her baby to a myriad of doctors, but they still don't know what is wrong with her. The baby can hardly hold any food down and she hasn't grown much in her entire year of being alive, much to her parents' and the doctors' concern.

Finally, after a year of running from doctor to doctor, one of them concludes it has to be her heart, or *it could be her heart* are his exact words.

The diagnosis, even if it is vague, makes Penelope at ease finally. She is weary and tired of telling all the doctors that she believes something is wrong with the baby's heart, but no one believes her. They keep telling her the baby's heart is fine, but the heart palpitations and weight loss tell her a different story.

"So, what do we do next?" she asks the doctor. "Will surgery be necessary?"

The doctor lets out a deep sigh. "She is still so very young." He looks at the baby in her mother's arms. She is able to sit on her own, but no crawling or even standing up like other children her age. Her legs simply aren't strong enough yet. And she is way too sick to be moving around, let alone be with other children. It is too risky.

"We usually don't operate on children this young, if we can help it," he says. "But based on the tests we have so far, I'm thinking it might be necessary to do a heart catheterization procedure in time. In a child who has a congenital heart defect, a heart catheterization shows how the blood is flowing through the heart. The exact heart problem can be seen, and sometimes treated during the same procedure or a later one. If your child has a complex heart defect, he or she might need a combination of surgery and catheterization to treat it. But, as I said, it is very unusual to perform this procedure on such a young child. It has never been done before, as far as I have been informed. You might need to wait a few years till she is older."

"But, Doctor, we don't have a few years. If something is wrong with her heart, she needs the surgery now," Penelope argues.

She glances at the empty chair next to her where Peter is supposed to sit. He wasn't able to come with them this morning to get the results. He has lost too many hours at work running to doctors constantly. Penelope can't wait to tell him that, finally, she has found a doctor who believes her. Their baby is sick and she isn't just a hysterical mother.

The doctor looks at the baby again. "It's too risky," he says.

Penelope scoffs. "How can you say that? She might die if she doesn't get the surgery now! Look at her. She is very sick."

The doctor sighs again. He touches the bridge of his nose.

"I think we should wait and see, maybe give it six months, then run more tests. She needs to be at least three years old before I would dare to do a procedure like this on her."

Penelope stares at the doctor. How can he say that? Three years old? That is two years from now.

"But...but, Doctor...just this morning she threw up again. She can hardly hold anything down. She is so weak. I can't stand it. Please. Could you just perform the surgery? I'm willing to take the risk. Any risk. Anything to help my baby get better. Please, Doctor. I'm desperate here."

"I'm sorry. I can't. I won't risk her life. Come back in six months and we'll have a look at her and see how she's doing. We'll monitor her closely for the next couple of years. If she's not better by the age of three, we'll do the procedure."

"You can't risk her life?" Penelope says and stands up. "That is exactly what you're doing. If my baby dies, it's your fault."

The doctor gesticulates, resigned. "I'm sorry, but…"

Penelope snorts angrily as she opens the door. "Well, if you won't do it, then I'll find a doctor who will," she says and walks out.

34

September 2015

We end up getting drunk. Danny and I sneak outside on the porch to get away from the others and all their pity-looks. They mean well. We know they do, but it's just not what Danny needs right now.

Danny decides it is all right to get wasted, and he is in charge tonight. I find a bottle of whiskey in Alex's kitchen and start spicing our drinks up a little. I figure we both need it.

The more drunk Danny gets, the more he opens up to me about his marriage and how awful it was. It is a relief for me to hear and I can tell it helps him to talk about it.

"I wanted to leave her, Mary," he says. "I did. I thought about it so many times. But I was a wimp. I should have left her years ago. You want to know the funny part?"

"Sure," I say and pour each of us another whiskey. We both drink and he looks at me with his bloodshot eyes.

"I was afraid of her. Can you believe that? I was such a wimp, I didn't dare to leave her. I was terrified of what she would do. I was so scared she would keep Junior from me, you know? I would never be able to handle that."

"You probably shouldn't tell this to the police," I say, laughing. "It kind of gives you a motive."

Danny stares at me, then bursts into laughter. We laugh for a little while, then stop and sit in silence. Each lost in our own train of thought.

"So, how's Blake?" he finally asks.

In the distance, I can hear the waves crashing. I think about my dad and Laura. They are going to be pissed that we'll be getting back so late.

Screw them. I'm not a child anymore.

"Awful," I say. "He's in that terrible prison halfway to Orlando, and I don't think he will survive it. I've got to get him out somehow. The thing is, they have a murder weapon and a witness. Pretty solid case, if you ask me. I'm spending all my savings, the last of my money, on his lawyer."

"What do you mean the last of your money?" he asks. "I thought you were a big time reporter at *The New York Times*?"

I scoff. "Not anymore. I just got sacked a few days ago."

"What? You got fired?"

"Keep it down," I say, and look through the sliding glass-doors behind me. The others are sitting around the table. Alex's daughter, Ava, who I met earlier, is playing on an iPad. Three of Marcia's kids are sleeping on the couch, the last playing with a truck on the floor. Junior and Salter are watching TV.

"I haven't told anyone. Not even my dad and Laura."

I sip my whiskey and enjoy the burning sensation in my throat. I close my eyes, hoping it will make it all go away. My brother in jail, my separation from Joey, me fearing the future since I got fired, the terrible memories being brought back to life ever since I stepped into that house again. All of it. I just want it to be gone.

"There you both are. Hey, guys, they're out here!"

Marcia has opened the door and peeks out. "We were all wondering where you two were." She is holding a plastic cup in her hand. By the look of how she is swaying from side to side, it isn't soda she has inside of it.

Well, who am I to talk? I suddenly feel nausea overwhelm me. Danny doesn't look too well either.

"Maybe we should go inside," he says, and gets up from the small couch where we have been sitting.

When I rise to my feet, I feel dizzy and have to hold on to the wall behind me. "I think I've had enough," I say with a giggle. I am way more drunk than I had thought.

We follow Marcia inside, where the rest of the crew is sitting around all the food and chips. They're talking. Sandra smiles when she sees me. We used to be inseparable in high school.

"Come, join us," she says.

I shake my head. "I think I've had enough. We need to go home."

Danny stumbles towards me and gives me a heavy bear hug. I close my eyes and enjoy it. Danny has always been one of my favorites. Always so kind to others, so loving. It isn't fair that he has had such a lousy life as a grown-up.

"Let us know if there is anything we can do to help you with Blake," he says when he lets go. "Have you spoken to Olivia yet?"

I frown. "Olivia?"

Danny look surprised. "Blake didn't tell you about her?"

"No."

"He was seeing her. You remember Olivia, don't you? I think she is married now, right, Alex?"

Alex nods. "Yeah. To some general in the army. What's his name?"

"Hartman," Joey says.

"That's it." Alex snaps his fingers. "Olivia Hartman is her name now. It started out being all about the sex, but I think Blake was in over his head a little here."

"What do you mean?"

"He committed the only sin you cannot commit when being with a married woman," Danny says. "He fell in love with her."

35

March 1992

"Wow! Did you see the face on that woman?"

The four girls run down to the beach and hide in the dunes while they hear wailing sirens throughout the city. Ally's hands are shaking. She can't believe what just happened. What she has just done.

"Help. Help. Police," the girl with the Mohawk who calls herself AK says, imitating the woman. Then she laughs again.

AK is the leader of the group and impressing her means a great deal for Ally. Seeing the look in her eyes now makes Ally feel better about herself, about what she has just done.

"You're badass," she says to Ally. "I like you. From now on, we'll call you AL. Like in the song, right? *You can call me AL*?"

AK laughs. So do Double O and JJ. It is AK who has given them their street names, as she calls them, and apparently, Ally is now AL. Ally has been waiting for AK to give her a new name. She wonders if this means she is now officially part of the group. If it is enough.

The next day, the police arrive at the school and start asking questions about the students' whereabouts on the day of the attack on the tourists. Ally is worried that someone might rat her out, but to her surprise, the girls all stand up for each other and give each other alibis. The police suspect them, the girls all know they do, but they can't prove anything. AK even pays a teacher to tell the police that they were in class all day. AK always has a way of getting away with things. No matter how bad they are. Ally admires her for that. She admires her for many things. Her strength, her courage, her looks, the way she doesn't care what people think about her. She can terrorize the kids in the school without anyone daring to tell on her. Just by walking down the school hallway with her, Ally can hear the student's teeth clattering in fear. No one even dares to look at her directly. Kids flee from her presence. Even teachers fear her.

AK is one of those kids who has nothing to lose. She has no parents and lives in a home with other children that have no parents. She never thinks about the future or growing up or getting good grades. She knows she will never make it to college, since no one can pay for it, so there is no use in trying. No one believes in her, so why should she? She has a fire in her eyes that makes people tremble in her presence. Even the grown-ups.

AK is untouchable. And by being her friend, Ally becomes superior as well. Together, they kick the garbage cans in the school cafeteria and tip them over and throw garbage at the other kids. They terrorize students and tourists in the streets, they knock bicyclists off their bikes on A1A and make them fall, and then threaten to kill them if they ever tell anyone. They smoke cigarettes and place the burning butt on the arm of a woman if she tells them they can't smoke somewhere, then chase her off by threatening to burn down her house with her family inside of it.

That's who they have become now.

A few weeks after the incident with the tourists, AK approaches Ally in the schoolyard and tells her to walk with her during their lunch break.

"It was awesome what you did that day," she says, referring to the day when they beat the tourist. "I believe you're probably the strongest member we've had in our group. I believe in you a lot, but I need you to prove yourself to us. Your loyalty to our group," she says. She turns and looks Ally in the eyes. Ally sees the flame inside of them.

"I need to know that you're with us. With me. All the way."

"Of course I am. You know that I am, AK." How can she not know by now? With all they had done?

"Good. I need your complete loyalty. I have something I want you to do. With me. Just the two of us, alone."

AK then asks her to meet her at an address that coming Friday evening at midnight. She isn't allowed to ask any questions or to even speak to the other girls about it. Ally feels special sharing this secret, this upcoming event with AK.

Ally goes home that day, wondering what AK wants her to do. Will it be like some kind of initiation ritual? What will she have to do? Get drunk and run around town naked? She can do that. As a matter of fact, she is willing to do anything right now to be accepted by AK, to prove her loyalty. Moving around as much as she has while growing up, this is the first time she has actually made some friends, the first time she feels like she fits in. She will do anything to stay with these girls. To finally feel accepted.

36

September 2015

Blake was seeing a woman? Why didn't he tell me? Why has no one told me about this?

I am lying awake in my bed, staring at the ceiling of my father's house, wondering about my younger brother. I can't believe he hasn't told me anything about this. Maybe he thinks it isn't important, and maybe it isn't, but still.

I sit up and grab my laptop. I Google her name and find various articles about her husband and a lot of pictures of the two of them together. Apparently, they are sort of a celebrity couple within the military.

I grab the phone and call James Holland to hear how he is doing on the case. It is almost noon Monday and my head is throbbing heavily as I wait for his reply. I badly want to go down for a meeting, but he tells me there is no need to. Not yet.

"There is nothing new to tell, Miss Mills, I'm sorry."

"So, what do we do now?"

"We wait for the State Attorney to charge Blake. Once we know the charges, we can start to build our defense."

"So, let me rephrase. What can I do?"

"There isn't much you can do at this moment," he says. "We have to wait. I'm sorry, but that's all we can do right now."

Is that what I am paying you those big bucks for?

"Did you know anything about a woman he was seeing?" I ask.

James Holland scoffs. "No."

"I need help getting the details straight," I say. "Why doesn't he have an alibi for the night of the murder? It happened on a Thursday night, right? Thursday the week before he was arrested?"

"Yes. According to the eyewitness, Blake picked the two girls up at Grills Riverside in Melbourne and took them back to his studio, where they arrived at eleven o'clock at night. According to the eyewitness, they were all three of them engaged in some sex game and that suddenly Blake stabbed Jamilla Jenkins using the chisel. The eyewitness screamed and ran out of the studio and into the street, where she grabbed a taxi. Afraid that Blake might kill her as well, she kept quiet until it was all over the news that the body of her friend had been found. Then she came forward. She is still terrified of Blake and her name has been kept a secret so far."

"Could she be lying?" I ask.

He sighs. "It doesn't matter if she is. She's army, a decorated war hero from both Iraq and Afghanistan. No one will believe us if we claim she is lying."

"Alright. What else do we have? What has Blake told the police?"

"In his statement given to the police, Blake has declared that he *was* at the bar, the same bar where the girl claims he picked them both up, at Squid Lips in Melbourne on the evening of the murder. He was drinking heavily and was seen by a lot of people. People that have testified to seeing him drinking and dancing and being very loud, making quite the spectacle of himself. Apparently, the establishment was used to that from him. He is known around here as quite the party monkey. Anyway, the last thing he says he remembers is the band going on at seven o'clock. Some one-man-band named Johnny Danger took the stage. Your brother remembers it specifically because he loves Johnny Danger. The strange part is that after that he doesn't remember anything anymore. Not a single detail of what happened the rest of the night. It's all black, he says, which makes this case even harder. The problem is that is not unusual for your brother…to drink till he blacks out. He claims he woke up the next morning in his own bed. A week later, he goes to Starbucks to see his painting get hung up on the wall there. When he gets back to his own place, the police are waiting for him there. They found the bloody chisel under his sink. That and the eyewitness, who states she saw him stab Miss Jamilla Jenkins during a sex game the night before, is probably what they're basing their charges on."

"And the body? Where was it found? If I remember it right, there was no blood in the studio?"

"That's one thing I don't understand," he says. "The body was found in a hotel room at a Motel 6. How was Blake supposed to take her there, rent a room, and carry her inside after he stabbed her?"

"And, why would he do that?" I ask. "It's not like it's a great place to hide a dead body."

"Exactly. I have found no one at the motel that remembers him or her, neither is his name found anywhere. His credit card wasn't even used to pay for the room. It was paid with cash. There is no evidence in the car, no trace of blood, or even any of the girl's hair. That's the angle I'm working on right now. That's where the police's investigation is inconsistent. And that's all I can do with what I have."

I write everything down on my notepad, then tell James Holland I will be in touch before I hang up. I grumble while going through the details once again. I have been over it so many times and can't make it work. The part about the motel room is new to me. So is the girlfriend I never knew he had.

I circle the name Olivia Hartman a couple of times, wondering about her and Blake. I get that he has kept her a secret because she is married and all…to not get her in trouble. That makes a lot of sense. Especially if he really likes her. But he told Alex, Danny, and Joey about her, apparently. Why only them and not me? I can't help feeling a little offended. He and I aren't close, but we talk over the phone every now and then. Is he more comfortable talking to the boys? Is that what this is all about? Or is he bragging maybe? Maybe it's a boy thing that I wouldn't understand. Well, I can't blame him if he is bragging, I think to myself, looking at her picture on my computer screen. She is quite the beauty. But she is old. Much too old for him. I remember her vividly from when we were teenagers.

I decide to get moving, despite the headache and nausea. I, for one, am not going to sit here and wait for my brother to rot in that jail. I want to figure out what the heck is going on. I only have around eight days till Salter has to be back in school, and besides helping my brother get out of this mess, I have to find a new job. With the reputation I have by now, it could prove to be just as hard as getting my brother acquitted.

Salter has already walked Snowflake and comes back with a big smile on his face. I am just getting out of the shower. Snowflake jumps me and licks the water off my legs. His fur is filled with sand. I give Salter a look.

"Did you walk him on the beach?"

"Well…he…"

"You know you're not supposed to do that. Grandpa and Laura would kill you if they knew. And look at all that sand that he dragged inside the house. Oh, my God, Laura is going to kill me."

Salter is still smiling.

"What are you so happy about?" I ask.

"Dad called while you were sleeping. His job today on that roof has been pushed because of the high possibility of rain later today. So, he told me he would take me fishing again."

"That's great, honey," I say, longing for a cup of coffee to kill this hangover. "I'll drop you off on my way to Starbucks."

37

September 2015

I DROP Salter off outside his dad's place and don't bother to say hello to Joey. I don't want him to see me like this. He'd be able to tell right away that I am hung over. He knows me too well, and I would never hear the end of it. Besides, I am not in the mood for a new confrontation with him. I have no energy, nor the will to argue.

I park in front of the new Starbucks on State Road 520 and walk inside, still wearing my sunglasses. The girl behind the counter smiles at me and I order a pumpkin spice latte and a chocolate donut. I spot my brother's big painting on the wall and walk to it. *It is actually quite good*, I think to myself, while sipping my coffee and taking the first bite of the donut.

I grab a chair and sit down in front of the painting, admiring my brother's creativity. I have never been able to create anything but words on a piece of paper, and I have always found it astonishing what Blake can create. I never understood why he doesn't have more success. I know he has tried everything. At one point, he even painted cell phone cases for people, but he didn't make much on that either. My guess is that he still borrows money from my dad to get by, and I can't blame my father for being fed up with it. Especially with the lifestyle my brother has led the past years, ever since he got his art degree from college.

"You like the painting?"

It is the girl from behind the counter. She has come over to clean the table next to me. "It's for sale."

I chuckle. "Oh, I'm not looking to buy."

She picks up an empty cup, then stops in front of the painting. "It's really good, though," she says. "Too bad he won't be able to make more."

I almost choke on my donut. I swallow the bite that almost got stuck and look at her. "What do you mean?"

"Haven't you heard? He's going to jail. Apparently, he killed someone. Kind of hard to imagine him doing that, though. But that just shows…you never really know people, right? He seemed so nice."

"You know him?" I ask.

"Sure. He used to come here every day for his coffee. Then he would ask to talk to Ray, our manager. Every day for almost a year he asked him to let him put up one of his paintings for display. Finally, Ray got tired of saying no. He's pulling it down later today. Says he doesn't want some killer's painting in his shop. I'll miss it, though. I kind of like it."

"Say, did he ever come in here with anyone?" I ask. "Or was he always alone?"

"He was always alone," she says. "Until the day when we put up the painting. Someone was with him that day."

"Who? Was it a woman?"

"As a matter of fact, it was. I remember we talked about it, since we had never seen him with a woman before and some of us wondered if he was gay. I never thought he was, though. Just doesn't seem the type. He always flirted with me."

She makes a shy movement then returns to cleaning up. She throws out the cup. I pull out my phone and find a picture of Olivia Hartman, which I show to her. "Was this the woman who was with him that morning?"

The girl looks at it, then nods with surprise. "Yes. Yes. That was her. How did you know?"

I sigh and put my phone back. "Just a hunch. Say, did you notice if they left together?"

"They did. Drove in separate cars, though. Why?"

I finish my donut and grab my cup. "Tell your boss to not throw away the painting. I'll buy it and come for it later."

38

September 2015

THE DOOR to my brother's studio is decorated with black-and-yellow tape that says CRIME SCENE DO NOT CROSS.

I slide under it and through the door without breaking the seal. I enter his small studio. The place is a mess. Old beer bottles, cigarette stubs on dirty plates, food with mold on it. The studio is just one big room under the ceiling of the building. His bed is in one corner. Nothing but a mattress on the floor.

Who lives like this?

I pick up a sock from the floor, then realize there is nowhere I can put it, and let it fall to the wooden floor again. There is dust in the corners and on all his lamps; the floor needs to be washed. Shoes that have stepped in paint have left marks all over the wooden planks.

"Probably wouldn't count on getting that deposit back once you leave, dear brother," I mumble and walk into the kitchen. A chair is knocked over and I pick it up. I sit down on it and try to take in the room, wondering why I am even here.

"What happened, Blake?"

According to Holland, Blake was arrested right here on that morning he came back from Starbucks.

I want to go visit him again today or tomorrow, but the lawyer has told me not to talk about the case with him. They're still in a phase where they will be listening in and use anything he says against him. I know we have to be very careful now.

The crime scene investigators have swept the place. I see marks on the walls where they have dusted for fingerprints and same marks on the floors where they have taken footprints. The place doesn't look much like a crime scene. It's dirty and messy, yes, but there is no blood anywhere. The kitchen table is in an odd position, though…pushed up against the wall while the chairs are in the middle of the floor. I walk to it and look at the footprints on the floor. Someone stepped in blue paint. The prints are all over the floor underneath the table. What strikes me is the shape of the print. The print from the heel is very small, almost nonexistent. It can only have been made by a pair of high-heeled stilettos. The paint is fresh. I get some on my finger when I touch it.

Who wears stilettos to a crime scene?

I have been at my share of crime scene investigations, covering them as a reporter, and seen many female investigators and detectives, even sometimes the district attorney is female, but none of them ever wore high-heeled shoes, let alone stilettos.

I stare at the print and wonder, then take a picture of it with my phone.

I turn around and look at my brother's paintings. They are beautiful. I am surprised at how good he has become. I can actually say that I can see myself hanging one of them in my living room without lying anymore. Maybe I am not giving my dear brother enough credit. Maybe he isn't just some lazy parasite, sucking money out of our dad.

I sigh and walk around in this strange place he calls home. I am about to leave when I realize I need to pee. I walk to his bathroom and hope and pray there is toilet paper in there. Luckily, there is, and I do my business. I wash my hands and look at myself in the mirror, then get curious and open the cabinet. In it, I find Blake's toothbrush, mouthwash, toothpicks, and deodorant. I find his razor and inside of the case, next to the razor, I spot a ring. A silver ring with a beautiful green stone in it. I know nothing about jewelry, but I know enough to know that this is expensive. Completely out of Blake's price range. I grab it and put it in my pocket, even though I know it's a crime.

Just when I am about to leave the bathroom, I hear a voice. I pause and wait. The voice is coming closer. I peek out through the crack in the door and spot Detective Chris Fisher. He is one of the Cocoa Beach kids as well. I remember him. I saw him in the newspaper article in *Florida Today* where I read about my brother's arrest. I know he is the guy who took him in.

He has a phone to his ear and is speaking loudly while walking into my brother's studio.

"Yes, yes, of course I've got it under control," he says.

I hold my breath as Chris Fisher walks closer to the door leading to the bathroom, but then changes his mind and walks into the small kitchen instead.

"I know. I know," he says, while kneeling by the kitchen table. He is looking for something. I stand completely still and hold my breath. Me being there is an offense in itself. I stare at the front door and wonder if I can make a run for it. No. There is no way I can make it out without him seeing me. My heart is pounding in my chest.

I can't get caught here. He can't find me here!

"No, I'll find it. Don't worry," he says. "It must be here somewhere."

I feel the ring burning in my pocket. The detective is looking for something. Can it…Could it be…?

I don't want to take any chances. I pull the ring out of my pocket and place it on the sink when I see the handle on the door turn.

39

September 2015

The handle is moving and I manage to jump into the shower and hide behind the curtain. I hold my breath as detective Chris Fisher enters the bathroom and starts to look around. When he spots the ring on the sink, he lets out a small breath.

"There you are, little fella," he says and picks it up. "You had us all scared there for a second."

I watch him put it in his pocket, then rush out of the bathroom. I wait and listen as his footsteps walk across the wooden floors. I wait till they disappear. I don't dare to breathe until minutes later. Or, at least that's how it feels. I sit down in the tub until my heart is beating normally again. Then I get up and walk cautiously back into the studio.

As soon as I feel sure that the detective has left, I run across the floor and slide under the tape to get out into the hallway again. I take the stairs down and walk to the street, feeling like a criminal, like everyone's eyes are on me, that they have all seen what I just did. I jump into my car and drive off.

I can't believe what I just saw. Who was Detective Fisher talking to on the phone? His superior? Why was he looking for the ring?

Why hadn't they found it and brought it in when they searched the place after the arrest, if it was that important?

I don't understand it. That and the high-heeled prints have me wondering. Was Olivia there with Blake when he was arrested?

I think about going back to my father's house, but I don't want to. There is something I need to do first. An itch I need to scratch.

I park the car in front of Chloe's house and walk up the small driveway and ring the doorbell. It takes a while before she opens. She looks at me.

"Mary?"

"Do you have a minute? I need your help," I say.

She doesn't even think about it for a second before she steps aside and lets me in. "I was just making coffee," she says. "You look like you could use a cup."

"Thanks," I say, and follow her into her kitchen. I see many bottles of pills on the counter. And a tray with food half eaten.

"How's she doing?" I ask, thinking about how much I had always loved Chloe's mother. She was the cool mom around. The one who always listened when you spoke, like *really* listened to what you said and wanted to know how you were feeling. I spent many hours talking to her, while going through the hardest time of my life. She took care of me when I needed it the most.

"So-so," she says. "You know how it is. Some days are good, others are bad. You never know when it will be her last day, so we try to cherish every moment."

"That's nice," I say, and take the cup she hands me. The smell alone makes me feel better already. I could use something to eat as well, but don't say anything. I don't want to impose.

"She's asleep right now. She sleeps most of the day. So, what can I do for you?" Chloe finally asks.

We sit down in her kitchen. The smell of sickness is everywhere. The air in the house is stuffy. In the corner, I spot her old surfboard. It doesn't look like it has been in the water recently.

"You know about my brother, right?" I ask.

"Sure," she says, and sips her coffee. "He was arrested this Friday, right? I was shocked when I heard."

"Me too," I say. "But the thing is, I am beginning to think something is very wrong with this case."

"Like what?"

"Okay, first of all, they found the body in a motel room a week before they decided to arrest my brother. Why did it take so long? Second, there is nothing that indicates he was ever in that motel room; he never paid for it with any of his credit cards, nor did anyone see him there. Third, the eye-witness says she was with him and Jamilla Jenkins at his studio when he stabbed her, but there was no blood found in his studio or in his car."

Chloe nods and looks at me pensively. "Good points, but still… they might have needed a week to figure out it was him; it takes time to gather all the evidence and find the witness. He could have worn a disguise and paid cash, and he could have cleaned his place and the car afterwards. After all, he had an entire week to hide it."

I stare at her.

"Just playing the devil's advocate here," she says, gesticulating with her hands in the air.

"I know it's not much, but it's still enough for me to wonder. Why would he move the body to a hotel room? Why not throw it in the river or the ocean?" I ask.

"Maybe he figured someone else could take the blame. Maybe he thought they would react exactly the way you did. If the eyewitness hadn't stepped out, no one would have thought of him, the way I see it. Listen. I know he's your brother and we all love him and care for him, but you've got to admit he looks pretty guilty. They found the bloody chisel in his place, for Christ sake."

"I know," I say and drink my coffee, suddenly wishing it were something stronger. "I still think he's been framed. I just don't know how to prove it. I also believe he wasn't alone when he was arrested. Someone was with him. A woman. I need to know if she was there."

"And how do you plan on doing that?" Chloe asks.

I look at her while a smile spreads across my face.

40

September 2015

Cassie Morgan is waiting. Standing outside the door to the nursery, her ear pressed against it, she waits for the baby to start crying again. When it doesn't happen, she closes her eyes and lets out a deep sigh.

"I'm too old for this," she mumbles to herself.

She walks downstairs, cursing her husband, Ben. It was all his idea. *Let's have another baby. It'll be fun!*

Cassie thought she was done with all that, since the two others were teenagers now, but Ben kept asking her, begging her to have another one, one last baby. Cassie said no, but somehow he got his way anyway. Accidentally, she became pregnant and now they have started all over again.

"It'll be fun," she mumbles to herself, mocking her husband's voice. No wonder he thinks it is fun. He gets to do all the good stuff with the baby. It's not like he's the one who has to give up his job and his entire life for this.

Cassie places the receiver to the baby monitor on the counter in the kitchen and starts to empty the dishwasher. Just like every other morning. Cassie sighs and puts the dishes away, then the glasses and the silverware. With every fork she puts back in its place, she grumbles and curses her husband.

Cassie hates being a housewife. She loathes having to stay home and take care of the baby while everyone else gets to go out in the wide world and be with grownups and have grown up conversations. She misses her job like crazy, and with the age she is, there is no guarantee that she will get it back once she is ready for it. Ben wants her to take at least three years off, like she did with the others. But she doesn't want to spend three years like this, doing house chores and walking the baby in the stroller. She hates it. And, worst of all, there is no one her age with babies around here. All the other moms are in their early twenties. She has nothing in common with them. Nothing at all.

Cassie sighs again and closes the dishwasher. No. Life hasn't been any fun for many years. It's always about them and what they need and what activity she has to drive them to.

Cassie looks at the baby monitor and is filled with peace. It looks like the baby is finally really heavily asleep.

He sure needs the sleep, she thinks to herself. *After the night we had with him waking up every other hour. He must be exhausted.*

Cassie grabs her phone and smiles when she sees the picture of little Jared. She never admits it publicly, but of course, she is glad she had him. Even if it is a lot of trouble and a lot of work all over again, she loves him dearly. He's the only boy she ever had, and she is fonder of him than either of the others. There is no doubt about it. She would do anything for that little munchkin. It's the lack of sleep and the overload of work that gets to her.

But it'll pass. Just like it did with the others. It'll get better.

Cassie finds her friend in her contacts and calls her. Her friend is a stay at home mom as well, even though her children are all grown up. She never made it back to work. Now she is doing charity work and is in charge of the girl scouts.

"Hey, it's me. How's it going?" she asks.

"Great. Getting ready for the spook-tacular event next month. We're raising money for the orphanage in Titusville."

"Sounds exciting," Cassie says without meaning it. The friend throws these events every year to raise money for a charity of her choice, but it is really all about them getting together and getting drunk, just for a good cause.

"I've been thinking about getting some of Blake Mills' paintings for the auction," she says. "I think they will have great value this year."

"Oh, what an excellent idea," Cassie says. "The works of a local murderer. How very spook-tacular, indeed."

"I thought it might attract some attention."

Cassie agrees, then pauses and takes the phone away from her ear. She looks at the baby monitor.

"What's wrong?" her friend asks.

"Nothing. I just thought I heard Jared, but there is nothing on the monitor. You were saying?"

"I was just saying I wanted to find out who to ask to buy the paintings. I bet he has a lot."

"Maybe talk to his dad. I believe the old Mills still live on 7th Street right on the water. Maybe you could just drive down there and ask. I heard Mary is home too."

"I just don't want to impose, you know. I don't want to come out like a vulture."

"Wait a minute," Cassie says and looks at the monitor again. "I thought I heard something again, but it was nothing."

"Don't you have one of those with a camera?" her friend asks.

"Nah. I just have the old type with a light display." She looks at it again and sees the light moving.

"You should get one with a camera. That way, you always know if he is just turning over in bed."

"Well, there is definitely sound. I gotta go," she says and hangs up. The monitor is quiet now again, and Cassie stares at it. She feels like screaming at it for controlling every minute of her life. She really wants Jared to sleep longer.

He gets so cranky if he doesn't get enough sleep. It's going to ruin the rest of my day!

The monitor remains quiet and Cassie breathes a sigh of relief. Jared was probably just turning over in bed. She puts the monitor down, then walks to the kitchen to grab a soda from the fridge. She opens the door and peeks inside. Her hand is on the can of Coke when she hears something that makes her entire body start to tremble. It's the voice of someone singing, singing quietly, hauntingly.

Listening to the lyrics of her once favorite song *Cat's in the Cradle* being sung over the baby monitor immediately brings her back to her past, a past she has tried so hard to forget. A past with so many bad memories it makes her hands shake. She can no longer hold on to the can of Coke and drops it on the tiles. It explodes and sprays the floor and the cabinets. Normally, Cassie would be all over it to clean it up, but not in this moment. This time, she doesn't even notice. Not the stains it leaves on the cabinet doors, nor the pool of Coke on the tiles, not even how it soaks her socks. All she is thinking about is the baby.

Jared!

She grabs a knife, then storms up the stairs and stumbles on the last step; the fall buries her nose deep in the carpet. She gets up again and runs for the door to the nursery and opens it. Someone is in there. Someone is standing by the crib, her back turned toward Cassie while singing.

"Don't touch him!" Cassie groans. "Get away from the crib."

Cassie holds the knife out in front of her. It's shaking heavily. She can't make it stay still. The baby wakes up. He is crying.

"Get away from my baby!" she says.

The woman turns to look at her. She is wearing a surgical mask. She tilts her head slowly. She is still singing.

"*The Cat's in the Cradle…*"

"Stop!" Cassie yells. "Stop it! Stop singing that song!"

The woman stops singing. Jared is crying helplessly. Cassie takes in a deep breath. She wants to go to him, but doesn't dare to. She is still holding the knife out in front of her. "What do you want?" she asks. "Why have you come here?"

The woman takes a step closer.

"Don't!" Cassie yells. "Don't move!"

The woman pauses. She tilts her head once again.

"What do you want? Answer me!"

"Am I pretty?" she asks.

Cassie stares at her. Her mind is only on Jared, who is demanding her attention now. "What?"

"I asked: Am I pretty?" the woman repeats.

"What the heck…why? Get out of my house!"

The woman giggles, then suddenly changes expression and yells: "AM I PRETTY!"

"Yes!" Cassie yells back. "Yes, for crying out loud. Now get the hell out of my house!"

Jared screams loudly now, and Cassie runs to him. She looks at him and smiles, then caresses his head. "Shhh," she says.

When she glances back at the woman, she has taken off the mask. The sight makes Cassie gasp for air. She drops the knife in her hand and it makes a loud noise as it lands on the tiles.

"How about now?" the woman asks.

41

September 2015

"Oh, no! No. No. No!"

Chloe is raising her hand in the air like she is waving away an annoying fly. She is shaking her head at the same time. "I don't do that kind of stuff anymore," she says. "It's over. Caput. Finito. Done!"

"Come on, Chloe. It's me, Mary. Please, do it for me."

"No."

"Please?"

"I can't, Mary."

"Yes, you can. You can help me. You're the world famous Dr. Claw, remember? I helped you find the name?"

"Inspector Gadget's nemesis, yes," she says. "I still think the name is lame. That was your favorite cartoon. Not mine."

I chuckle. "I remember I thought it was so cool. Dr. Claw! Remember when they wrote about you in all the papers nationwide? You were world famous for that hack that gave you access to the White House, remember? You were so scared they'd find you. But they couldn't even track you to Florida. They even, at one point, believed you might be someone from Russia. You were that good."

Chloe laughs at the memory. So do I. What an innocent time it was. I can't believe how much has happened since then.

"Come on, Chloe. It's just a small peek into a police file, that's all," I say. "I know it'll be a walk in the park for you. No one will ever find out."

Chloe sighs. "But I'm done with that stuff. It's different now," she says. "This is what I do now." She points at her computer screen.

"Cyber-security for businesses?" I ask.

"Not that. That's just what I get paid to do. No, this is where my heart belongs," she says and taps on her laptop. She turns the screen so I can see better.

"Nochildporn.org?" I say.

"Yes. I founded it. It's an anti-child porn organization. We use a software that I created. Software that automatically gleans information from tens of thousands of suspected URLs and tracks those that are sending and receiving data with those websites. I share my information with the authorities once I have it, and they make sure to find and prosecute the bastards."

I stare at my old friend, not knowing what to say. I am impressed. More than that. I just don't know how to express it.

"Wow," I simply say.

She nods her head. "So, now you can understand why I can't help you hack into the Brevard County Sheriff's Office."

I grab her arm. "But you have to help me, Chloe. Please. It's important. You know my brother. He'll never survive jail."

Chloe hesitates when I mention Blake. He was only three when I moved away, but she has been here ever since. She has seen him grow up.

"Alright," she says. "For Blake, I'll do it. He's a good kid."

I wonder about her change of heart. Had Blake made such a deep impression on Chloe while growing up? I shake my head. It doesn't matter. As long as she does this for me.

Chloe gets up from her chair and finishes her coffee. I follow her. She looks at me.

"Remember the time when I changed your grades for you?" she asks with a mischievous smile.

"I will never forget that," I say. "I would never have gotten an A in Geometry if it wasn't for you."

Chloe laughs. "Especially not since you were always skipping classes to surf," she says.

42

March 1979

"Please, help us. Someone please help me."

Penelope storms into the ER with her baby girl in her arms. The child is throwing up. A nurse runs to Penelope.

"What's wrong?"

"She's been throwing up all morning," Penelope says anxiously. "It won't stop. And, suddenly, she seemed to have had a seizure of some sort, like a staring spell. I had no eye contact with her for at least three minutes. She was just gone." Penelope talks while panting from running. She has driven there on her own. Didn't want to wait for an ambulance.

"She does have problems with her heart," she says. "We're waiting for an operation."

The nurse takes the baby out of Penelope's hands. "I'll get her to a doctor immediately. Walk with me."

Penelope follows the nurse down the corridor, while all the eyes in the waiting room are on her. Penelope knows what they think.

Poor woman. It's always the worst when it's the little ones. So tough on the mother.

"How old is the girl?" the nurse asks while they walk.

"Two years old. She just turned two. We've known something was wrong since she was just a baby."

"Doctor," the nurse calls. "This child needs immediate attention," she says, as they approach a doctor.

"What seems to be the problem?" he asks.

The nurse opens her mouth to speak, but is drowned out by Penelope.

"Vomiting. Heavily all morning. And seizures. Staring spells. She was absent for at least three minutes. She has a heart problem. Might need a heart catheterization procedure."

The doctor stares at Penelope, then at the child. "Alright," he says. "Let me take a look at her."

Penelope breathes a sigh of relief. She follows the doctor into an examination room, where her child is put on a big bed. Penelope stands next to her and holds her hand.

"It's going to be fine, baby," she says with a smile. "The nice doctor will take good care of you. Don't worry." The girl, who is still very small for her age, chews on her binky.

"Doctor?" the child says and points at the man in the white coat, who is now looking into her eyes with a flashlight.

"Yes, doctor," Penelope repeats.

The nurse smiles. "That's a big word for such a small girl."

"I know. She has seen her share of doctors in her short life. It's her heart that is the issue."

"That is tough," the nurse says, and puts her hand on Penelope's shoulder.

Penelope nods with a sigh. "It is. It really is."

"You can tell she is used to it," the doctor says, and tries her reflexes. The girl's leg reacts like it's supposed to. "Usually, I need the mother to hold a two-year old still for examination. But not this girl. She sits nice and quiet through it all."

After the initial examination, the doctor pulls Penelope aside and speaks with a low voice. "We'll be running a series of tests, and I will try and get a hold of Dr. Mussels, our pediatric neurologist, and have her take a look at her. It's the part about the seizure that makes me nervous. You say she was out for at least three minutes? That's a very long time. And she has a history of heart problems?"

"Yes. We're waiting for an operation, but no one has wanted to perform it because she is so young. I have been to every heart-specialist in Central Florida. But they all believe I am mad for wanting to perform heart surgery on this young a child. I just want to do what is best for her, Doctor. I just want her to be well."

The doctor places his hand on her arm and Penelope relaxes finally.

"We'll get to the bottom of this. Whatever is causing the vomiting and the seizures, we'll find it and make her well. Don't you worry about it. You're not alone with this."

43

September 2015

THEY MAKE it look so easy in the movies, but it really isn't. I realize that as I wait for Chloe to hack into the server at the sheriff's office. It takes hours.

Meanwhile, I go and say hello to Chloe's mom, Mrs. Edwards. She is awake for just long enough to hear my story. I hold her hand in mine and tell her how Joey and I grew apart, how I was fired, and how I am trying to get my brother acquitted. Even this sick, she still listens to everything I say.

"It'll all work out," she finally says, right before she dozes off again. "Eventually it will. It always does. Just don't worry too much."

Hearing her comforting words makes me feel a lot better. When she is heavily asleep, I walk to Chloe's kitchen and find some Oreos in the cabinet. I eat them while waiting. When the box is empty, I make us some more coffee. I call Joey and ask if Salter can stay with him for the night. They both make a thrilled cheering sound, and I am certain I hear them doing fist bumps. They're getting close. That's good. Why do I feel so awful about it? Because I am left out? Am I that selfish?

Apparently.

I sigh and look at Chloe, who is sitting in front of her many screens, working the numbers and running her fingers across her keyboards. I have no clue what she is doing, but I am fascinated, and very impressed.

"There you go," she suddenly says.

I jump up. "You're in?"

"Almost. I found a hole. They all have one if they don't have someone like me to secure their systems. Now, I'll be able to use this hole…"

She taps eagerly, the tip of her tongue sticking out between her lips. I smile to myself because I remember she always used to do that when she was younger too. Some things never change. I know she doesn't notice it, so I say nothing.

"…and I am in."

Chloe leans back in her chair with her hands behind her head with a victorious smile. "Here you go."

I pull up a chair and sit next to her, while she opens the file containing the police report of Blake's arrest. I pull my chair close to better see, and together we read through it. Most of it is a lot of technicalities written in police lingo that I don't think is important. I ask her to go further down to the description of the arrest, and then read through it. I shake my head and read it again.

"There is nothing there," I say. "Not a word about any woman being with him. I was so sure…"

"Why did you think someone was with him when he was arrested?" Chloe asks.

"I found footprints in the studio, high-heeled footprints. And he was seen with this woman at Starbucks right before he was arrested," I say, and pull out my picture of Olivia Hartman.

Chloe whistles when she sees her. "Blake was involved with Olivia?"

"That's what the boys have told me. Apparently, he told Joey, Danny and Alex, but not me."

Chloe goes quiet. I look at her. "Did he tell you?"

"What? No. No. We never spoke about his personal life."

"But you spoke of other things?" I ask surprised.

"Well…no…I mean, yes…sometimes."

"I need the full story, please," I say.

Chloe avoids looking me directly in the eyes. "Okay. Okay. I helped him set up his webpage for his paintings and the other stuff he creates, to make it easier for him to sell them. You know he did coffee tables too and sculptures, and wanted a page where people could order exactly what they wanted, like ordering a pizza. We talked a lot. One thing led to another…He hung out here several days during the week. It only lasted for about a month. It was nothing, really."

"You're kidding me, right? You do realize you're fifteen years older than him, right?"

Chloe blushes. "Of course. But, so is she," she says, and points at Olivia Hartman. "What was it they called her back then?"

"Double O," I say.

Chloe nods. "Because her last name was Owens, that's right. I guess your brother has a thing for us older ladies, huh?"

44

March 1992

They meet on 7th Street at midnight. Ally has butterflies in her stomach. Her mother is travelling again, so she doesn't even know she is out. Not that she would notice if she was home anyway. She is always wrapped up in her work. Always on the phone, always occupied, even when Ally walks into her study and asks her something.

"I'm swamped here. I had a rough day. Can't you solve this yourself? You're a big girl, right?" is her standard answer. Even on the day when Ally wanted to tell her she got an A on her math test. Even on the day when Ally was seven and had been bitten on her arm by the neighbor's dog and she came in to tell her. Even then, she had no time.

"You're late," AK says. She hands her something. "Put this on."

AK pulls her ski mask over her head and covers her face. Ally does the same. AK told her to wear black from top to toe. To make sure she isn't seen in the night. Ally wonders what they are going to do. She still hopes she is just supposed to get drunk and do something stupid, but she has a feeling that is not it. AK points at the house next to them, the one they usually do the campfire in front of. AK has something against the family living there, but she has never told Ally what it is. She always talks about how much she hates them. She once wrote a message for them using their empty beer cans after a long night of drinking.

AK stares at the house. Ally can sense her anger, her hatred. It frightens her slightly.

"Follow me closely," AK whispers. "Don't make a sound. If we get caught, it'll be your fault, and I'll tell the police you put me up to this, that it was all your idea, all right? So you better do it right."

Ally swallows hard, then nods. She doesn't dare to do anything else. She knows AK will do it. A big part of her wants to run away, to get the hell out of there, but she doesn't dare to. She would lose everything. She would lose all of her new friends…all the trust she had worked so hard to gain. She would never have a friend in this town again.

"All right. Let's go AL," AK says. She lights up her face with her flashlight like she was telling a scary story, and Ally can tell by her eyes that she is excited. Her eyes look a little mad. Ally wonders if she is.

AK shuts off the flashlight, then signals for Ally to follow her. They sneak up towards the gate and crawl over the fence. Ally wonders if they have cameras or alarms on the house. But she can't hear anything.

She follows AK up the driveway towards the main entrance, but AK walks past it. She stops at a small window on the side of the house.

"It's broken," she whispers. "It can't lock."

Then she pulls it hard and it opens without making a sound. She looks at Ally triumphantly. "Told you so."

Soundlessly, AK slides through. From the inside, she signals Ally to follow her. Ally sticks her legs through and slides in as well. She lands on the floor with a thud. AK gives her a look. She wants to say she is sorry, but decides it's better to not speak.

AK seems to know her way around the house. She sneaks through the hallways, opening drawers, pulling out jewelry and cash that she apparently knows exactly where is stashed away. She fills her pockets with the valuables, then glides on to the next room. In the kitchen, she finds a checkbook that she steals and a wallet, where she takes a credit card and some more cash. She has a bag that she fills with CDs from the living room. Ally watches her, but doesn't want to take anything. She grabs a photo from above the fireplace and looks at it, then lets out a small gasp. She recognizes the girl in the photo, standing between what can only be her parents. AK sneaks up behind her and looks at it too. Then she pulls it out from between Ally's hands and throws it at the floor. She steps on it with the heel of her black boot, and the glass breaks. It makes a loud sound and the light upstairs is turned on.

"Is someone down there?" a voice asks.

45

September 2015

I DON'T LEAVE Chloe's house completely empty-handed. Before I go, I find out everything there is in the report about the deceased, Jamilla Jenkins, and I get the name of the witness who claims she saw my brother stab her to death. I know it's illegal, but I don't care. I want to know who she is.

I tell Chloe thank you and run up 7th Street towards my dad's house. The sun has set and it is dark now. I can't stop thinking about poor Snowflake, who has been alone in that room all day. I have completely forgotten about him and the fact that Salter isn't there to walk him.

I open the front door and run upstairs. Snowflake attacks me when I open the door to our room. He is wagging his tail and licking my ears. I giggle and sit on the floor until he stops whimpering.

Then, I spot it.

Right there on the middle of the white, thick, very expensive carpet is a big round yellow spot the size of a paperback. I sigh and look at Snowflake.

"Now what do we do?" I ask him.

He looks at me and wags his tail intently, then creeps up between my legs and hides his head. I can't stop laughing.

"Is that you, Mary?" I hear a voice in the hallway outside the room.

It's Laura! Think fast!

I turn and grab my son's T-shirt from the bed, then let it fall to the carpet. It lands in the second she enters and covers the spot. I smile. I know it must look phony, but she is used to that from me.

"Hi," she says, showing her fake teeth in just as fake of a smile. "I haven't seen you all day. I was beginning to think you wouldn't come home to spend the night. But then I thought, well she can't stay out all night because she has a dog to take care of," she says with a light laugh. "Silly me. Where is Salter?"

"He's staying with his dad tonight. A little bonding time. They need it. He never sees his dad. You know how it is. " It's way more information than I usually give her about anything. It sounds suspicious, even to my own ears.

"How nice," she says, and looks at the T-shirt on the floor next to me. "Maybe you could use the time off from your motherly duties to clean up a little." She sniffs the air and makes me think of a poodle I once knew. Even her hair looks like it. "It's getting a little stuffy in here."

Can she smell the pee?

I can tell that the T-shirt on the floor bothers her. She wants to pick it up herself, but holds herself back. She lets out a sigh.

"I guess you should take the dog out first. It hasn't been out since this morning. It probably needs to…take care of its business."

"Yes. Yes. Come on, Snowflake," I say, and find his leash. "Let me take you out for a little walk. We don't want any accidents to happen, now do we?"

I put the leash on, then walk towards Laura, who is still staring at the T-shirt on the floor. I know she wants me to pick it up, but I don't.

"Excuse me," I say. "I kind of need you to move in order to get out."

"Yes. Of course," she says and moves to the side. "I'll just grab this…"

Before I can stop her, she moves past me, reaches down, and picks up the T-shirt from the floor.

Uh-oh.

I close my eyes, and when I open them, she is staring at the big spot on her nice carpet.

"That's funny," she says, her lips tightened. "I don't recall having a spot on the carpet right there." She looks to me for an answer, then down at the dog. She turns pale, as the realization sinks in. There isn't anything I can say or do anymore. It's over.

Laura doesn't speak another word. She holds a hand to her chest, then storms right past me. She disappears into another room, her own bedroom that she shares with my father, for the most part, when he is not sleeping in one of the other rooms. I hear her yell. Then my dad talks quietly.

Seconds later, my dad comes out. "I'm sorry," he says. "I need you to find somewhere else to stay while you're here. We can't have that dog here."

Even the way he says *that dog*, makes me want to scream.

46

September 2015

Sandra is looking through her book. She stops at a picture of her on the cover of *Elle*. It is one of her favorites if not *the* favorite. It is hard to determine. Every one of these pictures has their story to tell, and right now they are telling the story of Sandra's life. In the beginning, it was mostly surfing brands that wanted to use her. Swimsuits, clothing, surfboards. She had posed with it all. Oh, my, how incredibly young she was back then.

How I miss those days. How I miss looking that young.

Sandra sighs deeply, then puts the book down. Now what? She has never wondered about the future before. Things simply just happened to her when she was younger. She never had the time to wonder what to do when it was all over. Is she getting closer to *that* point now?

Of course she is. She gets older every day, and lately there has been less demand for her. But, can she live without it? She loves the work, loves the way she is pampered and looked at. It is hard work; it's no walk in the park. A photo shoot is many hours spent getting it just right, so it's not something that anyone can just do, you have to be cut out for it. But it has its benefits. It certainly does. Sandra loves the travelling. She loves going places she would never go otherwise.

She loves how everything is taken care of when she arrives, the hotel is booked, the people are already there waiting just for her. She is the star. And she does love seeing the end results once the magazine or the commercial comes out. She likes to look at herself and how beautiful they can make her look. Sometimes, she hardly recognizes herself.

Sandra looks at her face in the mirror. She places a hand on each side of her face and pulls the skin back to smoothen out the fine lines. Every day now, it seems they're getting bigger and more plentiful. There is no way of reversing it or even stopping it from happening. Every day, she gets closer to being done in the business. And then what? Is she just going to hang out here in Cocoa Beach with Ryan? He has his business. He is gone all day. There really isn't anything here for her.

"You'll get bored after a week," she tells her own reflection.

She could always go back to surfing full time. But the waves aren't always good, and it would get boring too eventually.

As she is looking at herself, thinking it is all over, her cell phone rings. Sandra picks it up.

"I've got a great job for you, girl," her agent from the agency in New York chirps from the other end.

Yes! I am not done yet!

"It's not until two weeks from now, but it's *Vogue*, so it's worth the wait."

"*Vogue*?" she asks smiling from ear to ear.

If Vogue *wants me I am definitely not done yet.*

"Yes, baby. They want both the cover and three pages inside."

"The cover? You're kidding me?" Sandra asks. It was ages since she last did one of the big magazines…and then the cover on top of it?

"Nope. They love you. They asked for you specifically. I didn't even have to pitch you to them. You're getting hot up here. Once the word is out that you're doing *Vogue* next month they'll be calling from all over for the rest of the year. You're back, baby."

"Really? I'm hot right now?"

"Sure. Retro is in right now. They're bringing in all the faces from the nineties these days. It's hot."

Sandra hangs up, feeling like her life has been turned upside down. She can't stop smiling. Just as she thought it was over, she gets a new life in the business. She had not expected that.

Sandra sits down, staring at her phone. *Florida Today* is on the table underneath. She barely notices the small note on the front page when she puts the phone down on top of the paper. Her eyes pass it, hardly taking it in.

MAN HOSPITALIZED AFTER DRINKING DRAIN CLEANER

At first, her mind is on how stupid people can be. How do you accidentally drink drain cleaner—could he not see the label—or see that the bottle doesn't look like anything else you would drink from? But then, as though a fist suddenly bursts from the page and hits her in the face, she looks again. The picture, the man's name, is it…? Well, yes, it is.

47

September 2015

I MOVE in with Joey the next morning. I called him after my little chat with my father the night before and he told me he could take me in. Salter is still there and his eyes sparkle when he opens the door for me. I know he loves having all of us together again. Of course he does.

"You can sleep in here," Joey says, and shows me into the bedroom. "I put new sheets on and everything."

"B-but that's your bedroom," I say, slightly confused.

"That's alright," he says. "I'll sleep on the couch downstairs."

"I can't throw you out of your own bed," I say. "I can sleep on the floor in Salter's room."

Joey smiles. "Just take it, okay?"

I nod. "Okay. That is very nice of you."

"You can thank me later," he says with a mischievous smile.

I throw a pillow at him. Meanwhile, I hope he doesn't think this means anything more than me needing a place to crash. I am beginning to long for Manhattan more and more. I don't know why I stay. Well, yes I do. I stay for my brother, because if I don't try and help him, no one else will and he'll get himself killed in jail. But still. I can't wait for this to be over.

Snowflake is already loving the place and running around in the small yard like crazy, playing wildly with Salter and Bonnie and Clyde. Salter is in heaven. So is Snowflake, it seems. He and the other animals seem to take an immediate liking to one another.

I let them play, then pull out my laptop and sit in Joey's kitchen. He places a cup of coffee in front of me. I look up and smile. Our eyes meet.

"You looked like you could use it," he says with that boyish smile of his. Even though he has just woken up, he is still cruelly handsome. I wonder if he is seeing anyone since we split up. I know the girls must be all over him.

"That is very kind of you. Thanks."

"What's all this?" he asks.

I draw in a deep breath. "My brother's case. I'm trying to piece all of it together. The lawyer says it's all about finding holes in the investigation now. If we can sow any doubts about the police doing their job properly, then we might have a chance. Something like that. I'm not a lawyer, obviously."

"Obviously."

Joey grabs a chair and sits on it the wrong way. *He is such a cowboy*, I think to myself.

"Tell me what you've got," he says. "Who was the girl?"

"Her name was Jamilla Jenkins," I say, and open the file on my desktop. I had written down everything the night before, while snorting and heavily cursing my dad.

"She was a military girl, lived on base. She was thirty-three when she died. Her parents were both in the military as well, and she grew up on bases all over the world. I guess it was the world she knew, and therefore it was only natural for her to stay in it once she grew up. She served three times in Iraq and once in Afghanistan. She is a decorated war hero."

"Ouch, that makes it even harder on Blake."

"Tell me about it. The woman testifying against him, claiming she saw him kill Jenkins is also military. Who's going to believe Blake's word over hers?"

"Him, a local artist who never held a real job in his life and who never served his country or risked his life for our freedom or them. That's going to be difficult."

I nod and look at the screen with my notes. I try to picture the two girls standing at the bar in Squid Lips, listening to the band, maybe even dancing and drinking some beers. Witnesses in the bar stated in the file that they saw all of them. They saw the two girls and they saw my brother. They were all hanging out at the bar. Even Blake admits to having been there, sitting at the bar, but he doesn't remember the girls. There were a lot of girls that night, he is quoted saying. He was drunk. He doesn't remember. That isn't new for my brother.

I groan and lean back in my chair. I lift my cup to drink more coffee, but it is empty. I put it down a little too hard. I feel so frustrated.

"Who am I kidding?" I ask. "I'm no investigator. There is no way I can figure out what really happened."

"Have you asked this one?" he says and points at the picture on the table.

"Olivia Hartman?" I ask. "She wasn't there that night. They were just screwing around."

"No, but she is also military. She must know these other two. Maybe Blake told her something. Maybe she knows something. It's worth a try."

"Yeah, but the thing is, she lives on base as well, and there is no way I can get in there," I say.

Joey looks pensively at me. "I might know a guy."

48

March 1979

THEY KEEP the child at the hospital for two days. Penelope never leaves her side. When she needs water, she brings it to her, when she is sad, Penelope strokes her head gently and sings to her. She does everything a good mother is supposed to do. When she has a break, she walks to the payphone and calls Peter, who is still swamped by his work.

On the morning of the second day, the doctor asks Penelope to step outside with him.

Penelope feels anxious as she follows him out into the hallway, where nurses walk by with quick and urgent steps.

"Any news, Doctor?" she asks.

"We have now performed a variety of tests," he says.

She can tell from his face that he is tired.

"And?"

"We tested her blood sugar and blood calcium, we did a urine culture, a lumbar puncture, X-rays, and an intravenous pyleogram, but the tests revealed no abnormalities whatsoever. Neither does the cardiovascular exam that we performed. I did have Dr. Neuhart, our ear, nose and throat specialist, examine her, and he found evidence of a low-grade infection, and because of her previous ear infection,

I will recommend an operation called a myringotomy, which entails removal of fluid from the ear drums."

"An ear infection?" Penelope asks. "But…but her heart? What about her heart? What about the vomiting, the staring spells, the seizures?"

"It could all have been caused by the infection she is battling," the doctor says.

Penelope shakes her head. "No. No. Something is wrong with her heart. I had a specialist tell me so. He told me she needs surgery. Her physician told us her heart is sick…"

The doctor places a hand on Penelope's shoulder. "Her heart is fine," he says. "We've run all these tests, and all she has is an ear infection. That's it."

But Penelope is not convinced. She shakes her head again and again, desperately, on the verge of breaking into tears. Her pointer finger is waving in the air.

"No. No. No. You promised me you'd get to the bottom of this. You promised me. It's her heart. I just know it is. Why won't anyone listen to me? I can't believe I can never reach you people."

The doctor looks at her, then at his watch. "I have to go. I will schedule the myringotomy for later today. After the operation is done, I will discharge your child within forty-eight hours."

The doctor turns on his heels and leaves Penelope standing in the hallway. She watches him as he leaves. She doesn't understand. Why won't they listen? How is she supposed to take the child home now? She'll only get sick again. She'll have more seizures, and then they'll have to start all over again. Why can't they figure out what is wrong with her?

Penelope walks back to her child, who is now smiling and seems much better. She strokes her hair gently, then leans over and kisses her. The child is visibly happy to see her mother. The nurse soon brings her breakfast.

"Someone seems to be feeling better," she says, as she places the tray in front of the child.

Penelope smiles and nods. "Yes, she is better. The doctor told us they will remove the fluids in her ears later today, and then we'll be discharged."

"That is excellent news," the nurse says, then leaves.

Penelope waits for her footprints to disappear in the hallway, then reaches into her bag, and pulls out the jar of salt. She pours three handfuls into the child's milk and uses the spoon to mix it. Then she smiles and hands the child the cup.

"Now, finish up, baby girl. Just like last time. You have to drink it all."

49

September 2015

Of course Joey knows a guy who can help us get on the base. Joey knows everyone. And, somehow, they all always owe him a favor. It turns out this guy is actually in security and that he can help us get one day passes to the base, even though we can't say we actually have business there.

Admittedly, I am impressed.

Joey drives the car; Salter sits in the back as we approach the gate. A guy in a uniform comes out. I break a sweat. I always do that when people in uniform approach me, especially the police. I can pass a police car in the street, not having done anything at all wrong, and I still find myself shaking, my heart racing, and my hands get clammy. I don't know why. That's just how I am. I hate authorities and I assume they always have it in for me as well. It's not like we're about to do anything illegal. We're just going to talk to someone.

"That's Tim," Joey says, and rolls down the window.

"Hello," he says, then hands us the passes through the window. He looks inside the car, like he is probably supposed to. He looks tough and serious. "We're even now," he says, addressed to Joey. "If anyone asks, you didn't get these passes from me, alright?"

All three of us nod. Tim pulls his head out from the car and signals someone that we are cleared. With my heart in my throat, we drive through the security gate with the many guards following our every move. At least that's what I feel they're doing…watching us closely.

We drive past a big sign welcoming us. We are in. We're inside the base they call *the control center for Cape Canaveral Air Station, America's gateway to space.*

We find the road taking us to the South housing areas. We drive along the big runway for the airplanes, and I watch as a big one takes off into the air. There is water on both sides of the base, since it is located on a thin area of the barrier island. Many of the houses have views over the Intracoastal waters.

Before we left, I called Chloe and had her find the general's address for me. I am holding the piece of paper in front of me where the address is written. I feel nervous, but also determined. I want to find Olivia Hartman and ask her about my brother, about her relationship to him, and if she knows anything that might help us. I pray and hope this pays off somehow.

"It's here," Joey says. "Number 1145, right?"

"Right," I say, and fold the paper with the address on it. I put it in my pocket, then take in a deep breath as Joey parks the car in front of the house.

"Do you want me to go with you?" he asks.

I think about it for a second, and then tell him I can do this on my own. I get out of the car and walk up to the front door and ring the doorbell. It doesn't take long for it to open. There she is. The famous Olivia Hartman. The woman whose picture I have been staring at ever since I found out she was seeing my brother. She is just as beautiful as her picture, and a lot more so than back in high school. Some people age better than others.

"Mary?" she says.

I nod. "We need to talk."

She looks behind me and around us to make sure nobody is looking, then tells me to come inside. I follow her into the house. It's big. Two stories with great views of the Intracoastal. It's nicely decorated as well. Double O has good taste. Expensive as well.

We sit down in her living room. The couch is soft and delicate. The fabric is white. It is obvious they have no children. She looks at me with a sigh.

"I guess I know why you're here."

50

September 2015

Liz can't believe her eyes. Did she just see Mary Mills on the base? Did she just see her drive up to the general's house and walk up to the entrance? Yes, she did. She watched it all when she got back from her run at the track. She saw her ring the doorbell and Olivia Hartman open the door. She can't believe the general's wife actually let her inside.

Liz feels a pinch of worry. What is the bitch doing here, and why is Olivia letting her inside her home?

Liz is doing jumping jacks in front of her own driveway. She is panting and groaning, mostly with anger, and a little with worry. She waits and watches. Waits and watches patiently. When Mary doesn't come back out, Liz decides to go inside her house. She searches through her things frantically and pulls out her gun. She looks at the clock on the wall. She is off until 1300 hours. There is still time. She feels the cold gun between her hands when she loads it. She grumbles in anger.

How the hell is she supposed to do this? She's on base, for crying out loud. If she fires a gun, she'll get caught. She can't escape. Not from the base. Can she pull it off somehow anyway?

Liz growls and looks out the window. The car is still there, parked in the general's driveway. There is no way she can go into the general's house and fire a gun and get away with it. No way. But she can't let her go either, can she? No, she has to do something. Anything.

You should have hit her with your car when you had the chance, you idiot. Now she is here, who knows what she is up to, how she will destroy everything for you again.

Just thinking about Mary makes everything turn inside of Liz. The anger hasn't decreased over the years. On the contrary. She feels it much stronger now than back then. Back when...Argh, just thinking about it makes her want to just go over there and shoot her in the head, not caring one bit about what will happen afterwards. Heck, she could shoot them all if she wants to. She can get away with it, can't she? She has gotten away with so many things so far.

No, it's too dangerous.

Liz looks at the car. It looks like someone is sitting inside of it. Who is it? It looks like a child in the back seat. Is that Mary's child? It looks like it. Could she use him, maybe? But wait. There is someone else in the car. It looks like a man.

Damn it!

Liz sighs, frustrated. She isn't good with spontaneous decisions. She likes to be in control. She likes to plan ahead and then act. Like the day with Billy the Kid. She had planned what she wanted to do and bought the drain cleaner. The past few days she has thought long and hard about what to do about Mary, now that she is back, and she believes she has come up with an idea that will be her best to date. But now this happens? Liz doesn't know what to do. She lifts the gun and walks to the window, pointing it at the car. Liz is an excellent shot. Always hits her target. Never misses a single shot when in the field. She always gets her man.

Or woman.

Liz knows she can shoot the boy from where she is standing. They're less than a mile away. Her 9mm can make the shot. But then what? She needs to think about her escape as well. Maybe she can think about that later. Her desire to hurt Mary drowns out all other thoughts. Right now, she is blinded by it. By her rage.

God, how I hate her. How I loathe everything about her.

But she wants her to suffer. To feel pain, to be hurt. That is when it hits her. That is when the idea comes to her mind like lightning from a clear blue sky.

What hurts the most?

Liz laughs at her own cleverness. She looks at the car across the street and is filled by a triumphant sensation.

51

September 2015

"I NEED you to tell me everything you know about my brother," I say.

Olivia, or Double O, looks at me. I know she doesn't want me there; in fact, I am probably the last person she wants in her house right now. But I am not leaving. Not until I get some answers.

"And don't tell me you don't know him, 'cause I know you two were seeing each other."

Olivia's green eyes stare at me. To my surprise, she seems frightened. Maybe she is just acting.

"I...I don't know what to tell you." She sighs and looks away. "Yes, we met at a party at the Officer's Club, and we have had some fun, that's all."

"Fun?" I ask feeling, anger rise inside of me. Was that all my brother was to her? A toy?

She shakes her head; her eyes search the floor. "I don't know what to say."

"Start by telling me what happened. Why is he in jail right now?" I ask.

Olivia looks up again and our eyes meet. Hers are full of regret.

"You should go...if my husband finds out...he has eyes and ears everywhere here. It was very dangerous of you to come here."

"I don't care about your husband or who he is. I demand to know what happened to my brother. You were with him, weren't you? You were with him when he was arrested, weren't you?"

Olivia shakes her head. I can tell she is lying. She is not a very good liar.

"Come on!" I say. "You were seen at Starbucks together. You were seen leaving together. Did you go back to his place to have sex, huh? To have some of your *fun*, huh?"

Olivia's eyes are growing wider.

"You can't lie to me, Olivia. I know you were there. I saw your shoeprint in his studio. You stepped in some blue paint. I just can't seem to figure out why that part was left out of the police report. Are they working together? Is the detective in the general's pocket?"

I can tell by the look in her eyes that I am right. "So, they framed him, huh? They framed my brother because he was sleeping with you." I look down at her hand and spot the ring with the green stone from my brother's bathroom. "Nice ring, by the way."

Olivia reaches out and grabs my arm with a gasp. "You've got to be careful, Mary. These people are capable of anything. Yes, they framed Blake. They even forced me to place the bloody chisel under the sink so the police would find it. The general found out about us weeks ago and has been planning this all along. He'll do anything. He'll get rid of you as well if he knows that you know."

"I am not scared of him," I snort.

"You should be. And now you must leave. The word about you being here must have reached my husband by now."

I stare at the woman whom I used to go to school with and wonder what happened to her. Back then, she had been so strong. So tough. Now she was reduced to this shadow of her former self.

That's when I notice the bruises on her arm. She sees it in my eyes and rolls down her sleeve. Even though Olivia has never been and will never be my favorite person, I feel bad for her all of a sudden.

"You should get out of here," I say. "Why don't you leave him?"

Her eyes turn moist. I can tell she is terrified just by the thought.

"Don't you think I've tried? I love your brother. I wanted to leave the general for him. It was more than just a fling to me. Blake was…well…it doesn't matter anymore. There is no way out for me. Now you must go before they get here."

I rise to my feet. I walk towards the door when I turn and look at her again. "If you planted the evidence that framed my brother, then who killed Jamilla Jenkins?"

Olivia shakes her head. "I don't know. Now, please. Leave."

52

September 2015

I WALK BACK to the car and get in. Everything inside of me is pumping like crazy. I feel so angry, yet so frustrated at the same time.

"What happened?" Joey asks. He puts down the phone. I can tell he has been playing Candy Crush. Salter is on his iPad. My pulse is throbbing in my throat. I feel like crying. Or screaming. Maybe both.

"He was framed," I say. "Olivia told me they framed him. She was in on it. Because of the affair. The general has it in for my brother and he has got the police working for him."

"Wow. That was a lot of information you got from that brief meeting," Joey says.

I sigh. "Yes, but what can I use it for? If the police have decided that Blake is guilty, they'll make sure to prove it. They have all the evidence in the world. And there is no way I am ever going to get Olivia to tell the truth in a courtroom. The woman was terrified just to talk to me. Yet, she is the only one who knows the real story." I hit my hand a few times hard on the dashboard. "Damn you, Blake!"

Joey puts a hand on my shoulder like he always used to when I was upset.

"I don't want to calm down," I say to him. "I am entitled to be angry. He messed with the wrong people, Joey. And now he is paying the price. But it's a price that is much too high. It'll end up killing him. And there is nothing I can do to help him."

"So, if they planted the evidence, then who killed the girl?" Joey asks all of a sudden.

"That's what I asked," I say. "Olivia said she doesn't know. I believe her. She's a bad liar."

"So, let me get this straight. They had Olivia plant the chisel, but what about the witness? They had her lie too?"

I shrug. "Yeah, sure. She's an army girl too. They're all in on it."

"Do you have a name?"

"Sure. Jamie Barley, why?"

"Why not pay her a visit while we're here? There's a guy walking over there. I bet he knows where she lives."

Before I can protest, Joey jumps out of the car and runs to a man in uniform. I think about what Olivia said about the general having people everywhere. If that is true, then this guy is probably one of them. Joey talks to him and I watch as they chitchat. I can tell by Joey's body language that he is getting what he wants. He smiles when he returns to the car.

"She lives further down the road and to the right. I got the address," he says, and gets in.

We drive down the road and find the address. I walk up to the door and ring the doorbell. I can't help but look around me constantly. I feel like there are eyes on me everywhere.

The door is opened immediately. But it is not Jamie Barley that is in the doorway. It's a man. A uniformed man.

"Hi. I'm looking for Jamie Barley," I say, trying to sound like I'm not terrified, but my eyes give me away. I smile awkwardly. The guy is quite intimidating. He looks at me and doesn't smile back. He grabs my arm and leans over and speaks with a very low voice, almost a whisper, in my ear.

"If you know what's best for you, you get the hell out of here. You are not welcome here. Go back to your son, your dog, and husband and take them with you back to New York before it's too late."

He lets go of my arm and I gasp because it hurts so badly. Now he smiles. Widely.

"A message from the general," he adds.

53

September 2015

"Let's get out of here."

I get in the car and avoid looking at Joey.

"What happened? You're all pale," he says.

I shake my head. "I…I think I was just threatened by someone working for the general."

Joey turns the engine over and starts driving. I can't figure out what I am feeling. I am angry. I am so angry I could explode, but I am also terrified. I have never been threatened like that before. If it was only me, it would be different, but I have responsibilities. I have to think about my child. Still, I have to help Blake, right? I can't leave him like this.

I have no idea what to do. Where to go from here.

"So, I take it you didn't get to talk to Jamie Barley?" Joey says, as we leave the housing quarters. I am sweating heavily. I feel so paranoid, thinking they are watching us, watching our every move.

"No," I say. "Only the guy that said he had a message from the general. He basically told us to leave town because we weren't safe or welcome here. It scared the crap out of me. He even knew we lived in New York. And that we had a dog. Look, I still have goose bumps and I'm not cold. On the contrary, I'm sweating."

Joey hits his hand onto the dashboard in anger. "I shouldn't have let you go in there alone. I knew it. I just knew it. They can't do this to you. They can't threaten you like that. I just wanna…I wanna go back and…Scaring you like that. Who do these people think they are?"

"Well, in here, they're the people in charge. But they're not getting to me. I might be leaving the base, but I am not going anywhere. I am not stopping. I will find out what happened to Jamilla Jenkins and have my brother acquitted. I feel more determined than ever. After what Olivia told me, there is no doubt in my heart that my brother is innocent, and I will do whatever it takes to prove it," I say, as we approach the exit of the base.

We have to wait in a line to get out. Soldiers are picking out random cars for a more thorough check. Making sure people don't take out anything they're not supposed to.

Joey looks at me while we wait for it to be our turn. I can tell he is scared. "You're not doing this alone," he says. "I'll be with you, and I am sure the rest of the crew will as well."

"Me too, Mom," I hear Salter say, just as the soldier at the gate points at our car and pulls us aside. They ask us to get out because they are doing a random search and our car has been chosen.

Yeah right! Random!

We wait while they split the car to pieces. They even take out the seats. I have to really focus to keep calm. I want to tell them how I feel about all this, but Joey's arm around my shoulder keeps me from doing it. I look at him and he smiles from ear to ear and thanks the soldiers for doing their duty. I want to pull his hair out, but know that he is right. That it is the only way to go about this, even though I hate it. This is their territory, and they have the power to make us wait all day if they like.

It takes forty-five minutes before they are done and we can finally leave the base. I feel a huge relief as we drive out into A1A, where it no longer feels like a thousand eyes are constantly examining us.

I still have this feeling of extreme unease as we drive back into Cocoa Beach. We stop at the gas station and buy some candy for

Salter and me. I am in desperate need of something sweet to make me feel better. I buy a bag of chips as well, and some sodas for later. Joey fills up the car while Salter and I fill up on goodies. I open a chocolate bar right away while we walk back to the car. Sirens are wailing and a huge fire truck drives past us on A1A. Joey points.

"Looks like there's a big fire somewhere," he says.

I see the smoke in the distance, but take no further notice of it. Neither does Salter or Joey. We get in the car and drive off. As we get further up A1A, we realize the fire is getting closer. As we reach 10th Street, my heart drops and I stop breathing.

"Oh, my God," Joey exclaims. "The fire. It's at your dad's house! The fire is in your father's house!"

54

March 1992

Ally looks to AK for a signal, a sign, anything to tell her what to do. Mary Mills is standing at the top of the stairs looking down at them. She has seen them, but still she is not saying anything. It's like she and AK are staring at each other, sizing each other up.

Ally is waiting for Mary to scream and for AK to run, but nothing happens. They are just staring at each other. Does Mary know it is AK? Does she recognize her behind the mask?

"What do you want?" Mary finally asks.

AK doesn't answer. She is staring at Mary, her body trembling. It's like she is paralyzed. Ally has never seen her like this before.

"Why have you come here?" Mary asks.

There are more steps coming from upstairs and a door is opened. A man comes out and stands behind Mary. Ally guesses it's her father. It's the same man from the picture that AK just smashed. The one that is scattered all over the floor.

"What's going on?" he asks. "Who is this? What are you doing in my house?" he yells.

Mary turns to look at him. "It's her," she says. "It's Anne-Katelyn."

The man calms down. His shoulders fall back into place. "Oh."

Ally is surprised. She had never heard AK's real name before. She is stunned that Mary knows it. Mary's dad reaches out his arms.

"Katie," he says.

"Don't," AK suddenly yells. "Don't call me that. You have no right to call me that. And don't come any closer!"

Then she says something that makes Ally's blood freeze.

"I have a gun!"

"Katie," Mary says. "I know you don't want to hurt anyone."

"Yes! Yes, I do," AK yells, then pulls out the gun and points it at them. "I want to hurt all of you."

Ally gasps and pulls back. She has never seen a real gun before. She can tell by AK's voice that she is desperate. It scares her. It terrifies her to her core. She doesn't know what AK is capable of. Could she kill someone?

This is not going to end well.

"AK…maybe we should…" She tries to speak to her, but AK doesn't listen. It's like she is in this trance of anger that she can't escape. Ally can't reach her.

The gun is shaking in AK's hand. She is sniffling behind her mask.

"We never meant to hurt you, Katie," the dad says.

"We only did what was best," Mary says.

Ally tries hard to figure out what the heck is going on. She has no idea what they're talking about, how they know each other. She feels like crying. She wants to get out of there so badly. She looks towards the entrance door and wonders if AK would shoot her if she tried to escape.

Probably.

Ally doesn't dare to try. She stands completely still and hopes AK will calm down and come to her senses.

"Katie. We…" The dad tries to say something, but he doesn't get any further before AK interrupts him.

"You know what hurts the most?" she yells with bitterness to her voice. "That I was so close. I was so damn close."

"What is going on out here?"

A woman Ally recognizes from the picture as the mother comes out of the door and approaches the others.

"Who is yelling? You're waking the baby."

When the gun goes off, the bullet moves so fast that Ally only sees the mother freeze in the air before the blood spurts out of her stomach. While Mary screams, the woman tumbles down the stairs, one step at a time.

55

September 2015

"MY FATHER's house is on fire!"

I storm out of the car. A fire truck has just pulled up and they're trying to get the fire under control. I spot Danny among them and run up to him. He grabs my shoulders and looks into my eyes.

"Is there anyone in there, Mary?"

"I…I don't know," I say. They're usually home at this time. I think. Can't you send anyone inside to check?"

He shakes his head. "It's way too dangerous right now. The fire has gotten to the roof, and it's going to crash in a matter of seconds."

I am desperate now. As we speak, a car drives up, and a woman jumps out. She screams. I turn and look at her. It's Laura. She is cupping her mouth and screaming. I run to her.

"Laura, where is my dad? Laura!"

She doesn't even look at me. She points at the fire and simply screams in shock.

"Laura!" I yell. "Is my dad in there?"

She looks at me and nods. My heart stops.

"H-h-he was taking a n-n-nap," she stutters. "I went to Publix for just half an hour."

I turn to look at Danny, then I scream at the top of my lungs while running to him.

"My dad is in there! My dad is in the house!"

As I yell, I am drowned out by a loud crash when the roof collapses. I fall to my knees and scream.

"NOOOOO!"

Joey grabs me in his arms and tries to pull me away from the fire. The firefighters are yelling at each other and at people to stay back. They're yelling at me and Joey to get out of there. I can hardly hear them anymore. It's all a blur. The smoke, the people, the screams. I can't take it anymore. Joey is pulling me, but I can't let him. I can't just go away. I refuse to give up.

I pull myself free of him, then storm towards a window on the side of the house that hasn't popped yet. I see nothing but smoke on the other side, but I also know this is my father's study, his favorite room to work in and nap in his chair.

"No! Mary, no!" Joey yells.

"It's too late!" Danny yells.

While everyone is screaming behind me, I jump. Like Superman, I jump through the glass window. Glass is everywhere. I cut myself on my hands and face before I land on the floor inside. Fire is licking up the walls in the room and I stay low to not inhale too much smoke.

"Daaaad?" I scream, while beams are falling on all sides of me. I realize I can't breathe and start to cough heavily, when suddenly I hear something. The adrenalin is rushing through my veins as I spot my dad. He's on the floor, so close to the window, lying flat on his stomach, his arm stretched out like he is reaching for the window, for the outside.

You almost made it, didn't you?

He is stuck underneath a fallen beam. It's still on fire, so I can't touch it. Instead, I kick it with all I have, while pieces of the roof are still falling around my ears. I get him free, then grab his arm and pull him up on my back. As I approach the window, I scream.

"Heeeelp!"

I see something. Through the smoke, I see movement. I carry

my dad closer, hoping and praying we won't be hit by anything falling, when I spot Danny jumping through the window, wearing all his gear. He spots us when he lands, then runs to us. He's got a couple of big wet blankets that he throws on top of us, then he grabs my dad and lifts him up, while I run forward, my arms covering my head, holding the blanket over my back. I manage to get myself back out the window, cutting my leg and ripping my dress. When I am outside, I throw myself on the ground. Exhausted, out of breath, coughing, and scared to death.

Joey runs up to me and helps me get to my feet. I watch as the firefighters help Danny carry my father out of the window and towards the paramedics. They're all over him. I try to get close.

"Is he alive?" I ask.

No one answers. I try hard not to cry.

Please, dear God. Please, don't take him too.

"We've got a pulse," I hear someone say, then fall to my knees and let it all go.

56

September 2015

I GO with the ambulance to the hospital in Cape Canaveral. Joey drives Salter there and they meet me in the waiting room. Salter runs into my arms and holds me tight.

"That was really dangerous, Mommy," he says.

"You gave us quite a scare," Joey says and hugs me as well. We hold each other like we used to, back when we were still a family. "I thought I was going to lose you."

"I am sorry," I say, crying and holding my loved ones close. Gone is all the hurt; gone is all the pain. It doesn't matter anymore. These are the people I love and I am so grateful to still be alive and to have them in my life. So happy I can still hold them in my arms.

"I am so sorry," I say through tears. "I just couldn't leave him in there to die. I just couldn't."

We let go of each other and sit down to wait. Salter keeps ahold of my hand. Joey has a hard time holding back his tears.

"Have they checked you?" he asks, biting his lip. "You could have suffered from smoke inhalation injury or something. They need to check you."

I nod. "I know," I say and cough.

"Is Grandpa going to be alright?" Salter asks with concern.

I pull him closer and kiss the top of his head. "We don't know yet, sweetheart. We don't know. But I do have hope."

A doctor enters the room and I get up. "Any news about my father?" I ask, but he shakes his head.

"We're doing all we can to save him, but we need to take a look at you as well. Right now. Smoke inhalation is a serious thing."

I follow the doctor and they put me in a bed. They do a chest X-ray to determine if there is lung injury. They attach a probe to my finger to determine the degree of oxygen in my blood. They run a series of blood tests and finally they hook me up with an oxygen tank. I am hoarse and I do find it hard to breathe on my own, so I am happy to be in good hands. But several hours later, I still don't know how my dad is doing. I am terrified of losing him.

Finally, a doctor comes to my bedside. He tells me I have suffered a minor smoke inhalation injury and that there may still be shortness of breath with minimal exertion in the coming days.

"It may take time for your lungs to fully heal, and some people may have scarring and shortness of breath for the rest of their lives. It's important to avoid triggering factors, such as cigarette smoke. You'll need to have follow up visits with your own doctor, but other than that, I'll recommend you'll be discharged tomorrow morning. Seek medical help if your symptoms worsen," he says.

I pull off the oxygen mask to speak. I still have shortness of breath, and speaking makes me tired.

"How is he?" I ask, not caring one bit about what he is telling me about myself. "Is he alive?"

"Your father is alive, yes. He is still in critical condition. It's too early to say."

"But he's still alive?" I say.

"Yes."

The doctor leaves and I lean back in my bed. Minutes later, Salter and Joey peek in.

"How's the patient?" Joey asks.

I can tell that Salter is scared.

"I'm fine," I say, sounding more cheerful than I feel. I didn't like the look on the doctor's face when he told me about my father. It wasn't hopeful.

I ask Salter to come closer, then have him sit on the edge of my bed. I look into his eyes. "Mommy will be fine, alright? The doctor just told me so."

"Why do you have all that, then?" he asks and points at the oxygen mask that I have pulled down to be able to speak.

"Ah, this old thing? It's just to help me breathe better, they say. I don't really need it. They're just being very overprotective around here."

I end the sentence with a deep cough and have to pull the mask back on to breathe. I take in a few deep breaths, then pull it off again. Salter looks at me, worried. I try to smile.

"There's someone else here to see you," Joey says, and opens the door.

In comes first Danny carrying a fistful of balloons. Then Alex, Sandra, Marcia, and Chloe follow him.

It melts my heart to see all of them here, and now I start to really cry.

"Aw, you guys."

57

January 1984

"HERE'S YOUR DAUGHTER. She is a little shy."

The lady from the adoption agency kneels next to the young girl. "There's no need to be scared," she says to her. "These are your new parents."

The young girl looks up at Penelope and Peter. She is seven years of age, the agency has told them. Just like their own daughter.

"Oh, Peter, she is perfect," Penelope says, smiling. She is happy. They both are. After years of trying to have a second child, it was the right decision to adopt.

"We've wanted another child for so long," Penelope says to the lady from the adoption agency.

The lady smiles. "I'm sure you'll all be very happy together. I understand there is another child in the family?"

"Yes, we have another daughter. She is actually the exact same age. I hope they'll have so much fun together. It's going to be almost like having twins."

"Where is your daughter now?" the lady asks.

Peter's smile stiffens.

"She is not well," Penelope says. "She had an emergency last night and had to be taken to the hospital. We'll go there now and see her with her new sister."

The lady from the adoption agency looks at Penelope. "Oh, I am so sorry," she says. "Will she be alright?"

"We hope so. The doctors simply can't figure out what is wrong. It is frustrating."

"That must be very hard on you both."

Peter doesn't say anything. Penelope nods her head. "It is. It's always tough when it's the little ones, you know? You want so badly to make them feel better, but there isn't anything we can do. That reminds me. We should get going. They're running more tests this afternoon."

Penelope looks at the little girl and reaches out her hand. "Hi there, sweetheart. What beautiful eyes you have. How do you feel about going to the hospital to meet your sister?"

The girl looks at Penelope, terrified. Penelope knows her story and knows she has to be careful with her. She has to gain her trust.

"I understand she has moved around a lot?" Peter asks.

"Yes. As you know from the file we sent you, she lost her parents when she was three, and since then she has been moving around to different foster homes and families, and it has just been a mess for her. I do hope it'll work out with you. She needs a stable family now."

"Oh, we can provide that for her," Penelope chirps. "Come with us."

The girl is still staring at Penelope's hand with skeptical eyes.

"And you do know about the last family she was with, don't you?" the lady asks.

Penelope nods. "Yes. Awful story. To think that they would have those orgies at their house with the child there; it's painful."

"And you must know that she was abused by several of the members of their satanic cult. That was why we had to remove her."

"Well, you won't see any of that stuff around here," Penelope says. "We're good old God-loving church-going folks."

Then she laughs. Peter chuckles along. The little girl stares at them still, while she makes her decision.

"Come on," Penelope says, and moves her hand closer. Finally, the girl decides to grab it.

Penelope smiles. "We'll take good care of you. Don't you worry."

58

September 2015

"We're still working on the site, but I wanted to tell you in person that we're ruling it arson."

Danny is standing at my bedside, looking seriously at me. "The electrical wiring, the appliances, and all other potential accidental causes of a fire have been ruled out. The burn patterns show the fire was set in a back room of the house with the use of an accelerant—gasoline. I have seen it enough times in my professional life to be sure."

"So, you're telling me someone broke into my father's house and set it on fire?" I ask.

"Yes. That's what we believe."

"With him inside of it!" I exclaim, feeling the anger build.

Joey grabs my hand in his. I pull away. I am angry right now. I am entitled to be. I don't want comfort or pity. I want whoever did this to pay, to go to jail.

"Have you informed the police?" I ask.

"We will. As soon as the investigation is done."

"Good."

Sandra approaches me, her head slightly tilted, pity in her eyes.

"I am so sorry," she says. "It's terrible what has happened to you and your father."

"Do you have any idea who might have wanted to hurt your father?" Danny asks.

I look to Joey. Our eyes meet. He knows what I think.

"No," I say. "But I do have an idea who wants to hurt me."

Joey tells them about our visit to the base and the threat from the man in Jamie Barley's house.

"You really think they would go this far?" Marcia asks. She seems more present than usual. She doesn't smell like alcohol, but her eyes tell me she is on something else.

I shrug and look to Joey again. "I didn't hear the threat," he says. "I was in the car, but you were pretty shaken up when you came back. These people are dangerous."

"They're the ones who framed Blake," I say.

All eyes turn to look at me.

"What?" Sandra asks.

"What are you saying?" Chloe asks, stepping closer to me.

I take a deep breath of oxygen through the mask to better be able to speak. The sound reminds me of the time when I went scuba diving in the Keys. "I spoke to Olivia Hartman earlier today. You all remember her, right? Double O?"

They all nod. Alex and Danny look at each other while nodding, and I can tell they still find her hot. "Well, she was seeing Blake. Some of you already know this, but they had an affair. I have a feeling it has been going on for quite some time. She is married to General Hartman, and he apparently found out about them, then decided to get rid of Blake once and for all. Olivia told me that he forced her to put the bloody chisel under the sink and informed the police about it. Somehow, I believe Detective Chris Fisher is in his pocket, because when I went to Blake's studio, Chris Fisher came in and was looking for a ring. Olivia's ring. And when I visited her today, she was wearing it. I think Detective Fisher is in the general's pocket. He helped him frame Blake, told him where to find the body and the chisel, and provided a witness for him. Jamie Barley. It was at her house that I was threatened."

I stop to breathe in the mask again. I feel tired, but the anger still keeps me going. I can't believe the general would try to kill my dad just to scare me.

"So, Blake is innocent," Chloe says. "We know that for sure now. He just slept with the wrong woman."

"Yes," I say. "And I am determined to prove that."

"But how?" Sandra asks.

"I don't know yet. It's not like Olivia will testify. She's way too afraid of her husband. If only I could get to Jamie Barley, the witness, and talk to her. Or if I could somehow figure out who really killed Jamilla Jenkins."

I sigh and put on the mask again. My throat is sore and I am hoarse. I can feel the aftermath of the smoke inhalation injury now. The doctor told me it would happen, that I would feel tired and short of breath. I look at Danny and grab his hand.

"How are you doing?" I ask. "Any news about the investigation?"

He shakes his head, then looks down.

"There was another one," Alex says.

"What?"

Danny nods in agreement. "It's true. Someone else was killed yesterday in her home here in Cocoa Beach by the same killer as Jean."

"How do you know it was the same killer?" I ask, baffled.

"She was found in her home with a pair of scissors in her throat," Alex says. "Just like Jean."

"The strange part is that it is another person we know from high school," Danny says.

"Who?"

59

September 2015

CASSIE MORGAN? Cassie is dead? I can't believe what they are telling me. I am breathing hard in my mask now, sucking all the oxygen I can out of it, while trying to calm myself down. What the heck is going on here? Another woman from my high school who has been murdered? Is someone targeting people from my high school? Just going randomly through the yearbook or what? And why?

"They used to be friends," I say, once I remove the mask again. "Do you remember? Jean and Cassie?"

"Sure," Sandra says. "They always hung out together. Knew each other since preschool at FUMC."

Most of us actually went to the same preschool together, those of us that were born and raised in Cocoa Beach. I mostly remembered Joey from back then, since he had already decided that we were going to get married once we grew up, and told me once when his grandfather brought him into school one day.

He pointed at me and said: "This is the girl I want to marry."

All the grown-ups laughed, naturally. But Joey and I both took it very seriously. We remained friends all the way through elementary and surfed together constantly through high school. We even went away to college together, and that was when we started dating. We had always been together, always enjoyed hanging out so much. How could we have gone so wrong?

"Anyone else freaking out about this?" Marcia asks. "I mean, it is kind of creepy that two girls, two best friends that we grew up with have been killed. It doesn't sound like some burglary gone wrong or some psycho walking in randomly from the street. These girls have been murdered. Targeted and murdered. So, the question is…who is next? I, for one, am locking my doors tonight."

I nod pensively, thinking it is amazing that Cocoa Beach is still this small community where people don't lock their doors. After living in New York for a few years, I can't imagine not locking everything safely. But I get what she is saying. Something is off here.

"What do we know about Jamilla Jenkins?" Joey suddenly asks. "I mean, the only way we can help Blake is to figure out who killed her, or at least get the jury to doubt he could have done it. Like the lawyer told Mary, we need to show that the investigation wasn't done properly or thoroughly enough. Now that we know he was framed, there must be evidence out there that the police have overlooked."

I shrug. "Not much. She was a soldier. Was found in a motel room, Motel 6 on A1A, stabbed in her chest."

"Don't they have surveillance cameras on these places?" Chloe asks.

I shrug again. "Sounds like they should have."

"They do," Danny says. "At the front desk. There was a fire a few years ago in one of the rooms. It turned out to be an arsonist traveling through town, and they found his picture from the surveillance cameras when he checked in."

I look to Chloe. She nods. She knows what I am thinking. "I can give it a try. I might also be able to find a little on the girl from the army's database. It might not be usable for anything, but they have her files there. I can check them out."

"The army database?" Danny says. "That sounds like something you could go to jail for, for a long time."

Chloe shrugs. "They'll never know it's me. Patrick Air Force

Base is one of my clients. I work on securing their systems. I already have access."

"All right," I say. "I'll call the lawyer and tell him what I know so far."

"Do any of you remember Joanne?" Sandra suddenly says.

We all nod. Joanne is a girl who went to our school as well. She became pregnant at only sixteen and had to drop out of school. Most of us haven't seen her since. Except for Sandra, that is. They used to be good friends.

"I kept in touch with her over the years and helped her out with the baby. Her life changed completely and we drifted apart, but every now and then, when I came back from my trips I would go visit. Her son is now twenty-two. His name is Billy."

"Yeah. And?" Marcia asks impatiently.

"Well, yesterday I saw his picture in the paper. Apparently, he was hospitalized for drinking drain cleaner. I couldn't believe it was him and went to visit. He has suffered severe damage to his mouth and trachea, the windpipe. They don't know if he will be able to breathe on his own again."

"That's terrible," I say.

"The thing is, the doctor told Joanne that it looks like it was forced into his mouth. The way he was bruised around his mouth and the fact that it went into his windpipe and not the gullet shows that he was in distress, and therefore he hyperventilated and pulled the liquid into his lungs. Like he was panicking. Unfortunately, he is unable to speak to tell what happened. The police say they believed he drank it himself, that he tried to kill himself, but Joanne doesn't believe he would do that."

"That's odd," Joey says. "Who would be so cruel as to force him to drink that stuff?"

"That's what I was wondering," Sandra says. "I found it very strange. But the reason I mention it is that he was also found in a hotel room, at the International Palms Resort. The police say they don't want to spend resources on investigating it, but I thought, what if he wasn't alone? Maybe Chloe could find out who he went there with. Just to help out Joanne? For old time's sake."

60

September 2015

The next morning, I am being discharged. Joey has taken the morning off from work to come and pick me up. Salter is with him. They're smiling and have even brought me a box of chocolates. I open the box right away. Hospital food hasn't done much for me, and I'm craving something sweet.

We all go to see my dad. He is lying in his bed when we enter. Tubes and everything. His eyes are closed. It's just like the movies. Instruments are beeping, telling me he is in fact still alive, even if he seems more like he is dead.

I take in a deep breath. My throat is still sore. I walk to him and take his hand. Salter and Joey stay behind while I approach him. A nurse walks in and stands on the other side of him.

"He doesn't seem to react to anything," she says. "Maybe he will when he hears his daughter's voice."

My dad is still in a coma. He is severely burned on two thirds of his body. They had to transplant skin from other places of his body. He looks terrible. I start to cry and lean in over him.

"Oh, Dad. I am so so sorry. This is all my fault. I am so sorry. Please, don't give up. Please, come back to me. I need you. We never talked. We never made amends. We just let time pass. Why did we do that, Daddy? Why didn't we ever talk about what happened?"

Joey comes closer. I feel his hand on my back. He pulls me closer and hugs me. "Don't be so hard on yourself," he whispers.

I sob heavily. "I blamed him, Joey. I blamed him for everything. I always wanted to talk to him about what happened, but I never dared. Instead, I became angry with him. Bitter and angry. I can't blame him for running into the arms of Laura. I was a terrible teenager. When Mom died, I went completely mad and blamed it all on him. I never thought about how it affected him. He lost her too. So did Blake. I only thought about how bad I felt. And he was the only one I could take it out on."

"I know," Joey says. "I was there, remember?"

I look at him and chuckle. "True. You were always there. You have always been here by my side. What happened to us?"

Joey shrugs. "We grew up. We believed life would be a dance on roses once we got married and had a child. But it wasn't. It's not easy being a grown-up."

I chuckle again while Joey wipes away a couple of my tears. Our eyes meet and lock for just a second. I want him to kiss me, and then I don't. I am vulnerable right now and don't want to do anything I'll regret. I love him, yes. But do I trust him? Do I want to open that door again? I don't think so.

"We should go," Joey says. "I gotta get to work."

I nod and sob again. I grab my dad's hand in mine again and squeeze it. When I let go of it, it falls flat back on the bed. I touch his cheek. It feels cold. I wonder if he can hear anything in there behind those closed eyelids. The instruments keep telling me that he is alive, with their little beeps and dings, but I feel like I have lost him. Maybe I already did many years ago?

I lean over him and kiss him on the forehead. The nurse smiles at me when I draw back.

"We'll let you know immediately if anything happens," she says. "Hopefully, we'll have good news soon."

I nod. "Thank you. I appreciate it."

When we walk out of the room, I feel Joey's hand in mine. I let him take it because I need his care right now. I only hope that Salter doesn't believe that we're back together again.

When we're in the car, I find my phone and call James Holland, Blake's lawyer. Joey drives out on 520 and I have a lump in my throat, thinking about my dad, who is still back at the hospital all alone.

"We need to talk," I say, when the lawyer comes to the phone. "I have reason to believe Blake was framed. As a matter of fact, I spoke to someone who admitted to having placed the chisel in his studio to make sure he was arrested for it. Now, I can't convince her to testify. So what do you suggest we do?"

James Holland lets out a deep sigh from the other end. I don't understand why he doesn't sound happy.

"I wish you would have brought this to me a little sooner," he says.

"Why?"

"Yesterday, your brother declared himself guilty."

61

March 1992

The gun drops to the floor. AK is staring at the woman, who is no longer falling. She is lying at the bottom of the stairs, head first into the plush carpet, blood gushing out of her and coloring the carpet around her.

Ally's heart has stopped. She can't breathe. The sight of the woman lying lifeless on the stairs makes her sick to her stomach. She bends over and throws up. Meanwhile, Mary and her father rush down the stairs. There's a lot of screaming and crying and yelling. AK looks at Ally. Her eyes are terrified.

"Run," she yells through the chaos.

Ally shakes her head. "Where can we go?"

AK grabs Ally's arm and pulls. "I don't know. Just out of here."

Not knowing what else to do, Ally decides to follow AK out the front door and into the street. They throw their ski masks in a bush and run. When they hear sirens in the distance, they decide to go down to the beach and run instead. To not be seen. It's dark down there. Ally doesn't care. She's in shock. She doesn't know what else to do. So she just follows AK, tears rolling down her cheeks, wondering where they can go. There is nowhere to hide, nowhere for them to stay.

I just watched someone die. My God, what have I done?

They reach the lifeguard tower on 16th Street and Ally knows they're now leaving downtown Cocoa Beach. They can still hear sirens and they spot a police car drive past on the road. By now, everyone is looking for them. There is no way they can get away.

"What do we do?" Ally whispers with a pounding heart.

"We keep going," AK says.

They run across the sand. Ally is sweating and panting heavily. They pass Taco City and continue till they reach the last house on Cocoa Beach, where Ally knows the Air Force Base starts. She is tired now and can barely even walk anymore. AK is worn out too. But they have to. They have to keep moving.

That's when they spot the three houses. Three small houses on the beach that are owned by the Air Force, that they know are used to house military personnel.

"Come," AK says and pulls Ally's arm. "They look empty."

They choose the first one and walk up to it and look in the windows before AK breaks one of them with her elbow. She cries in pain and then crawls through. Ally feels sick again and throws up once more. She suddenly misses her mother more than ever.

What have I done? How will I ever get out of this?

AK opens the front door and grabs Ally's arm. She pulls her inside and closes the door. They both fall to the floor, panting heavily. Ally starts to cry. She pulls her knees up underneath her chin and cries while rocking back and forth. AK growls angrily at her.

"Stop it," she says.

"What have we done?" Ally asks. "What have you done? You shot that woman. You shot her and she…she fell."

"Shut up! Shut the fuck up!" AK says.

But Ally can't stop. Now that everything is quiet, her mind is spinning with all the scenarios.

"They're going to come for us, aren't they? They'll find us and bring us in. Oh, my God, we're going to be put away for life, aren't we? We're going to spend the rest of our lives in prison?"

"SHUT UP!"

AK is standing up now. She slaps a hand across Ally's face. "Shut up so I can think!"

"Who's in here?"

The voice is coming from one of the rooms. Ally gasps and looks. She sees a man come out of the darkness. She can't see his face because there is no light other than what comes from the streetlamp outside. But as he walks closer, she spots a gun between his hands.

62

September 2015

The police call me later in the day and ask me to come down. I take Salter with me and enter the small building next to City Hall. I glance at the new fire station that has just been built and wonder if Danny is at work.

Detective Chris Fisher greets me at the entrance and shows me into a small room. Salter is left to sit on a chair outside. I feel very uncomfortable as the detective sits down in front of me. He is a few years younger than me, and I remember him as a little punk.

"You want coffee or anything?" he asks.

I shake my head.

"We have donuts," he says with a smile. He is annoyingly nice to me. It pisses me off greatly.

"I'm good, but thanks," I say, even though every fiber of my body craves something sweet right now.

"First of all, I would like to tell you how deeply sorry I am for what happened to your father. I hope he'll get better. We're all praying for him. He is a big contributor to our small town. A very respected member of our community."

I always loathed the way they talk about Cocoa Beach like it was a sect or something. Now even more than ever, since the words are coming from his mouth.

The hypocrite.

Did you do it, huh? Did you set the house on fire for the general, did you?

"The reason I have called you down here is that I am in charge of the investigation of the fire. As you know, we believe it was arson. Since your dad was inside of the house, it has suddenly become an attempted murder investigation. I want to assure you we take this matter very seriously, and I intend to find whoever did this and make sure they are brought to justice."

All the right words.

"I appreciate it," I say, trying to stay calm.

"Do you know of anyone who might wish to harm your father or your family?" he asks.

"I was threatened yesterday," I say.

Chris Fisher looks surprised. "By whom?"

Like you don't know.

"By a soldier at the base. He told me he was giving me a message from General Hartman, told me to leave town if I knew what was best for me. Those were his exact words. An hour later, my dad's house was set on fire and he was almost killed."

I can feel how my voice is cracking as I speak the last words. I feel so much anger at this instant I can't hold it back. It's bigger than me.

Detective Chris Fisher stares at me, biting the end of his pen. "You mean to tell me the general actually threatened you? And that you believe he is responsible for the fire?"

He sounds like he is trying hard not to laugh. I want to slap him across his face and wipe the smirk off like I remember doing once when he was still in middle school and groped Sandra's boob at his sister's pool party.

"Yes. I don't believe he set the house on fire himself, but I do believe he had someone do it for him."

Detective Fisher is still staring at me. A smile is emerging slowly. He doesn't know what to say. I can tell he is looking for the words.

"You're kidding me, right?"

"I'm deadly serious. The general has it in for my brother and doesn't want me to help him. He is trying to keep me from finding out what really happened to Jamilla Jenkins. My brother had an affair with his wife. That's why."

Chris Fisher blows out air and whistles. "Wow. I don't know what to say to that, Mary. That's a lot of conspiracy right there. I never took you for being one of those. The general is a very well respected man."

I slam my palm on the table. "He threatened me, Chris."

He is still just staring at me and shaking his head. I can tell he is laughing on the inside.

"What did he do to you?" I ask. "Why do you work for him? Does he have something on you? Did you cheat on the wifey and did he threaten to tell her?"

I know I'm on thin ice now, but I can't help myself.

"I saw you, you know," I say. "In my brother's studio. You were looking for the ring. The ring that I later saw on Olivia Hartman's finger."

Chris Fisher stops smiling. "What?"

"I was in the studio when you got there, when you looked for the ring. I saw you grab it and take it. That's tampering with evidence, my friend."

Chris Fisher leans forward with a sigh. "I don't believe the ring was of importance. The general wanted it back; there is nothing wrong with that," he says. "It's a very expensive ring."

"Did you write Olivia out of the police-report as well? Did he tell you to?" I ask.

Chris Fisher's face turns red all of a sudden. He leans in and snorts at me. "I did him a favor. The general feared that it would come out in the open that his wife had an affair. He thought it was embarrassing to them. I can't blame him. His wife was sleeping around right under his nose. Humiliating the man. Yes, I helped him out when he asked me to. You'll never hear me admit it outside of this room, but yes, I did. I left Olivia out of the report, and when the general realized the ring was missing and Olivia told him where it might be, that your brother might have it in the apartment, then yes. I helped the guy out. He's an old friend of mine. We served together. I didn't destroy any evidence, nor did I ruin the investigation. Olivia had nothing to do with the murder of Jamilla Jenkins."

"And my brother did? Olivia placed the chisel in his studio. The general told her to."

Chris Fisher leans back in the chair. "What?"

"You heard me. She admitted it to me yesterday. That's why the general wanted me to leave town."

Chris Fisher runs a hand through his hair. "That is a serious accusation. You do realize that, right?"

"I can't prove it and she'll probably never admit it if you ask her again, but yes. She told me she did it. She placed the bloody chisel in the bucket under the sink because she had no other choice."

"But…but your brother just admitted his guilt?"

I let out a deep sigh. I feel so confused right now. Chris Fisher doesn't seem to be as bad as I expected him to be. I don't hate him. I feel like he is being honest with me. A lot more honest than I had ever expected. It confuses me deeply. He sounds sincere. He looks sincere. But I suspect he is only acting. Quite the actor he could have been.

"I know," I say with defeat in my voice.

"Why would he declare himself guilty now?"

"I don't know. That's what I intend to find out." I get up from my chair. "If you'll excuse me."

Detective Chris Fisher gets up as well. He looks at me intensely. He is handsome and it annoys me that I like him. I suspect he is still playing a little game with me, trying to be the nice guy and make me believe in him. I am not falling for it.

"Let me know if there is anything I can do," he says.

Ah! Come on!

63

September 2015

I AM STRUMMING my fingers on the table while I wait. I feel so frustrated, so confused and lost at the same time. I have left Salter at Sandra's house. I don't think he should be with me when I visit my brother in prison.

The door opens and my brother comes into the barren room. He looks pale and tired. He has lost weight. His cheeks are hollow, his eyes dark and sad. I feel like crying when I look into them, but hold it back by forcing a smile.

"Mary!" he exclaims.

"Blake. How are you?" I ask when he sits down. "Are you okay?"

Blake nods, but I can tell he is lying. "I'm good. I'll be alright."

"What's going on Blake?" I ask.

"What do you mean?"

"You plead guilty all of a sudden?"

Blake sighs. His eyes are avoiding mine. "Yeah, well…"

"Well what Blake? Explain it to me. I'm out there trying like crazy to get you acquitted, trying to help your lawyer make your case, and you go out and destroy everything?"

"Well, it's the truth. I did it."

I slam the palm of my hand onto the table. The guard watching us looks at me. I pull it back.

"Goddammit, Blake, why are you saying that?"

"Because it's the truth. I couldn't remember before, but now I do. I got my memory back the other day. I killed her, Mary. I should be punished for it. I belong in jail for what I have done. I am sick. When I get drunk, I do things I wouldn't ordinarily."

"Yes, like sleeping with a married woman or getting in a bar fight with someone, but you don't kill people, Blake. That's not who you are," I say, trying to keep my voice down. It is hard, though. I am so mad at him right now.

"What do you even know about who I am?" he says. "I was three years old when you left. A lot of years have passed since then. People change, Mary. I've changed. And I need to be responsible for my actions."

I stare into his eyes. I try to look for something, anything that tells me he is lying to me.

"I don't believe you," I say.

"Suit yourself. I can't help you with that."

"They got to you, didn't they?" I ask.

"Who?"

"The general, Detective Fisher. They got to you somehow. What did they do? Threaten you? Oh, I know. They threatened to kill Olivia, didn't they?"

I look deep into his eyes to see his reaction. I know he won't give it to me verbally because then the guard will hear it. I detect a flinch in his eyes when I mention Olivia's name. That's enough for me.

"That's it, isn't it? They came here and told you they would hurt Olivia if you didn't plead guilty. Am I right?"

He doesn't say more. He bites his lips. His eyes are flickering. He is right. I haven't known him much through his life, but he is still my brother.

"The bastards," I say and slam my hand onto the table again. The guard gives me a glare and I excuse myself. I lean back in the chair instead. "I can't believe them."

Blake leans in over the table. His chains rattle when he moves. "Mary. You need to leave it alone. I appreciate all you have done for me. But, for my sake. If you love me, you'll leave it alone."

64

September 2015

Leave it alone? Leave it alone? What the hell is he thinking? That I should just leave him to rot in jail?

I am angry as I drive back to Cocoa Beach. No, that's too mild. I am more than angry. I am furious. I don't have the words to describe it. I have come all the way down here to a place I'd rather never see again in my life, with so many bad memories that I have been busy trying to forget, just for him, just to help him out, and then this? Then he goes ahead and does this? He declares himself guilty and has the nerve to tell me to leave it alone.

"If you love me, you'll leave it alone," I say out loud, mocking him. I drive over the bridge leading to the islands. I take no notice of how fast I am going and once I reach the island and the entrance to Cocoa Beach, I get pulled over.

Crap.

The officer gives me a ticket and I drive on, growling and cursing even more than before. I drive to Joey's house and park in the driveway. Joey is back from work and is standing in the yard when I drive up. He is wearing nothing but shorts. He is dirty and sweaty and way too hot for me to handle right now. He waves as I approach him. He looks me in the eyes.

"Hey. What's wrong?"

Not knowing what to say or do, I stare at my gorgeous ex, who I could never quite live up to.

"I…I just had a real bad day," I say.

"Did you visit Blake?" he asks.

"Yeah. He pled guilty and he wants us to leave it alone. So, there you have it."

"We can't do that. He'll get life in prison. He'll never survive it," Joey says and wipes sweat off his forehead.

"That's what I said, but he won't listen. He ended up getting mad at me and that was it."

"You think someone threatened him?" Joey asks.

I nod. "They must have. Why else would he all of a sudden change his statement like that? When I visited him last time he told me he didn't remember anything and that he had never seen the girl before. I don't buy his crap about all of a sudden remembering everything. It's just too weird. But it changes everything, the lawyer says." I can feel the tears are pressing from behind my eyes. I can hardly speak for the lump in my throat. I sit down in one of his chairs on the porch. Joey disappears for a second, then returns with two beers. He hands me one. I open it and drink. It doesn't help much. I still feel like breaking down.

"What am I supposed to do?" I say.

Joey shrugs. "If he wants you to leave it alone, then maybe that's what you ought to do. Go back to New York with Salter. You probably have to be back soon anyway, right? I mean they can't live without you for long at the paper, can they?"

I scoff and lean back on his patio chair. I can hear the waves in the distance. I love that sound.

"I was sacked," I say.

"Excuse me?"

"Fired. They fired me."

Joey almost chokes on his beer. "You're kidding me?"

I shake my head. "Nope."

"You? Their star reporter? They fired you? How? Why?"

I sigh and drink my beer with my eyes closed. I am not sure I can cope with all this right now. Talking about it makes it all so real all of a sudden. I don't want it to be real. I want it to be a bad dream that I can forget about. Just like everything else in my life, I just want to close my eyes and make it all go away. But it never does, does it? It always comes back somehow to haunt you. The past never leaves you alone.

"It's a long story," I say.

He leans back in his chair. "I don't have to be anywhere."

I exhale deeply. I really don't want to talk about it. "Alright," I say. "To make a long story short, I wrote the wrong story. I pissed off some big shot people from a big medical company, Mirah, by revealing how they lied to the public about their results with a specific medicine that people are taking all over the U.S., but yet got it approved by the FDA. The FDA approved the medicine, a non-steroidal anti-inflammatory drug and a prescription painkiller, for use three years ago. I wrote the story of how the company was accused of misleading doctors and patients about the drug's safety, fabricating study results to suit the company's needs, continually thwarting an FDA scientist from revealing the drug's problems and skirting federal drug regulations. Last week, Mirah withdrew the drug from the market after a study revealed the drug more than doubled the risk of heart attacks and death. They had tried to keep this study a secret from the public, but I got my hands on it and published it. By that point, more than 8,000 deaths were already related to the use of the drug, and up to fifteen million Americans had taken the drug. The story went viral. People loved it, and hopefully we saved some lives because they were forced to withdraw the drug, but apparently both my editor and I had to pay a price. I don't know who is in the pocket of whom, but that's what happened."

"That's crazy," Joey says and finishes his beer. "They should give you an award instead."

I scoff. "Well, that is not how the world works, unfortunately."

"You should write about that," he says.

"About what?"

"About how you were fired. How they're all in bed with each

other. You could do it, you know. Now that you're famous for the article. People would listen to you. You have a voice."

I shake my head and finish my beer. "Nah. I'm in bad standing everywhere in the publishing world. The company says I violated the regulations for printing an article. Nobody will touch me after this. Who would publish it?"

"You could."

"Me?"

"Yes. Do it online. Create a blog and write about it. Have Chloe help you create it. She could probably give it a real cool design and everything. She knows what it takes."

"True, but still…come on," I say. "Why would I?"

"So they won't get away with it. Don't let them do that. Those bastards should pay for what they did to you. They deserve to pay big time. If you keep quiet, they've won. Do you want them to win? To keep you down? Do you want them to silence you?"

I look into Joey's blue eyes. *This is nice*, I think to myself. To sit with him like this again, just talking. Just the two of us. I can't remember the last time we did this. I miss him, I realize. I miss him so terribly. We were invincible when we were younger. Together, we could conquer the world. I am sick of feeling like I am defeated.

"That's not a bad idea, actually," I say with a smile. "Not bad at all."

65

September 2015

I WALK to Chloe's house with Joey. We have brought a twelve-pack of beer to smooth the way a little. Chloe likes beer. I knock on the door and she opens it.

"Good," she says. "I was about to call you. I have news. Come."

We walk to her room in the back. I feel like I am sent back to twenty-five years ago when I would visit her in that same house in that same room where she would be all cooped up behind her computer screens. The computers had changed, they had changed a lot, but Chloe was still the same. It amazed me how all of us were still pretty much the same. We quickly fell into the same roles as back then.

Chloe sat down in her chair behind the big screens. The room was dark and the curtains pulled, as always.

"First of all, I've been going through old cases," she says. "I went through criminal complaints and missing persons reports over the past fifteen years to see if I could find any similarities to what happened to Jean and Cassie."

I grab a chair and sit next to her. Joey does the same. The room is small and stuffy, but I like it there. I like hanging out with Chloe again. I have always been so impressed with her and her talent. I have never met anyone like her. And she is, by far, the most trustworthy person I know. Loyal to the bone.

"And?"

"And this is what I found," she says. She pulls up a document on the screen and opens it. "You remember CC?"

"Coraline, sure," I say and look at Joey. He shakes his head. He never remembers any names. He never forgets a face, but names he can't remember if his life depends on it.

"Coraline was found killed in 2004."

I gasp. "What?"

"She was found killed in a hotel room," she says. "A pair of scissors in her throat."

"Why haven't we heard about that?" I ask.

"It was in Orlando. Coraline Cane, married name Densley, moved to Winter Park in 1999. She was married to a senior pastor at some church there. According to the case file, she was supposed to meet someone at the hotel room, a man she had been seeing for years on the side. He was the one who found her lying on the bed with the scissors in her throat, blood everywhere. The killer was never found."

I swallow hard. I can't believe what I am hearing here. This is getting very strange. "Coraline was friends with Cassie and Jean," I say.

"Exactly," Chloe says. "They always hung out together."

"I don't remember that," Joey says.

"You don't remember them?" I ask. "They were this group of girls who were always causing trouble everywhere they went. It didn't last long, but for like a year, they were *the* troublemakers of Cocoa Beach High. Right before…"

"And that's what I'm getting at," Chloe says. "I think there might be a connection of some sort to what happened to Joanne's son, Billy, recently. I've read up on the story, and from the outside, from what they write in the papers, he tried to commit suicide, but I managed to pull the surveillance camera from the International Palms Resort," she says and touches the mouse. "From the night when Billy checked in. They have, like, the worst security in town, for your information. I could have pulled any credit-card information if that was what I wanted, but that's beside the point. I found these pictures," she says and clicks the mouse.

In the surveillance video, we watch as someone enters the lobby. There are five people. Four women and one man. I am guessing the man is Billy. The three women stay behind as the fourth woman grabs Billy's arm and puts it around her neck. They laugh and walk up to the woman behind the counter. They speak to her. I can tell Billy is not happy; he is not enjoying the situation. They check in and get the keycard to the room. As they're about to turn, Chloe pauses the movie. She looks at me. Her face is dead serious. It makes me uneasy.

"What is it?" I ask.

"I hope you're ready for this," she says with a deep exhale.

"Ready for what?"

"This," she says and zooms in the picture.

With my heart pounding in my throat, I watch as the picture of the woman next to Billy gets closer and clearer. Seconds later, I have a clear picture of her face.

My heart freezes to ice.

"You're kidding me, right?"

Chloe shakes her head. "Nope. It's her," she says. "She's back."

66

March 1992

"WHO ARE YOU!"

AK looks at the man with the gun pointing at them. Ally is shivering in fear. She wants to cry. She wants to go home so badly.

"No. You first," the voice says. "Who are you and what are you doing here?"

"I...We..." Ally tries to speak, but AK stops her with just one look.

"I'm sorry if we have intruded," AK says. "We didn't mean to. We just needed a place for the night, that's all."

The man steps closer. He finds a light switch and turns it on. He lowers the gun when he sees their faces. He is wearing a white T-shirt and jeans. Around his neck, Ally spots a military tag.

"What are you running from?" He looks out the window as more sirens howl by.

"Please, sir," AK pleads. "Please don't turn us in."

Ally is surprised to hear the soft tone in AK's voice.

"Why? What have you done?" the soldier asks.

"I...It...It was an accident," AK says. "Right, Ally?"

Ally nods with a whimper. The soldier suddenly smiles from ear to ear. "So, let me get this straight. You two did something tonight, something really bad, since the entire police force is looking for you, and now you want my help?"

AK nods cautiously. Ally doesn't say anything.

The soldier laughs loudly. "Ha! That's the best news I've heard in a long time."

Ally is confused. Why is this such good news? She doesn't understand. But she doesn't like the look in the man's eyes either. He is looking at them in a way that makes her feel uneasy.

He walks closer to AK with the gun in his hand. He lifts the gun and lets it slide slowly across her cheek.

"So, no one knows you're here, huh? I can have my way with you two. Any way I like. Sure sounds like a great deal for me."

He leans over and kisses AK on the neck. She gasps a little at first, but soon decides to roll with it. Ally stares at them, paralyzed, while the soldier puts his hand up under AK's shirt. He grabs her jeans and pulls them down, then opens his belt, bends her over the table, and has his way with her while Ally watches with terror. She wants to scream. She wants to stop him, to wake up from this terrible, terrible nightmare, but she can't. She can't move. The soldier stares at her while he grunts and growls and forces himself on AK, who is crying heavily underneath him. Ally feels desperate. She doesn't know what to do; still, she doesn't dare to move. Not even an inch. Yet she is desperate. She is crying, because she knows she is next.

"Two young girls running right into my arms, now there's a dream I never thought would come true."

When he is done with AK, he lets her go. AK sinks to the floor, crying and sobbing. The soldier looks at Ally. He walks to her and places the gun under her chin. Ally gasps. The gun feels cold against her skin. She is shivering all over.

"It might turn out to be your nightmare, though," he whispers.

Ally whimpers as he grasps her around the throat and applies pressure. She can hardly breathe and gasps for air.

"Please," she whispers.

The man laughs. "Please, what?" he says, while smelling the skin on her neck. Ally is scared. She has never been with a man. She doesn't know what it feels like. She is scared he will hurt her.

She can hardly speak. "Please, sir."

The soldier shakes the gun in front of her face. "No. No. That's not good enough, my little girl. You have to do better than that. It's please…*General.*"

67

September 2015

THE SIGHT of Anne-Katelyn on the screen in front of me makes the blood leave my head. I stand up, feeling sick to my stomach. So many emotions are awakened all of a sudden, so many memories. I feel dizzy and close my eyes. Voices in my head are screaming, crying. I see the stairs at my dad's house. I see my mom. I see her fall from the top of the stairs. I can still hear the sound of her body thumping down every step. Every time she hits a new step, it's like a knife to my heart. I am running, but I can't help her. There is blood smeared everywhere. I run to her and she is lifeless. She is dead. I look up, and there I see *her*. Those same eyes that I am staring at right now…looking into the camera at the International Palms Resort.

Anne-Katelyn, or AK as she liked to call herself, since it sounded more dangerous. I haven't seen those eyes since that night. That fatal night when she shot and killed my mother. The police never found her. She was never punished for what she did. And there she was. Once again, mocking me. Once again, causing trouble and doing what she does best, ruining people's lives.

"Are you alright?" Joey asks. He grabs my hand in his. They all know the story. They were there. They were a part of me back then.

A part of my life. When my mother died, it all ended. They all tried so hard to be there for me, but I simply couldn't stand this town anymore. I finished school, then left. But until I left, Joey was the only one who was allowed into my life. He was my strongest supporter. The rest of the crew, I couldn't deal with. They reminded me of what had happened, and I didn't want that. It wasn't their fault. It's just what happened. How I reacted. I pushed everyone away. Even my own father, whom I blamed for everything, for letting it happen. Shortly after, he threw himself into the arms of Laura, and after that, everything changed. Blake was just a baby, and he never really knew our mother, only Laura, who hardly wanted to know of him.

"I...I can't believe it's really her," I say, my voice cracking. "I mean it's...it has been so long and I...I never thought I'd see her again."

"But, here she is," Chloe says. "Alive and well. As soon as I saw her face, I ran a face recognition program, and here's what came up. See how she's dressed in an army uniform? Well, apparently, she has had quite the career in the army. Decorated and everything. Has served time in both Iraq and Afghanistan. But the interesting part is her profile. Apparently, her name is now Liz Hester."

I sink back into my chair with a heavy thud. "She changed her name?"

"She changed her entire identity. Liz Hester, with this social security number, didn't exist until April 1992. She enlisted two years later, in 1994, when she turned seventeen."

"I thought you were supposed to be eighteen to enlist?" I ask.

"Yes, usually, but you can do it earlier with parental consent," she says.

"Parental consent?" I ask. "But AK lived in a home? She had no parents," I say.

"According to this," Chloe says and pulls up another document on her screen. "Her enlistment papers were signed by a guardian, under the name of Henry Hartman."

Chloe looks up at me.

"*General* Henry Hartman," I say.

I stare at the screen, wondering what the heck this is supposed to mean. A thousand thoughts are running through my mind. I can't connect the dots. I can't figure out how this is related. If AK is responsible for what happened to Billy, is she then also responsible for what happened to Jamilla Jenkins, who was also found in a hotel room? And what about Coraline? And Jean and Cassie? They were all friends back then. Was she targeting her old friends? Killing them one by one? The thought made a chill run down my spine. If AK was responsible for any of this, there was one thing I could be sure of. At some point, she would be coming after me. Just like that night at my father's house. She had aimed that gun at me, but accidentally killed my mother. I had always been sure of that. She came for me that night, and she was going to come for me again.

68

September 2015

Olivia Hartman can't find rest. She is walking back and forth in her living room, nervously rubbing her hands together. It's getting dark outside and she is watching as the sun sets over the mainland. It's a beautiful sight, but Olivia doesn't notice.

She is way too afraid.

Ever since her old school friend, Blake's sister Mary had been to her house at the base, the general had been giving Olivia a hard time.

Now, it is getting late, and he will return within an hour, maybe less. She is terrified of what he might do to her. She is petrified of his anger.

She has thought about leaving, about simply running away all day, but where can she go?

Olivia sits down on the couch. She sits on the edge like she is ready to jump up and run if necessary. After a few seconds, she realizes she is biting her nails again. She has just been able to grow them long and nice, but now they're almost gone.

She still remembers with terror the night she came home after having spent the evening with Blake and he was sitting in the living room, on that same couch, waiting for her, fire in his eyes. She still remembers how she froze, how every cell in her body froze to ice. He had come home early from his trip, he told her. And what had he found? That she wasn't here. She wasn't at the house or even on the base.

"I was out with an old friend," she lied.

But he didn't buy it. He had her followed, he told her. Had been doing it for about two weeks now. And, guess what he learned? She didn't need to answer. She knew from the look on his face she was in deep trouble. Just like she knows it now. The general is always one step ahead of her. She is never going to get out of this mess. She is never going to be able to get the divorce she has been wanting for so long.

He'll have to die before you can be free.

Olivia lets out a deep sigh. She looks anxiously at the clock on top of the fireplace. It will not be long now.

She gets up from the couch and walks to the big window facing the Intracoastal waters. The sun is completely gone now. Bugs are swarming outside the windows, drawn by the light from her living room. Olivia wonders what will happen if she takes the neighbor's small boat and simply rows into the darkness. Will he find her? Of course he will. In minutes, he will have hundreds of men in helicopters and boats searching the area.

Of course he will.

She'll just have to stay here and take it like the big girl she is. She'll have to face his wrath like she did the day before.

"You have humiliated me! Do you understand? And now, they come running here on the base asking questions in front of everybody, and what do you do? You invite them into our home?"

Olivia exhales to calm herself down. She closes her eyes and tries to think of something nice. Her stomach is in knots. She hasn't eaten all day. She has been too nervous. And sad. She is sad because Blake is still in that awful prison. She misses him terribly. She wonders if she will ever see him again. She doubts it. The thought makes her want to cry.

A sound startles her. The sound continues, and she turns to look.

It sounds like a tapping on the big dark window. A continuing rhythmical tapping.

Tap-tap-tap

Tap-tap-tap

She chuckles lightly when she realizes it's just a big bug that keeps hitting the glass, probably thinking it can get through and swarm towards the desirable light. Olivia shakes her head thinking what a fool she is, to be scared of such a small bug. She, who used to be a fighter pilot, who used to beat all the boys in most of their training. How had she become this shaky shadow of herself?

You're being ridiculous. So what if the general is angry? What can he do to you?

Olivia takes in another deep breath and looks at the clock once again. Only a few minutes till he is usually home on a day like this.

Tap-tap-tap

Tap-tap-tap

The sound behind her is back. Olivia chuckles again and decides it's just the bug again. The sound is louder now and more persistent.

Tap-tap-tap

Tap-tap-tap

Tap-tap-tap

Thinking it has to be a really big bug this time, Olivia turns to look, then gasps. On the other side of the glass, her eyes meet those of her past. A set of eyes she thought and hoped she was never going to see again.

69

March 1984

"Help me!

Penelope runs into the emergency room holding her adopted daughter in her arms. A nurse approaches her. Penelope doesn't know this woman. She usually knows everyone, but this one is new.

"What's wrong?"

"She's been vomiting all morning; it won't stop. She has severe diarrhea and can't hold anything down," Penelope says, then adds. "It's the third time this week. I think it's her heart. Something is very wrong with her. She had seizures on our way here in the car that lasted about three minutes, and her eyes rolled back in her head. She is not responsive to any contact. You might want to do surgery right away on her heart."

The nurse nods, then takes the child out of Penelope's hands. "I'll get a doctor to take a look at her."

Penelope smiles vaguely, then nods. "Thank you."

A doctor is called and soon arrives. He knows Penelope and looks immediately at the unresponsive child.

"Doctor, you have to help her. She is in a very bad condition," Penelope says.

"This is not the same child," he says and starts examining her.

He lifts her eyelids and looks into her eyes with a small light. Penelope knows the procedure and knows what he will do next.

"She is adopted," Penelope says. "We brought her home only two months ago. Unfortunately, we don't know her family medical history, if there are heart problems among her close relatives," she says, sounding more like a doctor herself. "I am afraid surgery might be necessary."

The doctor finishes his initial examination, then admits the child to intensive care. Penelope waits all day in the hospital and lives on nothing but coffee and snacks from a vending machine. She calls home to Peter, who is with their other daughter. He was supposed to go to the office this morning, but decided to stay home and take care of their other daughter, who is still very sick and needs observation. Penelope only hopes he doesn't have to go to the office tomorrow, in case their daughter needs to stay for several days or even go through surgery. They'll have to understand at the office, won't they? Yes, of course. After all, they are only doing what they can for their children. It's not their fault they are very sick…both of them. It's just what happens. They'll understand. Of course they will. There really isn't anything else they can do. They're all doing the best they can.

A few hours later, the doctor comes out to Penelope. She stands up from her chair. He rubs the bridge of his nose and closes his eyes. Penelope has been with enough doctors to know their every little sign. The rubbing of the bridge of their nose is always bad news.

"Is it bad, Doctor? Tell it to me straight. I need to know. It's her heart, isn't it? She needs surgery, doesn't she?"

The doctor clears his throat and then looks at Penelope. "She is stable now. I have run several tests on your child and found nothing wrong with her heart."

"But…but, I was so sure…There were palpitations. Definitely. Maybe if you take another look."

The doctor interrupts. "But I did find her sodium levels to be highly elevated, beyond what is healthy in such a young child. Sodium in this amount in such a small body can be fatal."

"Sodium…but…I don't understand…"

The doctor sighs. "Penelope. I can't help but notice a lot of similarities with the symptoms your other daughter is suffering from. I hate to ask you this…but do they somehow have access to salt? Or have you maybe given her salt?"

Penelope stares at the doctor. She holds a hand to her chest. "What…what are you implying, Doctor? Are you saying I somehow did this to my child?" Her voice is breaking as she speaks. "Here I am, in the worst place a mother can be in, while her child is fighting for her life in there. I can't eat, I can't sleep, I can hardly breathe until she is better. Do you have any idea how hard this is on a mother? And…then you…then this? How can you be so heartless, Doctor?"

"There is a condition…I have been thinking about it as objectively as possible, I mean, these two girls are not related in any way and…it just seems incredible that they could even possibly have the same type of problem. I was recently at a pediatric staff conference where I heard about this condition. They call it Munchausen Syndrome by Proxy…"

"A condition?" Penelope asks, baffled. "You mean to say that something is wrong with me? How dare you…?

"As a doctor, I have to consider the possibility that your children are being poisoned. If that is the case, then it needs to stop immediately before one of the children dies. This is very serious."

Penelope snorts. She can't believe the doctor would talk to her like that. She turns on her heel, then walks right into the room where her child is lying in the bed, pulls out all tubes, and lifts her up in her arms. A nurse comes running in.

"What are you doing?"

"I'm taking her home," Penelope says.

70

September 2015

"We need to warn her."

I look at Joey. We're still sitting in Chloe's old bedroom. Chloe is upstairs feeding her mother. I feel so bad for Mrs. Edwards. She is eaten up by cancer. The doctors gave up on her years ago, and yet she is still alive.

"Who are you talking about?" he asks.

"Olivia Hartman. She was one of them back then. She was in the same group of friends as Coraline, Jean, and Cassie. Olivia might be in danger."

"So, you want to go back to the base?" Joey asks. "After the general threatened you? They're never going to let us in again. Besides, it looks like AK is in there somewhere as well. It's hardly safe for you."

I shrug. "You got another suggestion? If AK is in there, she can get to Olivia any time she wants."

"Call her?"

"Great. Do you have her number?" I ask.

He shakes his head. "Maybe Chloe can get it for us."

"Maybe Chloe can get what?" Chloe asks, as she walks into the room.

"We're thinking about calling Olivia Hartman," Joey says, "to let her know that most of her old friends have been killed and that she might be next. But we don't have her number. She lives on base, maybe you could find it somehow on your computer?"

"Sure," she says and sits down. Ten minutes later, she hands me the number. I am relieved that I don't have to go all the way back to the base for this, but still it feels really awkward to have to call her and give her a message like this. How do you begin?

I dial the number, but of course she doesn't pick up.

"Come on," I say, and try again. "Pick up, pick up, pick up."

The answering machine starts and I hang up again. "It's not working," I say. I look to Joey. "What do we do? I don't like it."

"I have a boat," Chloe says.

"A boat?" Joey says.

"It might work. Olivia's house is on the shores of the Intracoastal," I say. "It had a great view, and it also had a big flagpole in the back yard that I would be able to recognize from the waterside. The moon is pretty bright out there tonight. We might be able to see it even in the darkness. Banana River goes right past it."

Joey is shaking his head. "You're not serious, are you? You'll get arrested. Or shot. This is an army base. They're not going to let a boat come anywhere close to the shore."

Chloe looks at me. "We'll tell them we're tourists who took a wrong turn."

I nod. I think it's a brilliant idea. Joey, not so much. We don't care. Chloe and I have decided to do it. I have to warn Olivia, no matter how much I dislike her and always have. She deserves to know that her old friend has it in for her. I won't be able to live with myself if I haven't at least tried to warn her. It is worth getting arrested for. Maybe not shot, but I don't believe they'll try and shoot us; we could, after all, really be tourists or just some drunk people on their way back from a trip down the Intracoastal highway.

"We'll be fine," I say, and call Salter at Sandra's. I explain to her what we're up to and ask her if Salter can stay till we get back.

"Sure," she says. "It's no problem at all. He's a sweet kid. Be careful, though."

I hang up, wondering why Sandra never had any children of her own. She would be such a wonderful mother. Maybe if she had married Alex instead, then everything would have been different for her. Who knows?

"Are you ready?" Chloe asks and looks at the both of us.

"As ready as we'll ever be," I say.

Joey doesn't say anything. He only grunts, but still follows us out the door.

71

March 1992

Ally is panting. She is running across the dunes. She falls and the air is punched out of her lungs. She is crying. She can hear the general yelling behind her.

"Come back here, you little whore. I'll call the police if you don't get back here immediately. I'll tell them everything!"

But Ally is not going back. There is no way. She gets up from the dunes and continues to run. As fast as her legs can carry her through the heavy sand, she runs towards the city, towards the lights, leaving the three cabins on the beach behind her. She has a hard time breathing. Her cheek is hurting from the fist the general planted in her face before she managed to get out of his grip. Her nose is bleeding, but she doesn't care. She wipes it off and continues. All she can think of is getting the hell out of there. Anywhere is better than that cabin of hell and the rough hands of the general. AK is still back there. There is no way Ally can help her, but she can save herself. Anything is better than him. Even the police. Even prison.

She had kicked him. As hard as she had ever kicked anything or anyone. He was holding her down and had put the gun on the table, because he needed his hands to hold her down. She was screaming and squirming when he tried to pull off her pants. That was when she got the opening. Just as he was about to mount her, she had planted the kick right in his balls. She had managed to do it hard enough for him to fly through the air and land on the floor. It had given her enough time to storm to the door and run out. He had grabbed her leg as she did and started to pull her back into the cabin, but she had screamed and kicked, and finally hit him in the face. Then she had run for her life.

"I'll get you," he is yelling behind her.

She is getting tired now. So completely worn out of strength, she slows down unintentionally.

No, you can't. You have to keep going. He'll get you if you slow down. Keep running. Just keep running!

"Ha! I see you," he yells behind her. "Getting tired, are you? You will. But I won't. See, I'm a soldier. I can keep running like this for hours. You can't. Then I'll get you. And then I will kill you. See, no one knows you're here. They all think you're on the run from the police. They think you're hiding somewhere and they'll never think to look for your dead body buried under a house belonging to the Air Force Base, will they? No, they won't. Months will pass by and they'll give up searching for you. After a year, your parents won't even wonder anymore. They'll forget about you, thinking you just ran off with your little friend and maybe you're living on the streets somewhere or hiding in South America. And the best part is, they won't care. Why? Because you killed someone tonight. You did the inexcusable and robbed someone of her life. People don't look for murderers because they feel sorry for them or because they want to help them. They look for them because they want to see them hang or go to prison for life. When you kill someone, people stop caring about you."

Ally is gasping for air. Her lungs are hurting. That damn moist air makes it impossible to breathe properly and to get rid of the heat. Her face is boiling. She is crying and tears are streaming down her cheeks. She senses he is close now and wonders if she should simply give up. She can't run anymore. Her legs are so heavy they can hardly move. The general is whistling behind her. He is so close now; she can almost feel his breath.

There is no way out of this, she thinks to herself, seconds before she feels his hand on her neck. *This is it. This is the end.*

When her head hits the dunes, her mouth fills with sand. She is gasping for air, but getting nothing but sand. She can't breathe. Pressure on her neck makes it impossible for her to lift her head.

Oh, my God, he's holding you down. He's going to kill you right here.

Ally struggles all she can, but the hand doesn't move from the back of her head. Her nose and throat are filled with sand; she is gasping, but the little air she gets in her lungs is not enough. She is almost unconscious when she hears a voice in the distance.

"What's going on here?"

Finally, the pressure on her neck is lifted and she can raise her head into the air. A bright light hits her face.

"I am so glad you came, Officer," the general says. "I captured this girl and stopped her. I believe she is one of the two girls you are looking for. I saw it on the news earlier, and then spotted her down here on my evening walk."

"Thank you, General," the officer says, and grabs Ally by the arm. He helps her to her feet. She coughs and spits out sand.

"Well, little lady. Guess you're done running."

72

September 2015

"Go away."

Olivia waves violently at the woman on the other side of the window. "Get out of here."

But the woman doesn't move. The way she stares at Olivia makes her break a sweat. What is she doing here? She tilts her head still while staring at Olivia, and still tapping her fingernail rhythmically on the window.

Tap-tap-tap

Tap-tap-tap

It's driving Olivia insane. She opens the sliding door leading to the backyard and walks out. The woman keeps tapping while she turns to look at her.

"Enough with the tapping, would you?" Olivia says angrily. "It's driving me nuts."

The woman stops. Olivia forces a smile. "Now, get out of here," she says. "My husband is coming home soon. He won't be happy to find you here."

"Am I pretty?"

"What?" Olivia stares at the woman wearing the surgical mask covering the bottom part of her face. Does she really think no one will recognize her because she is wearing that thing?

"Am I pretty?" she repeats.

Olivia frowns.

What the heck is all this?

"What are you talking about? Go away. Go back to wherever you came from and leave me alone. I have enough to deal with as it is."

"AM I PRETTY?"

The woman yells so loud a dog starts to bark from one of the neighboring houses.

Oh, great. Now they'll start talking, and soon the general will know.

Olivia sighs. "What do you want? Can't you just tell me what it is so we can move on?" she asks.

"Am I pretty?" the woman repeats with a lower voice.

"What? Why do you keep asking me that? Sure, you're very pretty."

The woman grabs the surgical mask and pulls it off. Olivia can feel how her blood freezes when she sees what is underneath.

"How about now?" she asks.

Olivia can't speak. She stares at the woman like she is paralyzed. "I…I…I…"

She doesn't even notice the scissors in her hand until they're in the air and the woman is leaping towards her, moving almost unnaturally fast. But then, something else happens. Olivia is about to scream when she hears voices cutting through the darkness.

"Olivia!"

The woman is about to plunge the scissors into Olivia's throat, but the intruding voices coming from the river disturb her and she hits her arm instead. Olivia screams in pain as the scissors pierce through her right arm. The voices are coming closer as she falls to the ground, blood gushing out of her wound. Meanwhile, the woman runs around the corner of the house, dragging her long black coat after her. Olivia tries to speak as she watches Mary Mills' face come closer. She is flanked by two other faces that Olivia remembers well from school.

"Olivia, are you okay?" Mary yells. She leans down and sees the scissors in her upper arm. "We need an ambulance."

Olivia looks down, and, to her terror, watches as the blood colors the grass and she feels dizzy. She closes her eyes and tries to calm herself, but the dizziness soon takes over. She has no feeling of what is up and what is down, what is real and what is not. She can hear many voices and steps; she is certain she hears someone yell and others scream. She is even sure she can hear guns being pulled, and is that a helicopter? She doesn't know what is going on, and she hardly cares anymore. When she loses consciousness, she is certain she even hears the voice of the general.

She can't stop smiling, thinking at least he can't touch her now.

73

September 2015

"**Everybody stay still.**"

I am lying in the grass. I have someone's boot in my back. He says he is from the Military Police. I believe him. After all, I have just entered the military base from the waterside without permission. I know I am in trouble. There are weapons pointed at us from all sides. Even a helicopter swirling above us. But I am happy because I believe I saved Olivia Hartman's life. She was about to be killed, but my screaming as we approached shore in Chloe's boat disturbed her just enough to have AK miss her target and hit Olivia's arm instead. Olivia is passed out, but I have heard them call for an ambulance, and soon she will be in the hospital getting the treatment she needs. I, on the other hand, am in deep…over my head.

"I'll take this one from here," a voice says.

The knee is removed from my back and a pair of boots appears in front of my nose. I am pulled up by my hair and I look into the face of the man I know as the general.

"General Hartman, I presume," I say, and sit up on my knees.

The general stares at me. He is skinnier than in the articles I have read about him. I am guessing he keeps himself in great shape, the suntan tells me he might be one of those who constantly runs on the beach. He is maybe twenty years older than me. Just the sight of him fills me with disgust.

"And you must be Mary Mills," he says with a stiff upper lip. "Sister of the infamous Blake Mills."

"Can't say it's a pleasure to meet you," I say, and rise to my feet.

"What the hell are you doing here, breaking into a military base after nightfall? Do you realize I could have you shot and no one would lift an eyebrow?"

I wipe away some blood from my nose. I have hurt myself falling to the ground with that MP on my back.

"I'm saving your wife's life," I say. "Those scissors were about to land in her throat. Had we come a few seconds later, she would be gone by now."

I turn and look at Joey and Chloe, who are still face-down in the grass. Chloe's small speedboat is parked halfway on the lawn. We took that baby as fast as we could onto the ground, then jumped out. I feel a little like James Bond. Or Tom Cruise. Definitely Tom Cruise.

The general is looking at me, completely baffled. "You saved her...why?"

I am surprised he believes me. Something in his eyes, a look, tells me he loves her. It doesn't fit well with the picture I have of him.

"We went to school together. Three of her other friends from back then have been killed—with a pair of scissors stabbed in their throats. I believed Olivia might be next. Guess I was right. You're very welcome."

I can see the vein in the general's forehead grow. The porch light lights his face. I wonder if I should tell him whom I believe is behind this or if it would be a stupid idea. He is, after all, her guardian, or was when she was younger. I don't know what kind of relationship he has with AK, but I can't help wondering if he is in on it all as well. He looks like he could kill someone just by snapping his fingers. But again, he is a soldier, a general in the U.S. army, so of course he could. And he probably wouldn't even blink. I have to remember, he framed my brother.

The general growls and runs a hand through his hair. A soldier approaches him. "Sir. What shall we do with the prisoners, sir?"

The general sighs. I can feel my heart rate go up. I know the general wants me wiped off the surface of the earth along with my brother. I believe he is the one who set my dad's house on fire, or at least had someone do it for him. I hate his guts and I want to spit in his face, but I also know he is the one in control right now. He has the power to put me in jail for treason. My life is completely in his hands right now.

What will he do?

"Let them go," he says.

What??

"Let them go, soldier," he repeats. "They pose no threat to us. It was all just a mistake. A mistake that saved my wife." He turns and looks at me. I fight my urge to rethink my opinion of him.

He almost killed your father. He put Blake in jail.

"Now we're even," he says. "Remember that."

74

September 2015

I SLEEP in Joey's bed again while he takes the couch. I don't close an eye all night. I stare at the ceiling while going through everything in my mind. I feel so confused, so frustrated.

Why did he let me go? Why didn't he arrest us?

I don't understand. I thought the general had it out for me. Maybe he is really just angry at my brother for sleeping with his wife. I can't blame him. I wanted that coffee house girl gone from the planet once I found out about her and Joey. I couldn't even stand driving by the coffee house. It was like torture. I wanted her to get fired; I wanted her entire family to be fired and never work again. I wanted all the world's misery to come upon her and her descendants for all eternity. But, in reality, I knew it wasn't her fault. It was ours. We hadn't taken care of our marriage. We had lost touch with one another.

I think about us back then. Me and Sandra hanging out in the school cafeteria, Joey coming up to us with his tray between his hands and sitting next to me. Us talking about waves being good, talking about skipping a few hours of school this afternoon when the tide is going out. I think about AK and how she would always send me hateful looks when we passed each other in the hallways.

How she and her little gang would whisper as we walked by. She scared me back then. But I also felt sorry for her. Until she shot my mother.

Mommy, no! Mommy, no!

I see her in my inner eye as she falls down the stairs again and again. It makes me feel the sorrow that I felt back then, the emotions I had tried so hard to forget for so many years. I hate that I can't stop it, that I can't hold it back like I used to. A tear rolls from the corner of my eye onto my pillow. Another follows, and soon I am crying heavily, sobbing, pulling my legs up under my chin. So much sadness, so much anger. All these years.

Burn in Hell Mills!

I close my eyes and turn to the side while crying. I don't even notice when the door to my room opens and someone enters. A body creeps into bed with me. I feel his warmth, his arms around my waist, as he spoons me and caresses my hair. I can't stop crying. Not now that I have opened the faucets.

Joey is kissing my neck and holding me tight. I let him. I have missed him and his touch. I can't hold it back anymore. I can't pretend like I don't love him, like I don't want to be close to him.

I want this. I want to be with him again. What's the use in fighting it?

Joey moves his mouth to my ear. "Don't give up on us," he whispers.

I turn my head and look into his eyes. I see such deep intensity in them. It moves me. I touch his face, the rough edges, and the unshaved chin.

God, I love him! Why does it have to be so hard?

His eyes drop to my lips. I can tell he wants to kiss me. This is it; this is the moment when I make my decision. I want him to kiss me; I want it desperately. But everything inside of me screams that I can't. That I shouldn't. That it would be wrong of me.

He was the one who cheated on you, remember? You'll only get hurt again. Don't fall for it. Don't.

Yet, I close my eyes and pull him closer. He hesitates, then kisses me. Gently at first, then demanding, insisting. His hands are on me, on my body and soon my T-shirt is pulled over my head.

I'll explode if I don't let him.

It's like a surge of electricity that goes through my body when he enters me. I realize I have wanted this for so long, ever since I threw him out, ever since I found out about him and that coffee house girl. This is what I have craved…him, being close to him, feeling him inside of me again. I don't think of consequences, I simply give in to this urge of mine.

I surrender.

75

May 1986

"Sit still, sweetheart. It's going to be a long drive."

Penelope drives onto the highway leading to Miami. It's a four-hour drive, but it's going to be worth it. Next to her sits her daughter. Peter is at home with their adopted girl, who is still throwing up a lot. Penelope has told Peter to keep a close eye on the girl. If the vomiting continues, he has to take her to the hospital, she instructed him before she left. Once again, he had to stay home from the office. It's never popular when he does that, but Penelope has told him it's vital that he helps her out when they have two very sick children like they do.

"Will we be there soon?" her daughter asks. She is looking at the landscape passing by her window. She is skinny, and still way too small for her age.

"Just three more hours," Penelope says cheerfully. Today is a good day. "I am so happy we finally found a doctor to do your surgery," she says. "The nice doctor will make your heart much better, and then you'll be well. Doesn't that sound good? I think it does. I am excited."

"But…but, Mom…"

"No buts here, little missy. Once you have the surgery, you'll feel much better. I promise you. You'll be strong and healthy like your classmates."

Penelope turns on the radio and whistles along to *What's Love Got to Do With It* by Tina Turner. Her daughter keeps looking out the window.

"Are you alright?" Penelope asks when the song is over.

"I'm fine, Mom. I feel just fine. I keep telling you."

Penelope looks at her daughter's face briefly, then back at the road. She doesn't seem pale anymore. Come to think of it, she hardly seems like she is sick. It's been weeks since she last threw up. She has some color in her cheeks now, her eyes are sparkling, and she seems happy.

Almost like a normal nine-year-old.

"Mom, can I get ice cream when we get to Miami?" she asks.

"Ice cream? No, you most certainly cannot have ice cream," Penelope exclaims. "You're way too sick to have sweets."

"Mom. I feel fine. I don't feel sick at all."

"Don't let that fool you," Penelope says with a lifted finger. "Your heart isn't working properly; that's why you need surgery. Don't let one day of feeling better make you believe you're well now. It's just tricking you into believing that. You're still sick, even though you feel better right now. It's only temporarily. Make no mistake. It won't last."

"But…but…"

"Now, don't forget to tell the doctor how bad you feel when he asks, alright? Tell him how many years you have been sick, how much you throw up, and by all means, don't forget to tell him about the seizures you have all the time. Those are important. You have to really rub it on thick. Otherwise, he might not want to do the surgery, and that would be really bad. I've looked for a doctor who would do this for many, many years. Don't blow it, okay?"

The child lets out a deep sigh. "Okay."

When they arrive at the parking lot in front of the hospital in Miami, hours later, Penelope parks the car, then turns to look at her girl.

"Now, the paleness we can't get back. It's too late for that. But it is important that you look sick. And right now, you're smiling way too much; your eyes are way too bright. What can we do about that? Let me see…you haven't eaten in two days; I made sure of that. You should feel lightheaded and have heart palpitations. You do feel those things, don't you?"

The girl nods.

"Alright, that's good."

Penelope looks at her daughter, then leans over, grabs her head, and bangs it against the car window.

"Now, act sick, okay?" she hisses. "No smiling, no eating, and no laughing. You hear me?"

76

September 2015

When I wake up, I'm alone in the bed. I can hear Joey and Salter talking in the kitchen. I get up and walk out to them.

"Hey. Look who's finally awake," Joey exclaims.

"Mom!" Salter runs to me and hugs me. I feel overwhelmed. Salter has reached the age where mommy is mostly a source of constant embarrassment, and physical contact is kept to an absolute minimum. Suddenly, he is kissing me and hugging me like I have been gone for months.

"Dad made pancakes!"

Joey turns around with a smile. He knows how much I love to start my day with pancakes.

"I also made eggs," he says, and shows me the pan. "Cooked just the way you like them."

Someone is on the charm offensive. Or maybe he is just happy. I can't help feeling it a little too. It feels good to be a family again. But, is it enough? Do I dare to let him in again?

I am still not sure.

I sit down at the table and let him serve breakfast for me. Salter sits between us. He is smiling from ear to ear, looking at Joey, then back at me again. He's like a child at Christmas. I can't stand it. I mean, nothing thrills me more than seeing him like this, but I am not sure it's a good thing. I am afraid he might get disappointed again. And that is the last thing I would want for him.

"Let's eat," I say, and we all dig in simultaneously.

Joey has placed a jar of Nutella next to my plate, knowing how much I like to smear my pancakes with the chocolate. I chuckle when I see it.

"Seriously?"

He shrugs. "I think it is beyond disgusting, but hey, if you like it, you should have it."

I don't know what to say. Back in New York, when things were going bad between us, Joey had been on my case about my weight. He had criticized me for letting myself go. Where is that now? Has he simply parked it outside until later? I don't believe you can do that.

I smear my pancakes with Nutella and enjoy the food immensely. I don't have to make any decisions yet. Right now, I want to enjoy whatever it is we have. I want to enjoy Salter's happy face. I want to enjoy the feeling I have inside, the feeling of being where I belong.

After breakfast, I go and visit my dad. Joey doesn't have to go to work until ten, so I ask if Salter can stay with him. I have an hour. Laura is there by his side, and I give her an awkward hug. She seems smaller and very skinny, and I wonder if she has eaten at all since the fire.

"How are you holding up?" I ask.

She shrugs with a sob. "I'm doing my best."

"Where are you staying?"

"At the Hilton."

The Hilton. Of course.

"So, what are they saying?" I ask. "About his condition? What are the doctors telling you?"

"They say he is stable, but they're not sure he'll ever wake up again," she says with a loud sob. "I'm terrified that he won't, Mary. What if they ask me to make the decision to pull the plug on him? I don't think I can do that. On the other hand…this is no life for him, is it? He would have hated seeing himself like this. He would want me to do it."

I swallow hard and look at my stepmom. I know she is right. My dad would never want to be a vegetable. Better to end it. But the thing is, Laura and he never married. So, if it comes to that, the decision will have to be mine.

The thought gives me nausea. I feel like crying again. I can't lose him too. I simply can't. And it is all my fault he's lying there. If I hadn't pissed off the general.

I need to find proof that it was him. He might have gone easy on me last night, but I still loathe him. I want to nail him for what he has done. There must be a way of doing that. And AK. I have to get her too. She killed my mother in 1992. She is wanted for that murder, but how do I prove that she is who I believe she is? She has another identity now. Who will believe me? If I could somehow get her for the killing of Coraline, Jean, or Cassie… If only. If only I could somehow prove that she killed Jamilla Jenkins. In that way, I would get my brother back, as well as get AK. But who will believe me?

"Listen, I have to get back to Salter; Joey has work to do, so I need to go. But let me know if there is any news, all right? I'll try and be back later today or maybe tomorrow."

I speak fast. It's obvious I am trying to get out of there. I don't feel well all of a sudden. Watching my dad lie there fills me with such tremendous guilt. I can't breathe. The walls are closing in on me and I just need to get out of there. I don't wait for her answer. I storm out of the hospital, and don't stop running till I reach my car.

I need to fix this somehow. I have to fix it.

77

September 2015

I TAKE Salter with me to Chloe's house. I bring his iPad so he won't be too bored. His eyes grow wider than wide when he sees all her computers.

"Wow! It's just like the movies. Are you a famous YouTuber or something?" he asks.

Chloe laughs. I do too. In the world of a nine-year-old, the biggest stardom you can reach is to be a video game tester for a living and make videos about them on YouTube.

"No, but I do have Minecraft on the computer over there," she says, and points at an iMac in the corner.

"Oh, my God," I say. "You have no idea what a lifesaver that is. Salter has been so mad that he can't play his precious Minecraft down here, since all I brought was his iPad and my laptop, which he is not allowed to play on."

"Well, knock yourself out," Chloe says. "I think it is already turned on."

Salter exclaims happily, then rushes to the computer. Chloe hands him a set of headphones, and soon he is occupied in his own little world of bricks and stones. I never understood that game much, but I know it is Salter's entire world. He meets all of his friends on there, and they play for hours every day, talking on Skype while they play. It is a whole new generation of super nerds growing up. I don't mind him being a computer nerd and the fact that he speaks an entire language I don't understand at times, but I do worry that he doesn't get enough fresh air and real life human contact. Maybe I am just being a mother.

I decide to take him surfing this afternoon to make up for this morning. I know I probably won't do it, but it makes me feel better.

"I have something for you," Chloe says, as we sit down in front of her many computer screens. "I've been up all night going through old cases in the database, and look what I came up with. You might remember this."

I look at the screen. "Holly?"

"Holly Leslie. Born in 1977 like the rest of us. Moved to Cocoa Beach in 1990 with her family. Went to Cocoa Beach High School, friends with Jean, Olivia, Cassie, Coraline, and Anne-Katelyn."

"Has she also been killed?" I ask, agitated.

"No, but something else happened to her. In 1995. According to the police report, she was found on the side of the road at Lori Wilson Park. She had been cut several places on her body with a fishing knife and shot in the leg with a spear gun. According to this, her family never pressed charges. Holly refused to tell who was behind it. No one was ever arrested in the case."

"I remember her," I say. "She disappeared all of a sudden in the middle of the school year. I had several classes with her. There were a lot of rumors about her and what happened to her. Some people said they had met her at the mall months later, but that she didn't want to talk to them."

"It looks like she moved to Rockledge and she continued school there," Chloe said. "She graduated from Rockledge High School a year later."

"So they moved her because of the attack?" I ask.

"It sure looks like it."

"I need to talk to her," I say. "If for nothing else than to warn her about AK, and tell her that the others have been killed, in case she doesn't know."

Chloe glances at Salter. "I'll look after him while you're away. Seems like he's not going to cause much trouble."

I laugh and look at my son, who is completely in his own world, building castles and mining for diamonds.

"He won't," I say.

78

September 2015

I DRIVE up to the house in Rockledge and park in front of the garage. I haven't called first. I am afraid she will tell me to not come. I don't know if she is home. The house is a small one-story house with a porch in front. I walk up, open the screen door, and knock.

It takes a while before someone opens. I recognize her eyes right away. The face is older, the eyes filled with a sadness they didn't have then, but other than that she looks like herself. Except for the long scar on her cheek that I don't remember having seen before.

She looks at me for a long time. It's like she recognizes me, but isn't sure. Seeing me here seems to bring back memories.

"Mary Mills?"

I raise my hand in an awkward wave. "Hi, Holly."

"What are you doing here? Last thing I heard you were a big time reporter at CNN in Atlanta."

"I was…what feels like a lifetime ago," I say. "Can I come in?"

She looks surprised. "Sure."

She steps aside and lets me in. She limps when she walks. "If I had known you were coming, I would have cleaned up a little," she says, and picks up a toy from the floor. It looks like a dog toy. A pitbull in a crate in the living room tells me it is his toy. It snarls at me when I enter.

"Don't mind him," she says. "He helps me to feel safe. He guards the house. I keep him in the crate when I'm home. Sit down."

I sit on the couch. It is small, but very soft. It goes well with the small living room. I am guessing Holly hasn't had much success in her life.

"Do you want coffee? Or maybe a beer?" she asks.

"No, thank you. I'm good," I say. I don't want her to go through the trouble of making me coffee. "I already had two cups this morning."

She sits down with her hands in her lap. "So…what brings you here?" she asks and corrects her hair.

"1995," I say. I go directly to the point. I don't have time to beat around the bush. When I say the year, her face freezes completely. "I know it must be hard for you to talk about, but I need you to."

Holly's eyes drop to the ground. She touches her thigh on her bad leg. "It's such a long time ago," she says.

"I know. And I know it must be terrible for you to think back about, but things have started happening around Cocoa Beach, and I think you might be able to help me figure out why, or at least who is behind it. Three of your former friends from back then have died. Last night, the killer tried to kill Olivia as well, but was interrupted. I think someone is targeting your old group." I pause and wait for her reaction. It doesn't seem to surprise her. Then, I go in for the kill. "I think AK might be behind it."

Her eyes meet mine. She shakes her head. "AK? But how is that possible? No one has seen her since 1992. Since that night when… when she shot your mother."

I chuckle. "You're a terrible liar, Holly."

She sighs. "It's such a long time ago. Why do we have to start digging up these old stories again? I really don't want to…"

"Because they're not old stories. They're still here. They don't just go away because we stop thinking about them. They're real. We can't keep running from them. You have to tell me, Holly. Was AK among those who attacked you back then? Was she behind it?"

Holly clasps her mouth. I can tell that I am ripping up stuff she hasn't allowed herself to think about for years. I know how she feels. I know exactly how that feels, but sometimes it's necessary to dig up the past in order to not get stuck in it. It's like quicksand. The more you wriggle and try to get away from it, the more it pulls you back. Running from it will do you no good.

I slam the palm of my hand onto her coffee table. "Goddammit, Holly. Answer me! Was AK one of those that attacked you in 1995?!"

79

September 2015

"Yes! Yes, she was!"

Holly closes her eyes when she yells it at me. The words hit me like a punch in the face. It's what I wanted to hear, but it's also shocking. Back then, I believed AK was long gone, and now I realize that she was still here? Still right here? The police could have found her; they could have put her in jail for killing my mother and we could have moved on with our lives, feeling justice had been served. Instead, we walked around in this haze, this daze of anger and frustration. I lost my mother, my dad lost his wife, and since justice never came, we began blaming each other. We began loathing each other instead. Meanwhile, Blake had to grow up without a mother and with a father so distant he might as well not be there either. This thing destroyed us.

As I stare at Holly with my mouth wide open, I wonder if things could have been different, had AK gotten what she deserved back then. I had always believed it would.

"She was there," Holly says. "She was the one who started it."

"Tell me what happened," I say, suddenly wishing I had said yes to that coffee, or even the beer. I could use something strong right now.

Holly draws in a deep breath. She rubs her hands together. At the collar of her shirt, I spot another scar.

"I was so young," she says. "When I came to the school, I became friends with them. I hung out with them on the weekends doing all kinds of stuff, getting in trouble. I am not very proud of it today, but what can you do? What's done is done. I was just so incredibly naïve. Anyway, we were friends, and AK persuaded me to do all kinds of things that I didn't want to. But she can be very persuasive, you know? Suddenly, I was shoplifting and stealing bikes from the beach entrances. I did it to win their respect. I wanted AK to like me. If she liked you, then you were popular. You know how high school is. Anyway, I did a lot of stuff I wasn't very proud of. When AK went missing after that night…when she…well, you know, the police came to my door the next day. They took me to the station and asked me all kinds of questions about AK. I told them everything. My parents told me to. I told them everything we had done, how AK had led our group, and how we had bothered tourists downtown, and even sometimes attacked some of them, kicked them and stolen their belongings. I cried a lot when I told this. I hated that my parents had to hear this about me. I was never charged with anything, since I cooperated so willingly, they said. And I felt good about having told. It felt good to get it out and I pulled away from the rest of the group afterwards. When AK disappeared, the group kind of dissolved anyway. Without her, we were nothing. I think most of them were happy that she was gone."

Holly stops and takes in a deep breath before she continues. "I had a few very good years after that. But three years later, my doorbell rang one night when my parents were out of town. I went to open the door, and there she was."

"AK?"

"Her hair was different. It had been colored blonde and had grown long. She looked completely different. Her clothing was very different. But her eyes were the same. There was maybe even more anger in them."

"Was she alone?" I ask.

Holly shakes her head. "No. They were all there. All the girls from back then. They were right there next to her. I think they didn't really want to be there, but who says no to AK, right? They were terrified of her. She was out of control. If you said no, she would beat you up or cut you with the razorblade she often kept between her teeth. You just didn't say no."

"So, what did they want?" I ask.

"They were all giggling and laughing, and I think they were on something. They told me AK had come back to hang out with them tonight and that she would be gone in the morning. She told me she'd changed her name to Liz, I believe it was. That she lived far away now, but tonight she was back. *Let's go have some fun while I'm here*, I remember she said. While she spoke, she flashed her razorblade between her teeth, and I knew there was no saying no. It was too dangerous. They persuaded me to take them out on my dad's boat. They brought a lot of booze with them, and for a few hours we sailed the canals, drinking, listening to music, and fishing. For the first couple of hours, I thought I was going to be all right. That as long as I played along during this night, then AK would be gone in the morning, and I wouldn't have to see her again. But, of course, I was wrong. Suddenly, AK told me to take the boat to the ocean. I told her I had no clue how to do it, that you had to go through the lock system, and I wasn't sure you could do that at night. Nonsense, AK said. The lock is open till 9:30. Naturally, I had to give in to them, and we made it through right before the lock closed. We sailed into the ocean, and I was terrified, since I knew there was no way we could get back that same night. We would have to wait till it opened again at six in the morning. Were we going to be sailing the ocean until then, or what was their plan? I didn't dare to ask. I just went with what they told me to. I wasn't even sure there was enough gas in the boat to keep us going till the morning. The onshore winds were strong, and as soon as we sailed out of the canals, we hit rough seas. The boat was thrown back and forth in the waves. AK thought it was hilarious and wanted to start spearfishing. I told her she had to be in the ocean to do it, but she pulled one out from one of the compartments and aimed it at me for fun. They all laughed. AK drank heavily from a bottle of vodka and shot the gun out in the ocean. She didn't hit anything, but they all laughed, and she pulled back the spear. I tried to steer the boat and stay as close to shore as possible, so we could get in in case anything happened. I prayed and hoped the Coast Guard would find us. Maybe they would stop us. I was so afraid. When we had sailed down the coast in darkness for a little while, they suddenly surrounded me. AK was holding the spear gun and aiming it at me. *What are you doing?* I asked. *Getting rid of an unwanted smell around here*, she said. *And I am not talking about the stench of fish. No, it's the smell of betrayal!* I don't remember much of what happened after that, but I do remember someone coming up from behind me with a fishing knife, slicing my clothes into pieces, and cutting my back. Then I remember them pushing me to the floor of the boat and AK holding the knife, then stabbing me in the shoulder, and cutting me here on the throat and on the arm. They tied my legs and arms and cut off my pants. I remember screaming and the boat tipping back and forth. I remember somehow getting to my feet and jumping overboard, thinking I could swim to the shore. I was right. Luckily, the rope they tied around my hands came off in the water, so I could use my arms to swim. I thought I had lost them, that I had gotten away, but the girls followed me. They all abandoned the boat and jumped in the water. They came after me with the spear gun. I crawled on shore at Lori Wilson Park and ran across the parking lot, blood running from all my wounds. I almost made it to A1A when they shot the gun and it went straight through my leg. That's the last thing I remember. I woke up in the hospital and was told that a police officer had found me. I never dared to tell anyone what had really happened. Except my parents, who made sure we moved immediately afterwards. They too were scared that they might come back for me. Luckily, they never did."

I stare at Holly while she tells her story. I feel appalled. I am so angry with AK I can barely contain it.

"So, why do you think they did it? Why do you believe they turned on you like that? Because you spoke to the police?" I ask.

"Sure. I wasn't the only one who did, nor was I the only one who got punished for it," she says.

"What?"

"I have a feeling you remember Ally?"

80

September 2015

"We need to find Ally. Ally Meyer."

I am back at Chloe's house. Salter is still at the computer. I decide now is not the time to feel guilty for letting him play on the computer all day. There is no time for all that. It has to wait till later.

Chloe doesn't even look up at me. She stares at her screen and lets her fingers dance across the keyboard. "Ally Meyer?" she asks, surprised.

Chloe finally looks up at me. Her eyes are loaded with pity. I hate when people look at me like that. I used to see it all the time back then. That was one of the reasons I pulled away from my friends, from the crew.

"There's a name from our past I thought I'd never hear again," she says. "Are you sure you want to find her?"

"Yes," I say. "I have to."

"But…"

"I know. She was the one who was with AK when she shot my mother," I say. "They broke into our house. She was the only one who was captured. She told the police everything that happened. My dad decided to not press charges against her, since she wasn't the one who had fired the gun. She was just a kid, and she had, after all, cooperated with the police. He didn't want to ruin the rest of her life. All I know is that she and her mother moved after that. I don't know where to."

"And you're absolutely sure you want to find her, right?" Chloe asks.

"Yes. I need to talk to her. Holly told me she was attacked by AK and her gang in '95 like she was. As a punishment for having talked to the police. I've convinced Holly to testify against her and tell what happened. I want to do the same with Ally. I believe she owes me. I need to get to her before AK does. I believe she is killing off all witnesses from back then. Anyone who has something on her, anyone who might be able to testify against her…who knows her real identity. She is cleaning up."

"So that's why she killed Coraline, Jean, and Cassie as well?" Chloe asks.

"That's my theory, yes. I believe Jamilla Jenkins might have had something on her as well, maybe threatened to tell about what she's doing now. Like what she did to Joanne's son, Billy. She hasn't changed. Still leaves a trail of death and destruction behind her. I need to stop her. I believe she is coming for me as well. She's wanted me dead ever since…well, for as long as I can remember."

Chloe draws in a deep breath. She knows my story. I don't have to explain to her. She knows what I am up against.

"I got what I believe is her mother's address," she says. "They didn't move very far. Melbourne Beach. She bought a house there in 1992. It's worth a shot. Her mother's name is Janice Meyer."

I grab my purse and look at Chloe. "Could he stay here again?"

"Sure. But is it wise to go alone?" Chloe asks.

I hesitate. Is she right?

"I mean, you haven't seen her since back then, have you?" she says.

In the flash of a second, I see her again. Standing in my living room next to AK, who is holding the gun. I feel the anger; I feel the frustration all over again. "No, but that doesn't mean that I…"

"You're not going alone," Chloe says, and hands me her phone.

"Call Sandra. I believe she's not doing anything today. She can go with you and make sure you behave. It's okay to admit that you need someone, you know. No man is an island. Or woman."

I nod and grab the phone. Chloe is right. I hate to admit it, but she is. I call Sandra and she tells me she just needs to run to Publix first, then she'll be ready to go.

I pick her up half an hour later at her house. She has a bag in her hand. "I brought some supplies for our little road trip," she says with a smile. She opens the bag and shows its contents to me. I laugh.

"You remember how we used to munch on this when we went on surf trips to Sebastian Inlet, or when we went to all my competitions in Melbourne Beach? My God, it's a long time ago. You know what I remember? You were there every time. The others came now and then to cheer me on, but you, you were there every weekend to cheer for me. I'll never forget that."

"What can I say? I loved to watch you surf. Even more, I loved to see you kick those other kids' butts."

Sandra smiles and I start the car.

"Are you even allowed to have chips and root beer? Don't you have to keep to your strict model diet to keep you looking like a stick?" I ask teasingly. "Don't you have that big shoot coming up… who is it again, *Elle* magazine?"

Sandra shrugs. "It's *Vogue,* and yes, but what can I do? A girl's gotta live a little, right?"

81

September 2015

Liz rushes back to her house after her day is over. She feels so empowered, so strong after a day at the shooting range. Nothing beats a good day of shooting targets. And Liz is the best at it. The best on the entire base, as a matter of fact. That's what has given her this great career with the army for the past twenty years. She has been living on bases all over the world since she enlisted, or since the general enlisted her.

As she walks into her house, she thinks about the time she met him at that cabin on the beach. He saw something in her back then. He saw a potential that nobody else could, not even herself. When Ally escaped and he ran after her, Liz thought about running too. She was terrified of him, afraid he would hurt her, but something made her stay. Today, she still doesn't know if it was simply the fact that she had nowhere else to go, that the cabin was the best hiding place, or if it was because she liked the general even though he terrified her. But once he came back and told her Ally had been arrested, she was glad she had made the decision to stay.

"Now it's just you and me," the general said. "You can choose to leave like your friend, run into the arms of the police, or you can stay here with me. I think I can make something of you. But only if you want to."

Liz stayed at the cabin for a week. The general knew so many people, and soon he came back and provided an entire new identity for her.

"Your name is now Liz Hester. Here's your passport and your social security number. When you're seventeen, I'll enlist you in the army and you'll work for me. I'll make a soldier of you. I'll make an excellent soldier of you."

She never dared to ask where he got the new papers for her, and to this day, she didn't know.

Liz sits down in a chair in her living room. She doesn't have much furniture. She doesn't need it. There isn't much in life she needs. Still, she never feels satisfied, she never feels complete.

Liz walks to the kitchen and grabs a glass of water. She drinks it while looking out on the street. A neighbor walks her dog. She is one of the stay-at-home moms that Liz loathes so much. She wants to pick up her gun and use the woman as a target. Start with the dog. Liz shapes a gun with her fingers and pretends to shoot her.

Liz is sick of feeling this way, of trying to find satisfaction in what will never fulfill her. She knows what she needs to do. She knows there is only one way for her if she wants to feel complete. She has been thirsting for this for so long. Thirsting for her revenge. She knows all the things she does, the things she has done throughout her life have only been substitutes for what she really wanted to do, who she really wanted to hurt.

Her phone rings. She picks it up. It's the general. He is coming over, he says. Half an hour later, he is at her house. As usual, he grabs her by the throat and pushes her up against the wall as soon as she opens the door. Then he pulls down her pants and has sex with her up against the wall. Liz doesn't enjoy it. She never has. But she has to do it. It's part of the deal they made back then. It's why he protects her. She thought that it would stop when he married her old school friend Olivia, but it never did. Olivia is for show. She is there for him to bring to parties and official gatherings. She's his trophy. It's Liz he comes for when he has other needs. Liz doesn't protest, even though it has been going on for twenty-something years. This way, no one can ever touch her. Having the general on her side makes her invincible. If she gets herself in trouble, he fixes it. He makes sure it goes away. It's their deal, their understanding. Just like he made everything go away back when they first met at the cabin. He even beat his own wife when she said she knew who Liz really was and threatened to tell the police one day when they had an argument. The general can take care of anything. Nothing is too big. At least it hasn't been so far.

While he finishes himself, Liz wonders if he will be able to clean up after her this time. When she is done with her little plan.

Maybe it doesn't matter.

82

September 2015

It feels so good to be hanging out with Mary again. Sandra looks at her and smiles. It's been way too long. She misses her old friend. She has missed her terribly.

"Oh, my God, I absolutely love this song," Mary says, and turns up the radio really loud.

Nirvana and *Smells Like Teen Spirit* bursts out of the loudspeaker in the rental car. Immediately, they're both taken back in time. Mary starts to sing and Sandra chants along.

"*Hello, how low...Hello, how low...*"

Soon, they're both belting out loudly while memories flash in over them both. Sandra thinks about them driving in Danny's old beat up pick-up truck, all their surfboards in the back, the guys head banging with the long hair they had back then when everyone talked about grunge and wore flannel, even though it was way too hot in Florida. They would just cut off the sleeves and the guys wouldn't button their shirts.

Sandra chuckles at the memory. Then she remembers how in love she was with Alex. She wonders for a second why it never happened between them. Well, she knows. It's very simple, really. She chose her career over him. Fame and fortune. He would only hold her back, her parents said. The whole world was asking for her at that point. When she finally came back, he had married someone else. Maria. How Sandra loathes her. Not that she is entitled to. She made her choice.

She lets the thought go as Mary pulls up in front of a house and stops the engine.

"This should be it."

Sandra looks at the yellow two-story house across from the beach. On the porch, there is an old swing. Sandra always wanted that. She always dreamt about having a porch with a swing that she could sit on with all of her children and one day grandchildren. Suddenly, she can't remember why she never had children. It was her dream. It was what she wanted. But, it doesn't combine well with her career. Besides, Ryan isn't that interested in children.

"Let's go talk to them," Mary says, and gets out of the car.

Sandra follows her. She envies Mary so much for having both a career and a child. She even envies her for not having to care about her weight or how she looks. Sandra is sick of having to be on a constant diet. Right now, she eats nothing but raw food. It helps with her complexion and she needs to because of the shoot, but indulging herself in a bag of chips like she allowed herself to on the way here, felt so good. She misses it. She misses feeling alive. Misses enjoying her life.

Mary rings the doorbell, but no one answers. She rings it again, then opens the screen door and knocks on the door. Sandra can sense how it annoys her that no one answers.

"I don't think they're home," Sandra says.

They walk back to the car, Mary visibly annoyed, when someone walks towards them on the street with a dog on a leash. Sandra stops and pets the dog.

"Is it an Australian Shepherd?" she asks.

"Why, yes. As a matter of fact it is," the woman answers. "Not many people guess that."

"I love dogs. Have a Chihuahua at home."

"That's nice."

"Say, do you live around here?" Sandra asks.

"Yes, I do. I live right over there in the green house."

"We're looking for Janice Meyer. Do you know if she still lives in this house?" Sandra asks and points at the house behind her. Mary approaches them now, suddenly interested.

"Oh, she died five years back, I believe it was. Cancer. It spread. You know how it is."

Sandra nods in sympathy.

"Do you know what happened to her daughter?" Mary asks.

The woman smiles and nods. "Sure. She lives there now. Took over the house when her mother died. Keeps mostly to herself."

"Do you have any idea where we can find her?" Sandra asks.

"Oh, she's probably at work now. She drives one of those grooming vans. You know the ones that come to your house and groom your dog. It's very popular around here. *Groomers on Wheels*, I believe the company is called."

83

September 2015

I Google the name of the company while sitting in the car, still parked in Ally Meyer's driveway.

"Grooming on wheels," a singing voice says at the other end.

"Hello, I'm looking for Ally Meyer," I say.

"My. She is a popular woman today," the voice says. "Well, she is one of our best, so it's actually no surprise. What do you need to have done?"

"Eh, I need my Goldendoodle groomed. Does she have time today?" I ask, looking at Sandra, who shrugs.

I am not lying. Snowflake could really do with a trim.

"How long since his last grooming?"

"Three months."

"Three months on a Goldendoodle? That's a long time. It'll probably be a big job then. I don't know if Ally can make it today."

"It's not that big of a job. I've kept his fur brushed every day. He has hardly any mats," I lie. Snowflake seriously needs a grooming, and I haven't been brushing him every day as I should, like you have to do with a longhaired doodle. I lie because I feel like the woman is judging me, making me feel guilty. I wonder why I care.

"It will still be a big job," she says. "Let me see. Right now she is in Cocoa Beach. After that she is going to the base around four, but if you can wait till around six this evening, she might be able to make it. I know it's late, but it's all I got with this short notice. Where are you at?"

"I'm in Cocoa Beach. Did you say she has a job at the base, as in Patrick Air Force Base?" I ask.

Sandra's eyes meet mine.

"Yes. We have a lot of clients there," the woman says.

"Thank you," I say, and hang up.

"She has a job on the base at four o'clock," I say to Sandra.

"You think it's AK?"

"That's what I'm afraid of," I say, and start the car. "Last night, she tried to kill Olivia, and now she's going for Ally."

"So what do we do now?" Sandra asks.

I drive onto A1A and accelerate. "We get the crew together," I say. "Start calling them."

Half an hour later, we all meet at Joey's house. Snowflake is enjoying all the company, not to mention the attention and visits from person to person to get petted. Bonnie and Clyde follow in his trail. They seem to go wherever he goes.

Joey gets there last.

"So, what's going on?" Danny asks.

"We believe we know who killed Jean," Chloe says.

"We think someone is targeting a group of girls from our high school. Coraline Cane is dead, Cassie Morgan is dead, and so is Jean Schmidt. I spoke earlier today with Holly Leslie. I don't know if any of you remember her, but she was part of their little gang as well. She told me how she was attacked in 1995 by AK and the other girls and shot with a spear gun. She was lucky to get out of it alive. We believe AK is trying to kill all of them. Last night, there was an attempt to kill Olivia as well; someone tried to stab her in the throat with a pair of scissors, but we managed to stop her. It happened on base, and as we, or as Chloe has found out, AK lives on base where she is now called Liz Hester. We need your help to find AK's next target. I have reason to believe it is Ally Meyer. Sandra and I tried to locate her earlier today, but were told she was here in Cocoa Beach."

"Ally Meyer…?" Alex looks at me, then at the others.

Joey gives me a concerned look as well. "But…isn't that?"

I nod. "Yes. She is the one who was with AK when they broke into my house that night when AK shot my mother." I take in a deep breath, pushing back the memories and emotions. "I know what you're all thinking, and yes, I am pissed and I can't forgive her for what she did, but she still doesn't deserve to die. We need to stop AK or Liz or whatever her name is now, before she kills more people. For all we know, she might come after any one of us next. I know she has it in for me. We need to find Ally before she gets to her."

"How?" Danny asks. He is always the practical one. If there is a problem, he wants to find out how to solve it right away, instead of spending time discussing the issue. He has always been like that. I love that about him.

"She drives a grooming van for Groomers on Wheels. She has a client here in Cocoa Beach now, and then at four o'clock, she is going to the base. We have to get to her before she gets there."

Danny nods and finds his phone. "I'll tell the boys to look for her van. We can easily search the area if we bring out all the trucks."

"How about alerting the police?" Alex asks, while Danny leaves the room with the phone to his ear.

I look at him and wonder if he is right. I am just not certain I trust them. Especially not Chris Fisher. Besides, I am not sure they'll believe me.

"No police," Marcia says. "We don't need them. I'll take my bike and drive down to Minutemen. I know everyone that hangs out around there. I know every drunk, every homeless person in town. They usually have eyes on every corner. They'll know if she's here."

"I can get us access to the police's surveillance cameras on all the stoplights," Chloe says.

Sandra looks at me while everyone is scattered. "What do we do?"

I look at Joey, then back at Sandra. "The only thing we can do."

84

September 2015

"How short do you want it?"

Ally looks at the woman holding the poodle. The woman has been a client for two years. Ally can't stand her. Not her fancy home across from the country club, nor her spoiled poodle, and especially not her stiff upper lip that she always presents when Ally shows up in her van.

"Just like last time. Not too short, though," the woman says.

"And you want the nails clipped and the ears cleaned, right?"

"Yes."

"And the private parts."

"Yes. By all means. How much is it again that you charge for all that?"

As if you don't know.

"Seventy-five."

"That's a little much, don't you think?"

Here we go again!

"It's the standard price. I don't make them."

"I'll give you sixty-five," the woman says with a snort.

It's not like you can't afford it, lady!

Ally sighs. The first time she came to the woman's house, she agreed to the sixty-five, since she was new and afraid that the woman would take her business elsewhere. But the company made her pay the last ten out of her own paycheck, so she hasn't made that mistake again. And she isn't going to today either.

"It's the price. As I said, I don't make the prices."

The woman snorts again. "Okay then."

The woman hands Ally the leash and the dog walks to her reluctantly.

"I should have her back in less than an hour," Ally says.

She takes the poodle to the van and helps her get inside. The poodle tries to fight her, but Ally is a lot stronger, and soon she has the dog inside and can close the door behind them.

Ally sighs and sits down. She is tired. Sick and tired of dogs, and especially their owners. Driving a grooming van got you in contact with some of the worst of them. The rich upper class ones who just wanted everything done for basically no money at all. Why are the richest always the cheapest? Grooming dogs is hard work. Ally should be paid for it. She should be making a lot more than she does.

The poodle is not comfortable in the van. It knows what's going to happen. Ally turns on the water in the bathtub and puts in the soap. The dog squirms and tries to escape. Ally fights with it for a little while, hurts her hand in the process, then pulls out a syringe and injects a sedative in the dog. She waits a few seconds till the dog calms down before she finally manages to put it in the bathtub. The owners don't know that she sedates the dogs to make the grooming go smoother. Neither does the company. It was one of the other groomers that taught her the trick when Ally asked her how on earth she managed those troubled dogs. She even sells her the drug. It makes things a lot easier. The sedative is out of the dog's body within an hour, just in time to hand her back to the owner. She might be a little groggy afterwards, but not enough to make the owners suspect anything.

Ally bathes the now heavily sleeping dog, then grabs the shaver and cuts the hair. She cuts her around the eyes, then clips the nails, trims the ears and the private parts. She blow-dries the hair and looks at her work. It all takes about twenty minutes, then she waits till the dog wakes up again. The dog is big, and therefore wakes up before planned. Ally is happy to get out of there early.

She hands back the dog. The woman writes her a check for seventy-five dollars.

"See you in two months," Ally says, then leaves.

She gets into the van and looks at her list of today's clients. Only one more left. She starts the van and drives up Minutemen Causeway and soon finds herself on A1A, where she turns right. On her way, she passes three fire trucks, which strikes her as odd, but she doesn't take any more notice. On the passenger seat besides her lies her phone. It lights up, but is silenced, so she doesn't hear that it is ringing. Ally is whistling in the car when she continues on A1A towards the base and her last client of the day.

85

September 2015

"She's been spotted on Minutemen two minutes ago."

Marcia sounds agitated on the phone. "Johnny, who hangs out on the corner by City Hall, saw her drive onto A1A in the intersection."

"Two minutes ago?" I ask and look at my watch. "That means she is probably already down by 15th Street, maybe even further."

I hang up and look at Sandra. Joey is sitting in the back. We have been driving around our neighborhood and Snug Harbor to see if we could spot her somewhere around here. Meanwhile, I am debating with the woman at the groomer's main office on the phone. I want her to tell me where Ally is; I even tell her it's a matter of life and death, but she keeps telling me she is not allowed to give me the address. Instead, I tell her to call Ally on her cellphone and tell her to call me. I keep looking at my phone, hoping she will.

I hit A1A and speed up, when Danny calls. "She's been spotted at 16th a minute ago.

"16th! That means she is halfway to the base," I say, and hang up. I press the gas pedal down and exceed the thirty-five mile limit by...well, by a lot.

I pass 10th, then 11th, and when I reach 16th, I receive a text from Chloe. Sandra reads it to me.

"Her truck just stopped for a red light at the Officer's Club," she says.

The break in front of the Officer's Club is one of our old favorite surf spots. It is the first red light you meet after you leave Cocoa Beach, driving south towards the base. She is going faster than I expected. I have to accelerate, hoping the red light will hold her for a long enough time for me to catch up with her. If she makes it onto the base, then I can't get to her anymore; I can't help her.

"Hurry up," Sandra says.

"I'm trying to. But these cars won't get out of my way. I'm stuck." I honk the horn at the pickup truck blocking my way going twenty-five miles an hour. Next to him, a Toyota has parked on the inner lane. I can't get past them.

"If she's at the O Club, then there is only maybe thirty seconds till she reaches the base," Joey says.

I look at my clock. "She's early. By half an hour. She isn't supposed to be there until four. I had planned to go there just before four and stop her if we hadn't found her before," I say. "How was I supposed to know she would get there half an hour early?"

I growl and honk again. Finally, the car on the inside moves out of my way and I can go around the truck. I race past Summer Street, past Taco City and my favorite surf shop, Oceansports World.

I reach the O Club and realize the light has turned green. I speed up and think that I can spot the van in the distance.

"Is that her?" I ask Sandra. She has better eyes than me. "Is that the grooming van?"

"I...I don't know," Sandra says. She leans forward to better see, but still shakes her head. "It might be."

"We've got to get to her," I grunt. "We've got to stop her."

"Yes," Sandra suddenly exclaims. "I see it now. It's her. It's the van. It says *Grooming on Wheels* on the back. Hurry up. We're almost there. You can make it, Mary."

I literally stand on the pedal in order to press it to the bottom. I can see the van getting closer now.

"Almost there," Joey says.

"Almost," Sandra repeats.

I can see her now. I can see the van getting closer and closer. I realize she has stopped for another red light, at the intersection leading to the base. I have to reach her before the light turns green and she turns onto the base. I have to.

"Hurry, hurry," Sandra says.

"I'll make it. Once I get up to the side of her van, you roll down the window. Both of you. Then you yell at her, all right? Tell her to pull to the curb. All right? I need both of you to do it."

"Got it," they say in unison.

We can make it. I think we can. I know we can. Come on!

I manage to convince myself that we'll actually make it, when I hear the siren behind me.

86

September 2015

"It's the police! You've got to stop, Mary!"

Sandra is screaming now.

"No! You can't stop now," Joey yells. "We're so close."

The siren is wailing behind us. He is flashing his lights at me, trying to get me to stop. Meanwhile, the light turns green, and the van with Ally Meyer in it starts to go; it blinks to signal that it is turning, but holds back for oncoming traffic.

"You've got to stop," Sandra repeats. "I don't want to get shot. He will shoot. You know what they're like. Or he will hit our car with his to try and stop us. I don't want to die."

"You watch too many movies, Sandra," I say.

I keep going. I don't stop. The police car is getting closer to us. It has a stronger engine than my rental car. In a few seconds, it will be next to us.

"Stop! Mary, stop!" Sandra yells, and hides her face between her hands, just as I reach the van.

"Now!" I yell and turn the car to get up onto the side of it.

Joey is the only one who reacts. He rolls down the window. He yells and waves. "Stop! Stop the van! Don't go! STOP!!"

I have to keep looking at the road, so I can't see if she notices him. "Did she see you?" I ask.

"She saw me! She turned her head and looked at me," Joey says. "But…"

But she doesn't stop.

Our car screeches across the asphalt and lands in the grass, while her van continues through the gates of the base. She stops to talk to the guard shortly, but is let in within seconds. They know her.

I curse and growl. The police car has stopped behind us. The officer gets out of his car and walks to ours, pointing his gun at us, yelling for me to keep my hands on the wheel.

It takes maybe ten minutes, maybe fifteen, but finally I manage to convince him that I am not dangerous, that I am not drunk or intoxicated. I go through all the tests and don't fail even one. Not even the walking straight on a line, even though I am so agitated it is hard for me to focus.

He gives me a ticket for reckless driving, then tells Joey to take the wheel going back.

"Thank you, Officer," I say, trying to keep my cool. As soon as he is gone, I look at my friends, holding the ticket in my hand.

"Now what?" Joey says.

"I might have an idea," I say.

I grab my phone and call Danny. Meanwhile, Joey drives us to the nearest parking lot in front of the O Club. Danny arrives a few minutes later in his fire truck. It shines brightly in the sun.

"What's going on?" he asks and gets out. "Did you stop her?"

"No. She went in. I need you to get me onto the base," I say.

"No. No. No," he says and waves his finger at me.

"Yes. Yes. Yes," I say. "I know you can. In that thing. They'll never question a firefighter, a fellow hero. There's a fire station on base, right? Tell them you're here to visit your colleagues."

Danny looks at me.

"Please?" I say. "You're the hero here. You would want to save a life if you could, right? I should be the one hating Ally and not caring about her, but come on. She doesn't deserve to be killed. And we can't let AK get away with it. She has gotten away with way too much in her life. If we can get to Ally and get her to testify against AK, then maybe we could get her locked up. But we can't if she is dead."

"She's got a point, bro," Joey says.

Danny stares at me, then nods. "Alright then. I'll see what I can do. You can hide in the back. I can't promise you anything, though. Just pray that we don't get picked for a random search."

"Let me do it," Joey says. "It might be dangerous."

"No," I say. "I am the only one Ally will listen to. I am the one she wronged, remember? She owes me and she knows it."

I jump in and lay flat on the floor of the fire truck. Danny puts a blanket over me to cover me up. Sandra and Joey stay behind. Joey's and my eyes meet just before Danny closes the door. I can tell he is concerned.

Frankly, so am I.

87

September 2015

We're in luck. The guard at the gate buys Danny's story about paying his buddies a surprise visit. The guard calls the fire station and they're thrilled that Danny is stopping by.

We're let in. Once again, I have tricked my way onto the base.

As soon as we drive past the big signs and huge buildings, Danny tells me I can get up from the floor. I rise to my knees, and watch out the window as the base passes by.

"So, where are we going?" Danny asks, and I realize I have no clue. "We don't have long," he says. "The guys at the fire station will start to wonder where I am. Then they'll start looking for us."

"I know," I say. "I am trying to figure it out." I grab my phone and text Chloe. I ask her if she can find Liz Hester's address. It's my theory that AK has called the groomer and asked specifically for Ally to come to her home to take care of a dog that she probably doesn't even have.

Seconds later, she texts me back with an address.

What would I do without her?

I spot the van in front of the house as we approach the address and swallow hard.

"I hope we're not too late," I say.

Danny parks the truck in front of the house, then turns to look at me. "There's a box in the back, could you give it to me?"

I find the box and hand it to him. He opens it and reveals two guns. I know nothing about guns and have never even fired one. The mere sight of them makes me jump. Danny picks up one of them, then checks the holster, and then hands it to me. He grabs the other one himself.

"We have these for protection," he says. "Sometimes, we have to go into very dangerous neighborhoods. We need to protect ourselves."

"Of course," I say, and hold the gun in my hand. It looks so wrong. It feels so wrong. I am more terrified of accidentally shooting myself, but still I take it…just in case.

Danny tucks his into the back of his pants like in the movies, and I do the same. It feels strange and I try to walk carefully, afraid it might accidentally shoot me in the leg or worse.

We walk up to the house and stop at the front door. I ring the doorbell, then hear a loud crash coming from inside. I look at Danny, who takes out his gun. I do the same and watch while Danny walks back, then kicks the door in, like he is probably used to from his line of work.

The door slams to the ground and we enter. I steel myself. I tell myself I can do it. Of course I can.

Then we walk in.

I point the gun and walk after Danny inside the living room, my heart pounding in my chest. I can feel my pulse against my temples. I hold my breath.

"Hello?" Danny yells. "Is everyone okay in here?"

No answer. A noise comes from the kitchen. We hurry in there. Then we stop. On the kitchen floor is Ally; her face is smashed into the tiles. On top of her sits AK or Liz, whatever she goes by these days. She is holding a gun to her face, pressing it angrily against her temple.

I gasp.

"AK," Danny says.

AK looks up, and her eyes meet mine.

"Don't do it," I say. "Don't kill her."

AK grunts, then laughs while still staring at me. Her eyes are like needles on my body. She raises the gun and points it at me.

"Maybe I'll just kill you instead? How about that, huh?"

88

May 1986

Penelope takes her daughter into the lobby of the hospital. After fifteen minutes of waiting, a nurse tells them to come in for preparation. They put the girl in a bed and insert tubes and a drip.

"Now, this operation will take a few hours," the nurse tells Penelope. "She will need to have general anesthesia. Has she had that before?"

Penelope nods. "Yes. Once."

"So, she has no problem with it. That's great. It will take a few hours for her to wake up, and then we will need to monitor the heart for the next several months. Will you be able to come down here for check-ups, or do you want to have them done up in your own area? We can recommend a doctor if necessary. It is an awfully long drive. I couldn't blame you if you wanted to find someone closer to you."

"No. It's fine," Penelope says. "We've tried all the doctors up there, and they have proven to be quite incompetent. We will come here for her check-ups. It's no big deal; it really isn't."

The nurse stares at Penelope, then smiles. "Well, okay then. I'll make sure to set it up." She looks at the child, then smiles compassionately. "I'll take you to preparation now."

"I'll come too," Penelope says.

"I'm sorry," the nurse says. "Only the patient is allowed."

Penelope looks disappointed. "Really?"

"Sorry. Those are the rules here. We have a nice waiting area out in the back. There's a cafeteria where you can get something to eat and some couches with a TV and some newspapers to keep you busy. I know it's hard having to wait for this, but it's how the doctors want it. There is nothing I can do."

"Alright then," she says with a sigh.

She watches as the child is rolled away. The nurse takes her to an elevator, then takes her to the third floor, where she is rolled into her own room.

"Here. This will be where you wake up once you get out of the anesthesia. It's no hotel room, but I think it's pretty nice. Look at all the drawings on the walls from other children who have stayed here. They all had the same procedure that you're about to have. Now, you shouldn't worry. I can tell you're afraid. I've seen that look many times, but I tell you, the doctors here are the best. They'll take really good care of you and make that heart of yours work normally again."

The nurse taps the girl on her chest as she speaks. As she does, tears start to roll down the child's cheeks. The nurse sees it.

"No. Don't cry, little girl. It's all going to be just fine. Don't you worry. These doctors have done it so many times. You'll be just fine."

"But…" the girl says, then stops herself. She looks nervously at the nurse. "What are you going to do to me?"

"You mean you don't know?"

The girl shakes her head. More tears stream down her face. The nurse sits next to her on the bed, then caresses her hair. The girl's legs are dangling from the side of the bed.

"Well, the doctor will cut you open right here," she says and points at the girl's chest. "Then he will do a heart catheterization procedure."

The girl gasps and looks up at the nurse with terror in her eyes.

"Aw, don't worry," the nurse says. "You won't feel a thing. You'll be sleeping the entire time."

"She's making it up," the girl suddenly says with a small quiet voice.

"What's that, sweetie?"

"My mom. She's making it up," she says louder now.

The nurse laughs. "Now, don't go around saying stuff like that. I know it's an uncomfortable situation, but I'm sure your mom is nothing but a concerned mother."

The girl looks into the eyes of the nurse. The nurse suddenly senses the urgency. It scares her.

"No. I mean she is making it up. Really. She is," the girl says.

89

September 2015

I CAN'T BREATHE. The sight of the gun pointing at me makes me panic. I drop my own gun and raise my hands. I feel like an idiot. So stupid. Not so much Tom Cruise anymore. Danny puts down his gun as well.

"Don't do anything stupid," he says.

"It's quite the little reunion we have going here," AK says. "Are there any more of you people coming? I'm sorry I didn't put on a pot of coffee. I've been quite busy with this little monster here."

"AK," I say and walk closer. "It's me you're angry at. Why not let the others go? You know as well as I do that it's me you want. Am I right?"

AK stares at me like she is making up her mind. Then she shakes her head. "Sorry. No can do."

"Come on, AK," I say. "What has Ally done to you that is so bad?"

"Well, first of all, she's a snitch. She told everything to the police. If I hadn't run into the general that night, I would be in jail by now. She would have made sure I was put away for the rest of my life."

"But, AK. This is really about you and me," I say. "Come on, let's get it out in the open."

AK is still pointing the gun at me. Ally is growling underneath her. "Get off me," she yells. But AK doesn't move.

"So, you're mad at me," I say. "You've been mad for, what? Almost thirty years now? I am sorry. I am sorry for what I did."

"No, you're not," she says. "You're not the least bit sorry. I know you're not. I can tell. I know you better than you think, Mary."

"Alright. You got me. You're absolutely right. I am not the least bit sorry that I spoke up. I am not the least bit sorry that I stopped them from cutting my heart open when there was absolutely nothing wrong with me. I did it to save myself. And to save you, AK. My mother, *our* mother was killing the both of us. She wouldn't have stopped there if I hadn't spoken up. She would have continued. When I told the nurse that day at the hospital, she called the doctors and they immediately called the authorities. Why no one did that before, I don't know. I have wondered so many times, blamed so many people for closing their eyes. Munchausen Syndrome wasn't a well-known disease back then. But the thing is that once the authorities were informed, our mother finally received help. She was admitted. She received the help she needed to get better, and when she had Blake, she never did anything bad to him. So, no, I am not sorry for what I did. I saved you, AK. I saved your freaking life."

I can feel the tears rolling down my cheeks now. All the memories. All those days spent in bed, when I wasn't sick. All the doctors and nurses and emergency trips to the ER. The worry in my mother's eyes, the doctors constantly running tests, not knowing what to do. All that salt my mother shoved down my throat to make me throw up, all the crying for her to stop. I had thought it was normal…that this was how mothers were. That was just the way life was. I never questioned it until that day when she took me to the hospital in Miami and a nurse told me they would do surgery on my heart. That was when I couldn't take it anymore. That's when I finally spoke up, even though it killed me to defy my mother like that, to go against what she had told me to do.

"I am sorry, though," I continue, "about what happened to you.

I am sorry that the adoption agency took you back and placed you in that home. I am so sorry about that."

"You...you destroyed my life," AK says. She too has tears rolling down her cheeks now. The gun is shaking in her hands. "You have no idea what they did to me at that home. How my life was ruined. I had a family, Mary. When your parents adopted me, I finally had a family. I had a father and a sister. But most of all, I finally had a mother. A mother who cared about me. I had never had that before. Penelope cared so much for me. I have never had that, Mary. Never." AK wipes her face on her sleeve. "You don't know how much it hurt to get that close. And then to have it taken away from me? You haven't even a clue. You got your life back afterwards. You continued to live in that big house on the beach, having a mother and a father and even a brother later on. I had to watch you every day at school, see your happy face while my life was in ruins. You are so spoiled, Mary, and you don't even know it. That's why I wanted you to feel what it was like to not have any parents, to lose everything. So I killed your mother and set your father's house on fire. With him in it. How does it feel, huh? Seeing him in that bed at the hospital? I'm sure he won't survive. I bet you'll have to turn off his life-support soon, right? I can't think of a better way to take you down than this. You'll have to kill him yourself. Now, how do you like that?"

90

September 2015

"NO!!"

I am staring at AK, my nostrils flaring. I scream the word, right before I leap through the air. I don't care if she shoots me. I don't care if I get hurt anymore. Or even if I die. I am so angry now, I can't hold it back.

I hate her for what she has done.

My move takes her by surprise, and she doesn't shoot until it's too late. The shot hits the ceiling and ricochets back towards her. It hits her in the leg. Danny throws himself to the ground. I land on top of AK and pull her off of Ally's back. I manage to throw in a few punches while AK screams in pain.

"This is for my mother!" I scream, and throw in a punch in her face. "And this is for my father!"

I run my fist into her face again and again. AK is screaming and yelling. Blood is gushing out of her leg from where the bullet hit her. Meanwhile, Ally gets to her feet and stands next to me. I don't pay much attention to what else is going on in the room. I hardly even hear Danny screaming, *NO!*

I don't notice what's around me. Not until I hear another shot being fired and blood spurts into my face. AK's body goes limp beneath me. Her head has a hole in it and her blood is creating a pool around her.

I gasp and let go of her. Her blood is all over my hands.

I look up and into the eyes of Ally, who is standing with the smoking gun. She is still pointing it at me. On the floor behind her, I see a pair of scissors. That's when it hits me. That's when I finally realize what I should have a long time ago.

"You?" I say.

Ally nods. It's not until now I realize she's wearing a surgical mask covering half of her face.

"You killed Coraline, Jean, and Cassie? You tried to kill Olivia and now you've killed AK."

Ally nods again, still pointing the gun at me. Danny stays completely still in the corner.

"Why?" I ask.

"Because of what they did to me," she says.

Ally then grabs her surgical mask and pulls it off, revealing a mouth slit from ear to ear.

I gasp and clasp my mouth.

"They did that to you?"

"They came to my door in 1995," she says. "We had moved away. My mother and I lived in Melbourne. I thought AK was long gone. I thought she was out of my life for good. It had been three years since the night we…when we broke into your house. I had told the police everything. I had moved on with my life. Started a new school, made new friends, stayed out of trouble. I was a straight A student and doing so well for myself. I was back on track and determined to stay there. Until they rang my doorbell on that night in March. They attacked me at my house when I refused to go with them. They cut me with a knife. Do you have any idea how hard it is to get a job when you look like this? I had nothing for so many years. When my mother died, I had to find some way to make money. So I came up with the idea of grooming dogs. No one cares that I wear a mask. But I can never have a normal life. Never!"

"So, you killed them?"

I look at Danny, thinking it must be hard for him to hear all this.

Jean was his wife through almost twenty years and the mother of his son.

"Yes, I did. And now I have to kill you as well. Both of you."

Everything happens so fast. I believe I am the first to hear it. Footsteps outside closing in. And then…the piercing smash. Glass is shattered everywhere. Flying through the air is something, or maybe someone, crashing through the window.

I am thrown to the floor. All three of us fall down. Someone jumps over me. I scream while glass surrounds me. Someone is on top of Ally, holding her down. Chaos and shouting. Danny is pushed down. The person on top of Ally is struggling to hold her down. I blink my eyes. The man is in uniform. I recognize his face.

It's the general.

Ally is screaming. She reaches for the gun and grabs ahold of it. I don't think the general has seen it.

"She's still got the gun!" I yell.

Ally lifts the gun up in the air and I lunge forward to try and grab her, but I am not fast enough. She places the gun on her temple.

"NO!"

And then she pulls the trigger.

91

October 2015

Two weeks later, I am standing in front of the prison as my brother is let out. I see him and wave when he approaches the gate. The door makes a buzzing sound and he can finally step out.

As a free man.

"Yay!" I yell and run to him. I throw myself in his arms and hug him tightly. A tear leaves my eyes and ends its days on my lip before I wipe it away.

"Hey, sis," he says, and kisses my forehead. "Boy, it feels good to be out." He takes a deep breath of the intoxicating fresh air. He closes his eyes quickly, then looks at me again. "Thank you for never giving up."

"Let's get out of here," I say, and point at the car where Salter and Joey are waiting. Behind them is Sandra, parked in her Escalade. Inside sits Marcia, Chloe, Alex, and Danny. They poke their heads out of the windows.

"Hi, Blake! Welcome home!" Marcia yells. She holds a bottle of gin in her hand, which she gives to him. "Here. I bet you've missed this." Then she laughs with her hoarse voice.

"Everyone came?" Blake asks, looking at me.

"Well, we're almost family, right? Not one of us believed you were guilty."

"I'm moved, guys," Blake says.

"What are you waiting for?" Marcia says. "Let's get out of this dump. I have a beer with my name on it at the Beach Shack."

Blake gets in the car with me, Salter, and Joey. We all drive back to the beach. I, for one, am feeling grateful. I am so glad I finally managed to get my brother out. It wasn't easy. Ally was gone and couldn't admit to having killed Jamilla Jenkins. But once I got the general on my side, Chris Fisher finally listened to my story. The general told me he had received a phone call from the firefighters at the base telling him about Danny, who had announced his arrival, but never showed up. He immediately knew something had to be wrong and started a search. They found the truck parked outside of Liz's house. Worried about Liz, he looked through the window, where he saw Ally pointing a gun at us, and immediately took action. It was the general who made sure Chris Fisher would listen to what I had to say. I told him what Ally had told me and all the details about AK, alias Liz Hester. I told him how she admitted to having killed all the girls, but it bothered me that I had never asked about Jamilla Jenkins. I told him I had a feeling the four killings had to be connected, since they had many similarities, and asked him to look into it. Ten days later, he told me they had searched Ally's house and found Jamilla Jenkins' purse in her closet. They had also found out that Ally groomed Jamilla Jenkins' dog about a year ago, but they got into a fight over the price. The fight that was heard by many neighbors turned bad, and Ally Meyer ended up threatening Jamilla Jenkins. That was enough to drop the charges against my brother, and now he is finally free.

"Free as a bird. Boy, it feels good," he says, and stretches in his seat.

Blake rolls down the window while we drive across the bridges and sticks his head out like a dog. The rest of us laugh. It's such a relief for me. I can't believe I actually pulled it off, that I actually got him out.

We drive back to Joey's house, where Blake gets the bedroom

and I sleep with Joey on the couch. It can be pulled out, so it's big enough for the both of us.

"Are you guys…?" Blake asks the next morning when we eat our pancakes that Joey so generously made for all of us. I am smearing mine with Nutella when the question is asked.

I stop moving. I can feel Joey's eyes on me. I don't know what to answer. I have made no decisions yet. I don't want to. Right now, I just want to enjoy whatever it is we have. I don't want to think about the future. I really don't.

I avoid looking up. I don't want to look at anyone. I want them to stop staring at me. It makes me uncomfortable. I can't help it. I can't help myself. It starts as a giggle. Soon it turns into a loud laugh. I can't stop it. It overwhelms me.

Seconds later, the others laugh along with me.

92

October 2015

Blake is packing his suitcase. It's been three days since he left the prison. He has been to his studio once to grab his clothes and the few belongings he can't live without. His paintings, he has placed in Joey's garage. He'll ask Mary to try and sell them for him. She has put the one from Starbucks up in Joey's living room. He likes to look at it and sense how proud she is of him. He has no idea when he'll paint again, though. He's not going back to the studio. Too many bad memories. He needs to move on with his life. Jail was a bad experience. A real bad experience.

Mary steps in.

"So, Joey took Salter to work with him today. Guess it's just going to be you and me here." She pauses and looks at the suitcase. "What are you doing?"

He detects disappointment in her voice.

"I'm leaving, sis. Gotta get out of here, you know?"

She looks surprised. "You're leaving? But why? To go where?"

Blake shrugs. "Anywhere but here. I need to get away. I'm kind of tired of Cocoa Beach, if you know what I mean."

"But...but what about Dad?" she asks. "He might wake up soon."

Blake sighs. "Sis. Come on. The only reason he is alive is because of the machines breathing for him. You know it. I know it. He is not going to wake up. You have to let it go. The doctor even told you to shut off the life-support. I've already given my consent. Even Laura agrees. He's gone. You've gotta realize that."

Mary shakes her head. "I'm never going to shut him off. He'll wake up soon and then…then what?"

"You're hopeless," he says with a sigh. "I'm sure you'll take very good care of him. If it ever happens. "

Mary grunts and slams her hand onto the suitcase. "You can't just leave. Goddammit, Blake. You're the only family I have."

"You have Joey. You have Salter and Snowflake. Besides, you'll be going back to New York soon, and then what? I don't want to be left down here alone. I'm running off. Getting out while I can."

"I'm not sure we're going back," Mary says.

"What? What about your career?"

"I was fired. I didn't tell you because of all you were going through, but they sacked me. I have nothing to go back to. Salter doesn't even have a school anymore. He stayed down here for too long. They gave his spot to someone else. I can't pay for it anyway. I used all my money on a lawyer for you."

Blake sits down on the bed next to Mary. "Wow," he says.

"I know. It's bad. You can't leave too. You just can't. You're the only one I have here."

"What about Joey? What about the crew?"

"Alright, I have them as well. And I love them, but I don't know what to do about Joey. I love him, but I still don't know if I want to be with him or not. You know what I mean?"

"Sure."

"See. That's why I need you. You understand me."

Blake puts his arm around Mary's neck. He kisses her forehead. "I'll come visit."

She sniffles. "Do you even have any money?"

"Well, I don't. But Olivia does."

Mary stares at him, startled. "Olivia?"

"Yeah. She's leaving with me. The general agreed to a divorce."

"So, you're still together?" Mary asks.

"I guess so."

Mary smiles and looks at him. "As long as you're happy."

"Well, I am," Blake says, and gets to his feet again. He walks to the suitcase and grabs it with the intention of closing it.

Mary watches him. She gets up and walks to the door. On her way, she passes his phone on the dresser. It lights up. Before he can stop her, she picks it up.

"Olivia sent you a message," she says teasingly.

Blake opens his eyes wide. "Give it to me," he says. "It's private."

But she doesn't. She opens the message. "I'm your sister. You can't have any secrets from me. Not anymore. Let's see what she wrote…"

Blake lunges towards her, but it's too late. Mary stares at the phone, her mouth open. It looks like she is trying to scream, but no sound comes across her lips.

Shit!

93

October 2015

"What's this Blake?"

I stare at my brother. I can't believe my eyes. "What IS this?"

I yell in frustration. I am shaking all over while I stare at the picture of Jamilla Jenkins on the bed at the motel. Olivia is sitting next to her dead body with the chisel deep in her chest. Olivia is smiling and making a gesture like she is standing in front of the Statue of Liberty or another tourist attraction. I have never seen anything this appalling in my life.

"Why did she send you this picture? Can you tell me that? Blake?" I try to control my voice as I speak. "Why?"

Just like that, my brother's expression changes completely. He laughs, then walks to the door and shuts it. "Well, dear *Sis*, if you must know. *That*...is Jamilla Jenkins."

I drop the phone. I clasp my mouth with both my hands. I can't believe it. "You killed her? You killed her with...with Olivia?"

"Yes. Jamie Barley was there too. Just as she told the police she was. We picked them up at Squid Lips, then drove to the motel. To have some fun. They were very drunk. Apparently, Jamie was so drunk she believed we had gone back to my studio and not the motel. That was my luck, since it made it all so unbelievable, didn't it? Once you came down, you couldn't believe I would have moved the body, right?"

"But...but...Blake...why?"

"Let's just say Olivia and I like to play games. It went a little further than expected. When Olivia handed me the chisel, I didn't think I could do it, but she cheered me on, aroused me enough to do it. We cleaned the room, took the bloody sheet with us and burned it. Left nothing but the body. We knew we couldn't move it without someone seeing us. But we left no trace, no fingerprints, no DNA. I even used a condom and we took the chisel with us."

"So, the general didn't frame you? He didn't plant the chisel, nor did he pay off Jamie Barley to testify against you? He didn't do those things to get rid of you because you were screwing his wife?"

Blake laughs. "He certainly didn't. He only told Jamie to never talk about Olivia, but that wasn't hard, because they knew each other well. But it makes a good story, doesn't it? It is very believable that the big bad husband, a general in the army on top of it, would go to these lengths to get rid of me, doesn't it? I can see why you would believe that. So I played along."

"And...what about the confession?"

"All part of it. I had a feeling you could get me out somehow. And I was right. I knew you wouldn't let it go. Especially not if you believed the general was getting to me. I knew it would make you speed up the process. I had nothing to lose, did I?"

I can hardly breathe when I speak. I can't wrap my mind around this. It's too much. It's simply too much to cope with.

"And the purse at Ally's house?"

"Planted by Olivia. We had the purse all the time. Or Olivia did. It was easy for her to drive down there and plant it in the closet behind some clothes. It was our luck that it turned out that Jamilla Jenkins had also been Ally Meyer's client. That made things a little easier on us. So, I guess what I am saying here, *Sis*, is thank you. I owe you one."

"What?"

I stare at my brother, who is approaching me slowly. I don't like the look in his eyes. "But that's not you, Blake. This is not who you are!"

He tilts his head while walking closer. "And, just how do you know that, Sister dearest? You left when I was three years old. You have hardly seen me since. How do you even know who I am? How do you expect to know that when you were so far away and you left me all alone with that dad of ours and a stepmom who would rather see me fall off a cliff than have to deal with me. HOW do you expect to know ANYTHING about me?"

He is getting too close to me now, and I back up. What is he going to do?

"Blake…I…"

"Shhh. No more talk," he says, reaches out his hands, and grabs me around the throat.

94

October 2015

Sandra is whistling as she crosses the street with Lucky on his leash. She has just gotten back from three days in Germany doing a big runway show in Berlin with Heidi Klum. Tomorrow, she is off to New York for the shoot for *Vogue*. This morning, she just received a call saying that they want her in Milan next week.

It ain't over till it's over, she thinks to herself. *And I am definitely not over yet.*

She is beginning to think she might be able to keep doing this for years to come. The thought makes her happy. This is what she is good at; this is what she knows. So what if she never has any children? You never know how life will turn out for you, and hers turned out differently than others. Sandra likes to be different and not just go the same way everybody else does. She even went out surfing yesterday and people on the beach gathered to watch her, clapping when she did a 360 in the air. She still has it. Indeed she does. Even at the age of thirty-eight.

Children aren't for everyone.

Her whistling turns into humming. It's that old song again, the one by Nirvana. Sandra can't get it out of her mind again. Not after that day in the car with Mary. Sandra enjoys having her old friend back so much. She doesn't know how long Mary will stay in Cocoa Beach, so she is going to swing by Joey's townhouse and have a coffee with her, enjoy her while she is still here. Maybe it'll be their last for a long time.

You never know.

Sandra walks with quick steps, thinking she might burn a few extra calories before the shoot. She is terrified that they'll think she is too fat or too old. The last part, she can't do much about. She refuses to do Botox, even though it has been suggested a few times by her agency. That, she is never going to do. Ever. But losing a few pounds, she can do. That, she is actually very good at.

A young pool guy is working at the community pool at Joey's place. Sandra greets him as she walks past. She enjoys feeling his eyes examining her body as she walks by.

Yup! Still got it!

Maybe she will be able to work for another five years? It's certainly not impossible the way things are turning out for her right now. She's at the top of her game, her agency says. The demand for her is growing. They can hardly believe it. It never happens, they say. And the names asking are big. Versace wants her for the spring fashion show in Paris. Versace.

Sandra walks up to Joey's front door. She can hear voices coming from inside. Loud voices. She wonders if Mary and Joey are fighting again. Her heart drops at the thought. She sure hopes that is not the case. She loves Mary and Joey together. It has always been them. Sandra is rooting for them. They are the ones who did things right. They chose right. Sandra loves Ryan, she really does, but she often wonders what her life would have been like if she had married Alex instead.

It's all water under the bridge, Sandra. No use crying over spilt milk. You might never have gotten the career you have if he had been your boyfriend at the time. He would have held you back. He would have kept you in chains.

The voices calm down inside the house. Sandra stays outside, not knowing what to do. Mary is the one who called her this morning and asked her to stop by for coffee. She must be expecting her.

Sandra knocks on the door, but no one answers. The door is ajar, and when she touches it, it pushes open.

"Hello?"

95

October 2015

"Hello?"

Sandra's voice cuts through the air. I want to yell back, I want to tell her where I am, tell her to help me. I want to scream, but I can't. I can hardly breathe. Blake has me pinned up against the wall. He is holding my throat tightly between his hands. He is pressing hard, his face strained with the effort, his eyes flaming with anger and hatred. It hurts. It hurts really badly. I can't get free.

"Please," I manage to whisper. "Please…stop…you're…"

I can't anymore. I can't hold on. I am getting tired, the lack of oxygen is making me dizzy. My vision is blurry. I am only making gasping, spurting sounds. I am feeling a distinct tingling sensation in my legs and fingertips, my head is hurting badly; it feels like it's about to explode.

"Hello, Mary?"

I can still hear Sandra. She is entering the living room now.

Help! Sandra I'm in here! Help me!

"Are you home, Mary?"

Help me! Please help me!

It feels like I am about to slip. I can't hold on anymore. My vision is so blurry, I can hardly see Blake anymore. I can hear him. I can hear him grunting with effort as he puts further pressure on my throat.

As I am drifting in and out of consciousness, I suddenly remember something. A thing my mother always taught me as a child. What was it again?

Sandra's steps are on the stairs. She is coming closer. I can't determine where they're coming from anymore, nor can I sense what is up and what is down. It's all so fuzzy.

"Are you in here?" I hear her say. Her voice seems close now.

That's when I feel the grip on my throat loosen for just one second as Blake turns around. Just enough for me to get back to reality.

I hear Sandra gasp loudly.

"What are you doing, Blake? What are you DOING?!"

Go for the eyes. If someone ever attacks you, poke them in the eyes!

My mother's voice is loud and clear in my head. She taught this to both me and AK back then, when we had been a family. *A kick in the crotch followed by a poke in the eye, then run,* were her words.

"Stay out of this, Sandra!" he yells.

As Blake turns his face to look at me again, I have managed to lift my arm and poke two fingers forcefully into his eyes.

"My eyes!"

He screams in pain and lets go of me. I fall to the ground. I am gasping and coughing, making sounds I didn't know were even possible. Blake is yelling and screaming in pain. Sandra runs to me and helps me get up. I try to speak, but I can't. I get up and we start to run. My body is aching and hurting, but there is no other way if I want to survive. I gotta run. Get out of here as fast as I can.

We storm down the stairs. When we reach the door, Blake is yelling at us.

"Oh, no you don't!"

He is behind us quickly. Sandra lets out a scream. I open the door, and we rush out of the house, Blake right behind us. My vision is still blurry, my head dizzy, and it is hard for me to run. Sandra is in front of me as we enter the pool area. I slam the door to the fence after me, right when Blake reaches it, and he gets his hand stuck in it. Blake yells in pain and stops. I run across the pool area. The pool guy is standing with all his chemicals in big bottles, carefully measuring the acid in a small cup.

"Run, Sandra!" I yell.

But Blake is already over the fence. He is running the other way around the pool and cuts us off. The pool guy stops what he is doing and stares at us. Sandra and I both stop. Blake is standing in front of us, panting. His face is strained with anger. The pool guy remains clueless.

"Let us go, Blake," I say.

"You're not going anywhere! You'll only ruin this for me."

"If you mean that I am not letting you get away with murder, then you're damn right," I say. I know it's not tactically prudent, but I want him to know I would never let him get away with this. I can't believe how stupid I have been to let him trick me like this.

"Stop it, Blake," Sandra says. "You're never going to get away with this."

"Shut up!" he yells at her. "Just shut up!"

I look at the fence. It's not very tall. We can jump over it easily. I just want to get out of there, then call the police. I am ready to make a run for it. I grab Sandra's hand and start running. She follows me. I climb the fence and jump over it. Sandra is right behind me. As she is in the air, Blake grabs her foot and pulls her down. I watch as her face is slammed into the railing on the fence when he pulls her down.

"Sandra!" I yell.

Blake falls backwards and lands on his back. Sandra falls to the ground, face first. Next to her are the pool guy's containers. Blake is fast to get to his feet, then he grabs one of the containers, rips the lid off, and pours the liquid acid over Sandra.

After that, there is nothing but screams. Sandra's tormented screams.

Blake stares at her. He looks startled, then drops the container. I jump back over the fence and try to get her up.

"Water," the pool guy yells. "Get lots of water on her."

I manage to get her to the pool shower and hose her down. The pool guy pulls a hose and starts squirting her as well. Sandra doesn't stop screaming.

"My face! My face!"

While the pool guy fumbles with his phone and calls 911, I watch as Blake heads down the road, stops a car, pulls the driver out of the front seat, gets in, and drives off.

Epilogue

OCTOBER 2015

I AM ALREADY in the hospital when they call me. I am visiting Sandra. She is lying in her bed, her face all gauzed up. I am sitting in a chair next to her.

"I am so glad you're going home today," I say.

I look at what little of her face I can actually see. Her skin doesn't look good. I fear the worst for what it looks like underneath the gauze. A doctor comes in, along with a nurse, and gives the order to remove it.

Sandra tries to smile at me. Ryan is standing on the other side of her. I can tell by his face he is appalled by what he sees. I try to not let it show.

"Is it that bad?" she asks.

I shake my head. But it's a lie. The doctors have tried their best, but she still looks terrible.

"We had to transplant new skin from your back and thigh," the doctor says. "You're lucky it didn't get in your eyes," he continues. "At least it is all only cosmetic."

Only cosmetic? But that's her entire life! Her looks are her life!

"Is it really that bad?" she asks, looking at her husband. He is crying through his forced smile.

"We're just glad we didn't lose you," I say, and grab her hand.

"Can I see?"

"Are you sure you're ready for it?" Ryan asks.

"I have to at some point, right?" Sandra says. I can tell by her voice she is about to cry. She can't hold it together for much longer.

The doctor helps her get out of bed and walk to the bathroom, where she can look at herself in the mirror. I close my eyes as I hear her shriek.

"I'm…I'm hideous," she says.

I hold back the tears and walk up to her. "I am so sorry, Sandra," I say. "I am so, so sorry."

That's when my phone starts to ring. I pick it up. It's my dad's doctor.

"I have wonderful news," he says. "Your father just opened his eyes."

I look at Sandra as I hang up. "My dad's awake," I say through tears. "He's alive."

She tries to smile. "Go. Go see him."

"Are you sure you'll be alright?"

"Of course. Now go!"

I run down the hallway and find his room. I run inside, then stop. There he is. Still hooked up to all the instruments and tubes, but he is looking at me.

My dad is looking at me!

I walk to him and he follows me with his eyes. A tear escapes the corner and rolls down his cheek.

"Oh, Dad," I say, grabbing his hand. It feels limp.

"It doesn't appear that he can move it," the nurse says. "So far, there are no reactions in any parts of his body, except his eyes. He hasn't spoken yet."

I stare into his eyes, mine filling with tears. Right now, all that doesn't matter. All that I am thankful for is to be able to look into his eyes once again.

"I am so sorry, Daddy," I say. "I am so sorry for all this. It's all my fault. You were right. About Blake, I mean. He was guilty, and I wasted so much time trying to prove that he wasn't. You were right all along. Oh, Dad for so many years I blamed you for not doing anything when Mom was doing all those awful things to me while growing up. For so many years, I resented you for letting it happen to me. Only, the other day, I realized something." I hold his hand tight in mine and place the palm on my chest. "You didn't know, did you? You didn't realize what she was doing until it was too late."

I sniffle and wipe tears away from my cheeks. "I can't believe how badly I messed up. I came down here to straighten things out, to fix things, and look at what has happened. Look at everything that happened. You, Sandra..."

"It wasn't all bad," a voice says behind me. I turn and look at Joey and Salter. They're holding flowers and balloons. My dad's eyes light up when he sees them. Behind Joey, I spot Sandra and Ryan.

"I called them," Sandra says. "I hope it's okay. Oh, yeah, and I called a few others as well."

She walks in, and after her come Danny, Marcia, Alex, and Chloe. They all surround us.

"Thank you, Mary," Danny says. "For finding Jean's killer. For stopping Ally and for stopping AK."

"See. I told you. It wasn't all in vain," Joey says. "You stopped a serial killer."

I chuckle with tears in my eyes as the crew approaches me. We all hug for a little while. I am crying. I can't hold it back.

"You guys..." I say, and wipe my eyes.

"So, now what?" Alex asks. "Are you going back to new York?"

I look at Joey, who doesn't look at me. His eyes hit the floor. Salter looks at me in anticipation. I know what he wants me to say. I know what they all want me to say. And that is when I finally make the decision, because that is what I want too.

"Nah," I say. "I think we'll stay here for a little while. My dad has great insurance and the company agreed to build him a new house. He's going to need someone to take care of him. I have a feeling Laura isn't the nursing type. Besides, I have a blog I want to start writing, right Chloe?"

Chloe throws me a thumbs-up. "I already have the perfect design for it. Watch out, world!"

Joey's face lights up, along with Salter's. "So, we're staying, Mom? We're really staying?" my son yells, not even trying to hide his excitement.

"I guess so," I say. I look at Sandra. "We have work to do here. I intend to catch my little brother and have him pay for what he did to my best friend. And I am going to need all of your help to do it."

"Guess the 7th Street Crew is back together again, then?" Danny says.

I smile through tears.

"I guess so."

The End

WANT TO KNOW WHAT HAPPENS NEXT?

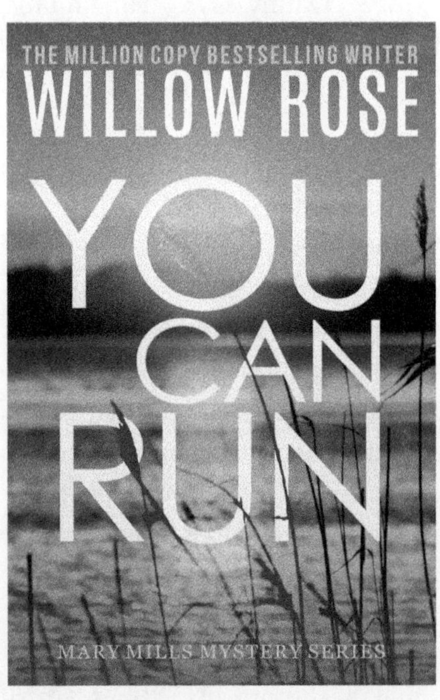

Afterword

Dear Reader,

Thank you for purchasing *What Hurts the Most.* I am so happy you did. This is the first in a series that I plan to write over the next many years. I am already so much in love with the characters, and I hope you are too. I am sure we'll hear a lot more about them in the future.

My inspiration for this story was—as many times before—taken from real life stories. Many of you might have heard about the disease Munchausen Syndrome by Proxy that Mary's mother, Penelope, suffers from. If not, you can read more here:

https://en.wikipedia.org/wiki/Munchausen_syndrome_by_proxy

It's an awful condition and the stories online of people growing up with this are plenty. It is often overlooked because many people don't believe a mother could do such terrible things to her child. It's not abnormal in these cases that the victim, the child, has organs removed before the reality is discovered. You can read one of the stories that I did when researching for my book here:

http://law.justia.com/cases/california/court-of-appeal/3d/122/69.html

or here:

http://www.cbsnews.com/news/prosecutor-lacey-spears-was-calculating-in-sons-salt-poisoning-death/

Furthermore, I was inspired for the girl gang led by AK, alias Liz Hester, when I stumbled over this article about a French girl gang who attacked a man and had him shop for them while humiliating him. You can read more about that here:

http://www.telegraph.co.uk/news/worldnews/europe/france/1396136/France-in-shock-at-girl-gang-who-tortured-youth.html

Lastly, the idea of a female killer with a slit mouth asking if she is pretty is taken from an old Japanese horror story. Read about the slit-mouthed woman here:

https://en.wikipedia.org/wiki/Kuchisake-onna

Thanks again for all your support. Don't forget to check out my other books if you haven't already read them. Just follow the links below. And don't forget to leave reviews, if you can.

Take care,

Willow

To be the first to hear about new releases and bargains from Willow Rose. Sign up to be on the VIP list below.

I promise not to share your email with anyone else, and I won't clutter your inbox.

- Go here to be on the VIP list:
https://readerlinks.com/l/415254

Tired of too many emails? Text the word: "willowrose" to 31996 to sign up to Willow's VIP text List to get a text alert with news about New Releases, Giveaways, Bargains and Free books from Willow.

About the Author

Willow Rose is a multi-million-copy best-selling Author and an Amazon ALL-star Author of more than 80 novels. Her books are sold all over the world.

She writes Mystery, Thriller, Paranormal, Romance, Suspense, Horror, Supernatural thrillers, and Fantasy.

Willow's books are fast-paced, nail-biting page-turners with twists you won't see coming. That's why her fans call her The Queen of Plot Twists.

Several of her books have reached the Kindle top 10 of ALL books in the US, UK, and Canada. She has sold more than three million books all over the world.

Willow lives on Florida's Space Coast with her husband and two daughters. When she is not writing or reading, you will find her surfing and watch the dolphins play in the waves of the Atlantic Ocean.

Tired of too many emails? Text the word: "willowrose" to 31996 to sign up to Willow's VIP Text List to get a text alert with news about New Releases, Giveaways, Bargains and Free books from Willow.

Printed in the USA
CPSIA information can be obtained
at www.ICGtesting.com
CBHW032104140624
10127CB00022B/333/J